1948

1948

A Critical and Creative Prequel to Orwell's 1984

BRIAN MAY

UNIVERSITY
of
EXETER
PRESS

First published in 2024 by
University of Exeter Press
Reed Hall, Streatham Drive
Exeter EX4 4QR, UK

www.exeterpress.co.uk

Copyright © 2024 Brian May

Paperback edition 2025

The right of Brian May to be identified as author of this
work has been asserted by him in accordance with
the Copyright, Designs and Patents Act 1988.

A CIP catalogue record for this book is available from the British Library.
This book is published under a Creative Commons Attribution Non-Commercial No
Derivatives 4.0 International licence (CC BY-NC-ND 4.0). This license requires that
reusers give credit to the creator. It allows reusers to copy and distribute the material
in any medium or format, for non-commercial purposes only. If others remix, adapt,
or build upon the material, they may not distribute the modified material.

https://doi.org/10.47788/EKND5658

Further details about Creative Commons licences are available
at http://creativecommons.org/licenses/

Any third-party material in this book is not covered by the book's Creative Commons
licence. Details of the copyright ownership and permitted use of third-party material
are given in the image (or extract) credit lines. If you would like to reuse any third-
party material, you will need to obtain permission directly from the copyright holder.

Every effort has been made to trace copyright holders and obtain permission
to reproduce the material included in this book. Please get in touch with any enquiries
or information relating to an image or the rights holder.
This Open Access publication was made possible through funds provided by Northern
Illinois University.

ISBN 978-1-80413-129-9 Hardback
ISBN 978-1-80413-228-9 Paperback
ISBN 978-1-80413-130-5 ePub
ISBN 978-1-80413-131-2 PDF

EU Authorised Representative: Easy Access System Europe – Mustamäe tee 50, 10621
Tallinn, Estonia, gpsr.requests@easproject.com

Typeset in Trade Gothic (1948) and Palatino (1949) by S4Carlisle Publishing Services,
Chennai, India

Main frontispiece: Sikorsky YR-5A/S-48 helicopter launch at Bridgeport, Connecticut,
29 November 1945, evocative of Orwell's helicopters in *1984*, by kind permission of
the Igor I. Sikorsky Historical Archives, Inc.

Novella frontispiece: Admiralty Chart No. 2326 Loch Crinan to the Firth of Lorne,
Published 1959 by United Kingdom Hydrographic Office (UKHO). The digital file is
licensed under the Creative Commons Attribution 4.0 International license.

Cover: Spiral vectors by Vecteezy. Background: https://indieground.net/licenses/

Contents

Acknowledgement		vi
I.	Introduction	1
II.	Novella: "From the Archives of Oceania"	19
III.	Teaching Supplement	105
IV.	Critical Supplement: "Orwell Agonistes"	111
Notes		165
Index		185

Acknowledgement

Warm thanks to my editor, the adroit and indefatigable Dr Anna Henderson, who helped me to see, and see to, difficulties in the book's design. By way of her patience and perspicacity, not to mention perspicuity, the book became more fathomable—less brash—brisker; in a word, better.

I. INTRODUCTION

Nineteen Eighty-Four is now being described as "probably the definitive novel of the 20th century," and its author, Eric Blair, better known as George Orwell, is being called "probably the best known twentieth-century English writer" and "the most widely read and influential serious writer of the twentieth century."[1] Unquestionably, he remains "nothing less than a cultural icon," an author of "enduring influence," even as the third decade of the twenty-first century comes into its own.[2] Indeed, Orwell's work, and most especially *1984*, as the novel is usually designated (enumerated?) in the United States (a choice that I sustain, for brevity's sake, on my title page), is now being read and reread with a new urgency; according to a recent *New York Times* headline, "George Orwell's '1984' Is Suddenly a Bestseller."[3] It may be that any time is a good time for a new book about Orwell. Nevertheless, "suddenly" the present time appears particularly ripe, being an era of such "Orwellian" phenomena as so-called alternative facts, Stop the Steal, widely available film clips of remotely controlled bombs going about their business, round-ups of the undocumented, signs of rising anti-Semitism across Europe and the USA, populist political insurgencies, America First, Brexit, Putin, Le Pen, Orban, Erdogan, Bolsonaro, Trump— Unreal.[4] As D. J. Taylor notes, "here in a world of demagogues, 'fake news,' and ever more intrusive technology, Orwell can seem very much alive."[5]

But this is not just another book about Orwell. For it is not just another work of literary criticism. Rather, it is a work of literary criticism-*plus*, one that balances its critical discussion with a creative intervention. Both critically and creatively, it is designed to illuminate, explore, and elaborate upon aspects of Orwell's post-war cultural moment *c.*1948, as well as Orwell's responses to it, which were likewise critical and creative. Structurally speaking, it is roughly one-half critical commentary ("Orwell Agonistes," a literary-critical essay of some 26,000 words), one-half fictional innovation (a novella, "From the Archives of Oceania," roughly 33,000 words). Its critical half does what all literary-critical discussions do, making arguments and claims about Orwell, his texts, and his era—claims conventionally delineated, logically arranged, and systematically defended. By contrast the novella, which precedes this critical discussion in the book's sequence, offers illuminations of these claims, extrapolations from them, creative explorations of them, superimpositions upon them.

"From the Archives" closely quotes, parodies and pastiches, figures and refigures, tropes, and trumps Orwell's *Diaries* even as it creates a kind of prequel to *Nineteen Eighty-Four*. If it does not quite "fabulate," certainly it fabricates; the implied but uncompleted pattern of these works, which is retraced in the second—conventionally critical—half of the book, is woven out in this creative portion into new events and episodes, scenes and settings, and even characters.[6] Though in appearance purely fictional, then, the novella possesses a critical dimension. A kind of "critical novella," it eschews unconstrained literary invention, hewing close to Orwellian intention, intimation, and implication. Orwell's preoccupations, in some cases Orwell's equivocations, inform it—its structure and sequence, its topics, issues, and themes, and its images and symbols. Not that it is a work of explanation; like most works of fiction, "From the Archives" does not present arguments, stating claims and furnishing evidence as if to construct warrants and grounds in the manner of a formal literary-critical essay.[7] But neither does it just make stuff up.[8] For it gets its evidence, rather, from Orwell. Its material has been strictly, fiercely located, having been found by and large in a certain circumscribed literary place: Orwell's later writings.

The fictional "From the Archives" thus follows Orwellian fact. Exploring the discursive ground lying on the uncertain border—more savannah than gulf—between the critical and the creative, it observes certain conventions of both literary-critical argumentation (quotation, eminently) and literary representation (for example, narration and characterization) even as it forgoes others. In so doing it moves beyond the freely fictional and the strictly literary critical alike into the space of a kind of critical semi-fiction. The aim is a mode of engagement at once interpretive and creative.

But if the fiction "From the Archives" follows Orwellian fact, it also follows Orwellian form. Orwell's wartime and post-war "Jura diaries" have provided its rhetorical and narrative structure. Indeed, the novella is a counterfactual extension and revision of them. Below (in "On Reading 'From the Archives'—and *Nineteen Eighty-Four*") I explain how "From the Archives" is best read with and against *Nineteen Eighty-Four*. Here, on the other hand, we may note how its most conspicuous formal quality follows from its rejecting the third-person limited narrative form of Orwell's final novel in favor of the first-person form found in most of Orwell's diaries as well as the diaries of others. "From the Archives" is something like the fiction that Orwell may have written had he recovered health subsequent to the composition of *Nineteen Eighty-Four* and decided that a part of its story still needed telling (in a word, the *whence*). Had he committed to the task of telling this untold part, he also may have decided that it could be told only by returning to the first-person narration of his previous novel, *Coming Up for Air* (1939), but with the first-person(s) under immediate and ongoing existential threat, a daily grind of personal and historical crisis. Hence the choice of diary form for "From the Archives," a non-fiction form that Orwell knew well here pressed into the service of fictional narrative.

Part cleft palette/palate, part roman-à-clef, "From the Archives" comprises a dual and dueling series of diary entries written by a renegade named Cedric B. O'Malley ("Winston Smith" but, as will be seen, not just Winston Smith) and by his sister, Avril (based upon Avril Blair, Eric Blair's younger sister). It includes one extended letter written by Cedric's spouse (they have recently married), Caroline Pretzel (a composite character based upon several of the widowed Blair's romantic targets but especially Sonia Orwell *née* Brownell), and addressed to Inez Holden (based upon Blair's longtime personal friend and confidant, the real English novelist Inez Holden). The story begins with the O'Malleys and Avril having some months ago fled a semi-fictional London that has suffered all that—and something worse than—the real, historical, Blitzed-out city did. They have taken refuge with their young adopted daughter,

Gillian O'Malley *née* Goldstein, in a cottage on the island of Jura in the Hebrides where they hope to be forgotten by the regime now in power and daily increasing its control of its citizenry. Nearby, the famous monster whirlpool Corryvreckan beckons—just as it beckoned to Blair/Orwell, who motored too close one curious day and nearly got himself and a boatload of others, including his adopted son, drowned.

But *why* such a book on Orwell, a composite or hybrid, one-half critical diary-novella and one-half critical essay? And why this sort of book on Orwell *now*?

WHY 1948?

This really involves two questions. On the one hand, why wax creative at all—why not just toe the conventional literary-critical line, as does "Orwell Agonistes," forgo the novella, and be done with it? On the other hand, if we accept the rationale for taking the creative approach, why have the novella stick so critically close to Orwell—why not just make use of Orwell as a springboard and thereby soon have done with *him*?

To address the first question, note that we have many books of literary criticism devoted to Orwell, works of explication and explanation; of works devoted to Orwellian implication, intimation, and equivocation, on the other hand, we have very few. We have many that clarify what Orwell said, as it were; we do not have many that address what Orwell did not quite say but came close to saying, or seemed to want to say but did not get around to saying, or said in part only, or said only to unsay, or only suggested, signaled, sighed, or whispered. [9] "From the Archives" is intended as just such a work: one in which Orwellian intimation finds expression. It is thus a piece of presumption, for it presumes that Orwellian intimation *deserves* expression—that Orwell's hints and hesitations and mere indications could prove as significant as his achieved meanings, as what he would have called his "message."[10] It also presumes that Orwell indeed does, often enough, merely intimate, that a number of significant issues, ideas, and images are introduced but not decided or developed in *Nineteen Eighty-Four* and elsewhere in his later works. And it presumes, finally, that such Orwellian intimation is better approached critically and creatively, or critically/creatively, than merely critically. The enabling presumption of "From the Archives," let us call it the premise, is that exploring and expressing what Orwell intimated but did not expound—a *what* that is both substantial and substantive, both weighty and worthy of attention—requires a certain degree of creative license, a degree not to be found in conventional literary-critical argumentation.

Does then Orwell merely intimate, often enough? May significant hints and hesitations, suggestions and intimations, be found in the later Orwell? Ghosts of ideas started from their alcoves but not pursued? As Robert McCrum explains in his pithy *Observer* account of "the writing of *Nineteen Eighty-Four*," the "circumstances surrounding" its composition "make a haunting narrative"; a look at "the original manuscript" reveals "obsessive rewriting, in different inks, that betrays ... extraordinary turmoil."[11] *Nineteen Eighty-Four* was, of course, the deathly ill Orwell's final book, and McCrum for one characterizes it as, rather than a swan song, "the masterpiece that killed" him.[12] Fatal as it may have proved, how final was it, career-wise? Issuing from "extraordinary turmoil," how finished was it, how complete, when regarded as an attempt at laying ghosts to rest?

Inarguably, Orwell was not done writing when done with— or done in by—this book. He had more books in him; Orwell on his death bed "told [his friend Malcolm Muggeridge] that he had five books in mind that he wanted to write" (at least one of which was a fiction).[13] It is an intriguing question of literary history, what he might have written subsequently. As I have noted, in trying to formulate an instance of exactly *that* I have gone by what he indeed wrote and by what may have been its lacks and deficiencies, its dilations and divagations, its incompletenesses, especially its ambiguities and ambivalences. The assumption is that such fissures and loose ends are there to be found—an assumption shared by Orwell himself. For the existence of such in his published novels was something that he himself was always ready to recognize; as Alex Zwerdling exclaims, "many of his works later struck him as failures."[14] Indeed, it is not just a question of whether he had completed this or that book, even the "masterpiece" (McCrum) *Nineteen Eighty-Four*, to his own satisfaction. Orwell verges upon declaring every book impossible to finish: "[w]riting a book is a horrible, exhausting struggle"; it is as if "one were … driven by some demon."[15] Such a creature would appear to be unappeasable.

"From the Archives" nonetheless attempts an act of appeasement. Its ambition is to give this "demon," or the part of it dissatisfied by the incompletion of *Nineteen Eighty-Four*, a voice; it aims to explore some of the concerns which drove Orwell to write his classic, the focus being on those which found only partial or otherwise imperfect expression therein and which, therefore, may have driven him to attempt another book. Its assumption is that such concerns exist, and that they are significant, even inspirational, at least potentially, and its method, accordingly, is to locate a vibrant bit of such unfinished business, some "demon[ically]" unresolved issue in the *Diaries* or in *Nineteen Eighty-Four*, usually by way of some one or few particularly intriguing passages. Having thus drawn upon close readerly—"critical"—attention, it then draws upon bold writerly—"creative"—intuition and imagination, in order to attempt to resolve it.

To the second question, why not—if one is going to sequel or prequel Orwell—keep it simple? Why not just be inspired to write something, well, essentially new? In part, the answer is: because so many have already been so inspired. If "From the Archives" is a composite, critical/creative meditation on Orwell, a response to Orwell that is neither strictly critical nor strictly creative, certainly we do not lack for the more expansively creative sort, any more than we do for the conventionally critical. Which is to say, and I will say it, that many of the former have been more inspired by than attentive to Orwellian substance. In such works *Nineteen Eighty-Four* is a rocket booster shed once it has done its job. Anthony Burgess's 1978 book *1985*, for example, is in part a novella that appears to be a sequel but that is not set in Oceania; it departs from Orwell's portrait of Oceania in most respects.[16] David Peace's *GB84* (2004) offers a deliberately Orwellian view of the miner's strike that took place in 1984; it has little to do with either Orwell's novel or his life.[17] Nor does the 2015 book by Andrew Ervin entitled *Burning Down George Orwell's House*, which has also been advertised as a sequel; it is in fact a book about Andrew Ervin.[18] These works divagate from Orwell, often brilliantly, but in so doing they sacrifice opportunities to point us readers at luminous Orwellian detail, opportunities that come with the more hybrid, critical-creative approach here attempted.

For all its magic realism, Dom Shaw's *Eric is Awake* (2013), on the other hand, may appear to fall outside of the category of such inspired divagations.[19] Like "From the Archives," it has a critical dimension. Despite its fantastical resurrection of Orwell as a twenty-first-century Quixote ("Eric") complete with a Sancho sidekick ("Pedro"), it is in places remarkably attentive to Orwellian substance. As in "From the Archives," its Orwell character has Orwell's history; moving back and forth in time and space between the near London future and Orwell's post-war past, it devotes a chapter to the Corryvreckan incident (also featured in "From the Archives"). *Eric is Awake* features bouts of critical scruple as well as of creative lark. But it tends not to combine but to alternate them. That is, the awakened, magical "Eric," quite a reach, is too often Orwell in template or caricature. Shaw's fidelity to the historical, quotidian Orwell as he composes *Nineteen Eighty-Four* in his grubby Jura cottage points away from the novel itself, which in these biographical chapters is kept largely separate, quiescent. Such an approach makes for a work different from the revisionary treatment here offered, an attempt at the sort of thing that Hermione Lee calls, speaking of Peter Carey's *Jack Maggs*, an "extrapolation" and "act of appropriation."[20] This inferential dimension of "From the Archives" is discussed below in "On Reading 'From the Archives'—and *Nineteen Eighty-Four*" under "Navigating *1948*."

If I have explained whence comes "From the Archives," a critical novella, a critical semi-fiction on Orwell and his *Nineteen Eighty-Four*, the question now becomes, whence comes "Orwell Agonistes," the conventionally critical second part of the book (or so it appears)? If we already have sheaves of such traditionally, strictly critical discussion of Orwell, and if—secondly—"From the Archives" offers a hybrid, critical-creative response that can stand alone, then why is such a critical commentary necessary here?

Yes, the archive of critical discussion devoted to Orwell, especially the later Orwell, is thick. But that is not to say that there is nothing contributive left to be said. Moreover, I have been overstating the degree to which "Orwell Agonistes" proceeds as if just another literary-critical investigation "toeing" the traditional literary-critical line. Its very commitment to the intimated-but-unexplored in Orwell distinguishes it from most works of Orwell exegesis, which have largely deplored Orwell's aporia, his nods, lapses, lacks, and absences, as flaws. By contrast, "Orwell Agonistes" treats them as Orwellian occasions of interest in their own right, ones less indicative of inconsistency or ineptness than of an intriguing, and significant, ambivalence.

"From the Archives" treats them as opportunities. Of course, it does not clarify exactly what they are and where they may be found; it does not name, explicate, and explain them. That is the business of "Orwell Agonistes." To cite just one such nod: in his later writings Orwell gives evidence here and there of misgiving about certain recognizable Enlightenment values; he also gives evidence that this dubiousness was not something he wrote about as such; it went largely unacknowledged and certainly undiscussed and unexplored. And, again, this and other such unexplored issues in the later Orwell are precisely what "From the Archives" narratively, figuratively, and in other fictive ways explores, expounds, "expresses." To expose and essay these same issues, on the other hand, is the precise task of "Orwell Agonistes."

But is such a task worth performing? Rather, is not such a task, such examination and exposition, after all, a *readerly* task? And should not readers, especially students, be left alone to perform it? They should be, and readers who read *seriatim* certainly will be, for much of the book; the critical account comes safely last in the book's sequence, the aim being to give readers space to formulate issues and answers on their own. Why then step in at all, even at the end? The premise of "Orwell Agonistes" is that inquisitive readers of "From the Archives" might, when all is said, like to compare notes with the author. Having been alerted to the novella's attempt to respond imaginatively to *unanswered* questions in Orwell, such readers may like to know at some point exactly what those questions are, according to the author; they might also like to know just how and where in Orwell's work they may be found. Thus "Orwell Agonistes" is offered as a critical *supplement* to "From the Archives," one that is if not necessary to an appreciation of the latter, nonetheless an optional extension. For within it are discussed a number of the Orwellian origins of important questions cropping up in the later Orwell—and which were drivers for the composition of "From the Archives." Determinedly eschewing spoilers, this terminally positioned supplement provides some illumination and explanation of "From the Archives."

"Orwell Agonistes" contains eight sections addressing in turn the issues of *rationality, sentiment, art, femininity, identity, prejudice, nature,* and *memory and history.* The question of Orwell's Enlightenment faith being taken up in the first and longest of the sections (section i), subsequent sections address various other lacunae in Orwell's "argument," whatever their provenance—a putative ideological blindness, mere writerly illness or fatigue (mere!), or something in between. The questions addressed in these additional sections include (ii) the question of Orwell's view of the nuclear family as social unit; (iii) the question of Orwell's (modernist?) conception of aesthetic expression and experience; (iv) questions of feminine individuality in Orwell's world of men—Cedric's sister Avril, as well as the composite figure, Caroline O'Malley *née* Pretzel, are based upon historical persons, the telling of whose stories, however obliquely, is here an end in itself; (v) the question of Orwell's individualism, his seemingly reflexive distrust of the collective; (vi) the question of his anti-Semitism; (vii) the question of what would now be called his "environmentalism" (his hardy, post-Romantic pastoralism); and (viii) questions of his historicism (his views of memory, autobiography, history-writing, and so forth).

Nothing should prevent readers from regarding this closing, avowedly supplementary discussion as a more-or-less freestanding entity unto itself, one dedicated to the task of delineating unresolved issues in the later Orwell irrespective of how they animate "From the Archives," and one that may be read profitably on its own.

WHY *1948 NOW?*

I addressed the question "why this particular book on Orwell?", but another question remains: why this particular book on Orwell *now*? Or perhaps it does not: few would need convincing that, for example, an author's concept of the feminine is a topic of ongoing literary-critical relevance in the era of #MeToo. One could discuss recent green initiatives—or the Biden-rescinded 2016–20 American truncation thereof by way of the US withdrawal from the Paris Agreement.[21] And so forth: at a time in which the phrase "fake news" has become a catchphrase, questions of historiography need no rehearsal, any more than do reports of the recent resurgence of anti-Semitism in Europe, in Eastern Europe especially.[22] Even the more philosophical issues taken up by *1948*, issues of individualism, aestheticism, and Enlightenment, either remain topical or have become such; note, for example, such recent attention to Enlightenment thought as may be found in Steven Pinker's 2018 book, *Enlightenment Now: The Case for Reason, Science, Humanism, and Progress*, or in "The Re:Enlightenment Project," an ongoing movement of "institutions and individuals who share a common purpose ... join[ing] together to pursue a historic opportunity: the transformation of our Enlightenment inheritance."[23] In a sense, then, *1948* is as much a product of 2020, the year of its completion, as of 1948.

FINALLY, *1948*—HOW? NAVIGATING *1948*

1948 has four parts: I, this introduction; II, the critical novella ("From the Archives"); III, a teaching supplement; and IV, a critical supplement ("Orwell Agonistes"). The assumption is that most readers will be quite familiar with Orwell's *Nineteen Eighty-Four* but will have read more cursorily if at all his diaries and probably—certainly?—will not have thought of the diaries as providing a possible shape for Orwell's next fiction. Thus below I cite the volume *George Orwell, Diaries*, identify the most pertinent diary entries, and provide a link to the Orwell Foundation website where many of them may be found; see "On the Diary Form of 'From the Archives'" below. With regard to sections III and IV, I have already explained why "Orwell Agonistes" follows rather than precedes the teaching supplement; it is designed to stir readers to explore their own independent sense of the connections between "From the Archives" and both the diaries and *Nineteen Eighty-Four*.

While the order is far from arbitrary, readers are invited to skip around, navigating the book as they see fit. The hope is that the parts prove to be mutually illuminating, whatever the sequence in which they are encountered. The hope also is that the two larger sections, "From the Archives" and "Orwell Agonistes," may be encountered as objects unto themselves and prove of independent as well as of supplementary or complementary interest.

On Reading "Orwell Agonistes"

As explained above, Part IV, "Orwell Agonistes," examines Orwellian ambivalence in the later writings, principally of the later 1940s. Its method is to seek out the most important intellectual pressure points in the later Orwell, areas in which Orwell exhibits second thoughts, unresolved conflicts, and mixed feelings. "Orwell Agonistes" I am calling a "critical supplement" because it is intended to discuss only those central Orwellian issues that inform and animate Part II, "From the Archives." However, the phrase "critical complement" may be equally appropriate. Supplements are of the supplemented—they add to it; augmenting or amplifying, they are more of the same or at least similar. Complements, by contrast, complete or enhance, but only by balancing a thing with its counterpart: "[i]f one thing *complements* another, it goes well with the other thing and makes its good qualities more noticeable" (*Collins Dictionary*).[24] "Orwell Agonistes" may be regarded as complementary rather than supplementary to the extent that it now and then contends for readerly interest with "From the Archives," exchanging places with it, so to speak, and thus rendering the novella the ancillary or adjuvant unit, itself claiming centre stage—for that moment, only to surrender it in another moment. The sense of complementarity may become acute, to the extent that those who begin with "Orwell Agonistes" or otherwise give it priority or privilege over "From the Archives" in the end turn back to the latter and foreground its creative dimension, perhaps by allowing the term "critical" to slip out of the phrase that I have been attaching to it ("critical/creative"). Hence would the critical complement the creative, and the creative, in turn, the critical.

But "Orwell Agonistes" may also now and again attain the status of an entirely freestanding commentary, a critical discussion of the later Orwell that is of interest above and beyond whatever light it might shed on—or have shed upon itself by—"From the Archives." As such it may strike the reader as a work or text which represents a fundamentally different kind of readerly response to Orwell, a mode of "reception" that is not just different from that which is represented by "From the Archives" but is its rival.[25]

In its treatment of Orwell's modernism, for example, "Orwell Agonistes" offers a commentary that builds upon the work of Martha C. Carpentier, Michael Levenson, Keith Williams, and Roger Fowler, literary critics who address the crucial question of what has come to be called Orwell's "divided aesthetic."[26] Rooted in a persistently "double sense" of the proper ends and means of literature and art in general, Orwell's Sentimental Modernism, as I would call it, sustained through the 1930s, comes to an end in *Nineteen Eighty-Four*.[27] As I argue, this final novel of Orwell's career indeed dramatizes a fantastical extirpation of all lingering Sentimental Modernism by means of an anti-Joyce—the totalitarian intellectual O'Brien, who roots it out (of Winston). It is as if the diseased Orwell decides to destroy or even disappear modernism, the better to punish himself for ever having entertained it as an aesthetic ideal and Joyce as a literary model.

On Reading "From the Archives"— and Nineteen Eighty-Four

How to read "From the Archives"? To read it best is to read it with and against *Nineteen Eighty-Four* and other works of the later Orwell, especially his wartime and Jura diaries. For the *revisionary* dimension of "From the Archives," noted above, is perhaps its most crucial dimension. I call it such because "From the Archives" instantiates what Caroline Rody terms "the revisionary paradigm"; it stands in what Lee calls an "extrapolat[ive]," critical-and-creative relation to certain of Orwell's texts, especially Orwell's *Nineteen Eighty-Four*, much as John Gardner's *Grendel* stands to *Beowulf*, or as J. M. Coetzee's *Foe* stands to Daniel Defoe's *Robinson Crusoe* and certain others of Defoe's works, or Aimé Césaire's *Une Tempête* stands to Shakespeare's *The Tempest*, or Jean Rhys's *Wide Sargasso Sea* to Charlotte Brontë's *Jane Eyre*, and so forth.[28] "From the Archives" in some moments hews more strictly to its Great Book host than these celebrated works tend to do. As mentioned above, it incorporates more or less verbatim individual phrases and lines and even longer passages; it is worth mentioning here that it does so perhaps in larger measure than do any of the other works. Even so, as readers will recognize eventually, perhaps eventfully, "From the Archives" may appear as happily "paradigm"-atic as any of them.

Indeed, the subtitle of "From the Archives" could be "A Monster Finds a Voice," a fitting subtitle for many of these well-known works, and those interested in the larger question of how the monstrous Grendels, Calibans, Berthas, and even the not-so-monstrous Fridays find their voices will be inclined to compare this book to these others. But knowledgeable readers of Orwell may be especially so inclined. Though "From the Archives" stands alone and should interest readers who do not know the Orwell *oeuvre* intimately, those who do know it well may be proportionately struck by its multifarious, sometimes comic (the material permitting), and sometimes rude engagement with its host.

On Teaching "From the Archives"—and Orwell

Part III, the "Teaching Supplement," could prove a crucial part of *1948* depending on the uses to which the book is put. It contains discussion prompts sorted into two groups.

Group one, under the subheading "Connecting 'From the Archives' and *Nineteen Eighty-Four*," presumes readerly familiarity with the latter text. It offers questions designed to direct readers' attention to the later Orwell by way of certain elements of "From the Archives"—and vice versa. For example, question #2 points to the glass paperweight in the novella with a view to disclosing new aspects and implications of its figurative use in *Nineteen Eighty-Four*. The aim is to prompt attention to Orwell's themes of art and of "the aesthetic," more broadly, as well as of the aesthetic faculty or imagination. The hope is that attention to how the glass paperweight is handled in "From the Archives" will disclose new aspects and implications of its role and purpose in Orwell's book, as well as uncover Orwellian hints about art that he does not here develop but that he might have explored in a subsequent book.

Group two, on the other hand, is made up of questions designed to point readers beyond Orwell proper to various cultural and intellectual contexts for interpretation and evaluation, a few of which belong to us twenty-first-century readers rather than to Orwell and his immediate post-war era. On the one hand, item #18, for example, invokes the Orwell-era (early to mid-twentieth-century) philosophical context of "logical atomism," a metaphysical theory which implies a certain theory of knowledge; as posited by Bertrand Russell, logical atomism indeed implies a certain definition of "fact," thereby putting the very notion of "fact" into question (a salutary measure in our own era of so-called "alternative facts"? [what Dan Rather calls "an Orwellian phrase"]).[29] An example of a *post*-Orwellian context, on the other hand, is that to which question #15 points, "reception theory." Drawing upon the "*Rezeptionsästhetik*" of the German critical theorist Hans Robert Jauss, this item invites readers to regard "From the Archives" as a particular sort of response to Orwell, that of what Jauss terms the "*auf Gipfelebene*" reader.[30] The aim is to introduce students and other readers to the practice of a so-called aesthetic of reception, one which prompts us to ask what we do when we read, listen to, view, or otherwise experience a work of art.

On the Diary Form of "From the Archives"

George Orwell, Diaries, which over its considerable course (597 pp.) presents the virtual entirety of Orwell's diary writings, was edited by Peter Davison and published in 2012 by Liveright Press.[31] Readers are, of course, hereby invited to explore the volume as an item of interest in itself. But this is also the moment to indicate those specific diary entries, or portions thereof, that the author found particularly inspiring and that, indeed, served as occasions for specific passages in "From the Archives."

From "War-Time Diary, May 28, 1940 – August 28, 1941"	From "The Jura Diaries"
20.6.40: Went to the office of, etc.	5.6.46: Very blustery all day, etc.
30.6.40: This afternoon a parade, etc.	25.7.46: Rather rainy in morning, etc.
	25.9.46: Fine and blowy, etc.

1.7.40: Newspapers now reduced, etc.
28.7.40: This evening I saw, etc.
29.8.40: Air-raid alarms during, etc.
10.9.40: Can't write much of the insanities, etc.
17.9.40: Heavy bombing in this area, etc.
21.9.40: Have been unable for some days, etc.
15.10.40: Writing this at Wallington, etc.
1.12.40: That bastard Chiappe, etc.
8.12.40: Broadcasting the night before last, etc.
29.12.40: From a newspaper account, etc.
2.1.41: The rightwing reaction, etc.
4.3.41: At Wallington. Crocuses, etc.
20.3.41: Fairly heavy raids, etc.
15.4.41: Last night went to the pub, etc.

20.6.47: Dense mist most of the day, etc.
6.7.47: Fine, blowy, not very warm, etc.
7.7.47: Coldish, blowy, overcast, etc.
21.7.47: Rain, almost continuous, etc.
22.7.47: A very few drops of rain, etc.
16.8.47: Fine hot day, little wind, etc.
19.8.47: Since 17.8.47 at Glengarrisdale, etc.

All of the "War-Time Diary" entries listed above (left column) have been made available on the Orwell Foundation website, which in 2012 began "'post-blogging' Orwell's domestic and political diaries, each entry [being] published seventy years to the day since it was written."[32]

Journal and diary novels alike create special challenges for literary narrative. The diarist's daily motive for sitting down to write, typically, is not to tell a story; often enough, rather, it is to report on notable events of the day that in their extraordinary quality represent a departure from the daily. A good example of the latter may be found in Orwell's brief account of the dangerous brush with the Corryvreckan whirlpool (discussed in Part IV, "Orwell Agonistes"), an account featured by

William Gass in his influential review of the Davison volume and a portion of which follows.[33]

> On return journey [from Glengarrisdale] today ran into the whirlpool & were all nearly drowned. Engine sucked off by the sea & went to the bottom. Just managed to keep the boat steady with the oars, & after going through the whirlpool twice, ran into smooth water & found ourselves only about 100 yards from Eilean Mor, so ran in quickly & managed to clamber ashore. HD jumped ashore first with the rope, then the boat overturned spilling LD, R & myself into the sea. R. trapped under the boat for a moment, but we managed to get him out... we managed to get my cigarette lighter dry & made a fire of dead grass & lumps of dry peat, prised off the surface, at which we dried out clothes. We were taken off about 3 hours later by the Ling fishermen who happened to be bringing picknickers round.[34]

Of course, the diarist may also enter daily observations on any number of issues or, alternatively, a select few abiding issues, the choice of which may seem arbitrary but attention to which immediately becomes obligatory. This applies to Orwell's own charming observance of the latter practice in his daily egg-count, examples of which occur in several of the target selections from "The Jura Diaries" (20.6.47 and several of the ones that follow); this habit is imitated in "From the Archives" in the nearly daily egg-count performed by Cedric and Avril both (for example, "*24 April*. **[First entry**.]... 4 eggs [210]").[35] Whatever the diarists' motive and method, in committing to diary discourse they undermine narrative urgency and even narrative continuity. On the one hand, counting eggs does not make for a lot of narrative suspense. On the other, "the journal form naturally creates opportunities for narrative disjunction ... creating daily entries results in a pastiche of subjects," often enough a hodgepodge of events and episodes, and a consequent "disjunction" in linear narrative sequence.[36] If a diary is authentic qua diary, then it should be difficult to read for the plot.

"From the Archives" does have a plot and does try to tell a story; its sequence has been constructed so as to sustain conventional readerly interest in a good yarn. Accordingly, it is perhaps best read *seriatim*. Nevertheless, with "From the Archives," as well as with the larger work of which it is part, *1948*, readers are invited to skip around the text. The diary/journal form may prompt—"naturally"—this more haphazard approach.

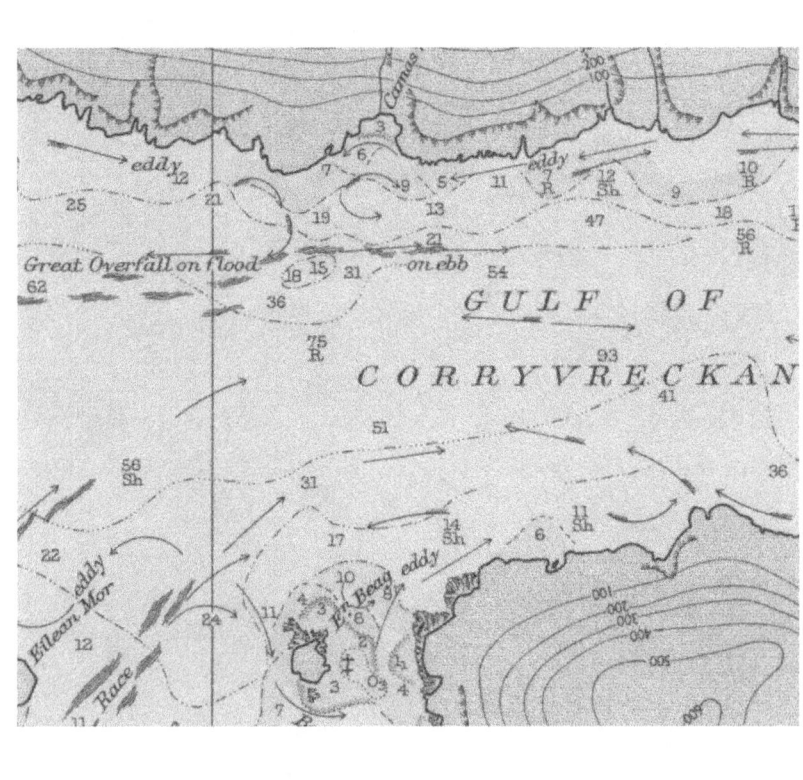

II. NOVELLA—"From the Archives of Oceania"

[Editor's Foreword]

Millions of the documents residing in the Archives of Oceania were destroyed in Trafalgar Square ("Victory Square," during the Oceanic era) in The Great Conflagration of 1987. This was the massive incineration of official records conducted in October of that year in reaction to the Inner Party ("IP") or so-called Blue Rebellion of 1986, the first of the three major rebellions constituting The Great Rebellion ending in 1989. Nevertheless, as we are now discovering, the "trafconflag" (*qua* Newspeak) proved less successful than has been assumed; many documents survived the blaze. The following fragment, composed by one of the senior Blue Rebels, is one such document, and it is of especial interest because it belongs to a class of documents that was specifically targeted for destruction: records of IP members' conversion experiences. In the face of a growing number of cases of ideological relapse among IP members during the eighties, it was decided that it had been a mistake to require members of the IP to engage in (that quaint 17th-century practice) "spiritual autobiography." This fragment, a portion of one such diary/journal, nonetheless has survived. Distinctively, it appears to relate to a prelapsarian period in which its author is attempting to save his "family" as well as himself. Having fled London for the Inner Hebrides and taken up residence in a secluded cottage, the fugitives spend their last summer together. In any event, herewith is it offered to the public for the first time.

***

[*The Diary of Cedric B. O'Malley*;
"Cedric O'Malley's Diary"
("Cedric's Diary"), selections]

24 April. [**First entry.**] Dirty weather. Smirred in the morning; rained throughout the rest of the day. Little could be done outdoors. Tried to make G—— a puzzle but could not; my coping-saw blade has broken. Towards evening the weather lightened a little, the sky brightened, & the wind picked up. Saw the eagle cruising rather low over the bay, which was rough. Often they soar. Looking for…? Evidently they just like the wind. Either way, I see it only when the wind is heavy. Not the usual noise of crows in array. Perhaps it is that the wind blows the crows away, clearing the coast for the eagle.

4 eggs. (210)

25 April. Heavy weather this morning, 'twas—the game being musical, as if a large number of iron & lead bullets the size of peas were dropping down in rhythm with the occasional cymbal-crash like a bell ringing in my ears. Or was it Something Large beating a tattoo on my roof? I am puzzled. Was it History reclaiming us? God forfend. Nature calling? God, rather? God at the keys?

God knows. Or Hegel does.

Mill wrote of the debauching influence of Hegel. I have been debauched but am a little better now.

The wind falling off about 10 o'clock, I was listening about for the Hag—Hagel?—& couldn't hear it, naturally, when I was thunderstruck, literally—the cottage rocked—pretty sure it was not a bomb (!), always a possibility these days that must be ruled out, even in the Hebrides, as History is my witness. Evidently it was only Nature, only lightning hitting the roof—only lightning! for God's sake—perhaps as I imagine fusing the encaustic tiles, turning them translucent… transparent? But a stone's throw from the sea, do I now live in a glass house? People who live in glass houses shouldn't… there are lots of things that they should not do. That's a thought, the thought of being seen, being watched: it puts one on the lookout. It opens the eyes—this thought of open eyes. The thought of ears, too, open wide. One wants to count one's curses. Incomparable, of course, is the sound of glass breaking, the stones being thrown by others.

Kristalltagesanbruch? A question. How many synagogues? As if the number mattered: somebody counted them up. Aufklarung. Establish the fact, qua Fact.

Broadening daylight, the blue sky above, it was morning, they say, precisely 9:11 am, in fact, that the Big Boy fell. Das Grobe Nummer. But I am this very day reminded of a different eye-opening, not to say Enlightening experience of a late afternoon some months ago from which, perhaps, a kind of thunder still sounds...

Boo-oooomp! Wooou-pooum!! Poum... poum... boummm...

Counterpointing, the casements fretted, she said, that different different time, yet longer ago. & how.

I couldn't see; I wasn't there; we were talking on the telephone.

—Oh, she said, it's only the window falling in.

She was a game one, the dear girl.

But that was a yet different day. But on this different day of days she, a different she—but no less game? (If often breathless...) But the game being different—she & G——— were removed to the country for a month & more.

& it was good job that they were. For like the wide thin slats of scrap sheetmetal that you as a child playing with your sister could barely spread-eagle & span & shake out & back out back out—whoop-ah, whoop-ah, whoop-ah—amplified immeasurably—that bombblast started something, a wind, a sound, a sensation, that could have been heard, could have been felt on the delicate skin of the cheek, as we were told later on—we were told lots of things, but this may have been true—it could have been felt a full mile off. It rounded corners, reverberated, a cannonball of force caroming from the west face of Senate House—the Ministry, that is—or that now was (!)—just as I, a Baffle Ball rolling in my own right, bounced on through the revolving door. I'd want to blame it on the Ministry, what with its later explosions & expulsions; more than one was snookered. But here & now sideways was I knocked, as it felt, & I did not so much walk as billiard homeward, veritably Blitzed. Ah, there it is—the verb, for all my sneering Daily Express-ed. Even I have succumbed; it was just a matter of time.

—Caw with the crowd, what ho. Whympspered. Aarronow, hell roast him. & a pest he was, indeed—inword—the, of our March Past.

But, of course, as I said—could have been heard—could. It was no whisper. The problem was that no one was paying attention, not even back then. Even I, I—being one who pays attention—one who spent that night on that hillside outside Madrid—even I did not hear for a long time a London bomb go off with the sort of bang that makes you feel you are personally involved. Of all the people who happened to be strolling in Regent's Park during a raid-warning at least half kept on strolling about, even as the sirens keened & the loose dogs bolted for home. & that's perhaps the sharpest memory of that time: how little attention was being paid, whatever one's class, save when a 500-pound guest like a loud political argument found its way uninvited to one's own kitchen table. Or a doodlebug sniffed one out even as one lay abed.

But that particular bolt out of the blue, mind—what with its poum & its boum—somehow impossibly I knew. I remember—I remember a lot—Memory—small memories on the wing flap & flit... they fly by. Or they hover sometimes, though not very often, rarely, really. Either way, I sit, or stroll, unhorsed, wingless & watch.

That particular vehicular bolt I personally remember well, I say—its thunder, which rolls on soundlessly, echoing stilly in all moments, vibrating, sounding yet however quietly to this very moment. In that moment I recall thinking that I must go to it, find a road to it, from the outside, from a remote distance, approaching it with slow, circuitous steps, thus circumnavigating the question of my home, the question of home itself, which is not after all much of one, as I was about to learn for myself. It had just been called into question, you see, veritably rocked, by the arrival of a rocket—thank God, when they were away in the country, where they would be staying for some time.

O City, City... O fallen unfellowed world!

Yes, I am still capable of such a cloudburst.

& what remained, what was tossed out lying there to be found nested in its wreckage? Was not it just another bombshell bringing light, this one as yet unexploded? A question. It would appear to be a delayed-action bomb, the worst sort of bomb—to adapt Avril, Tick Tick Tick... a Fact. An Atomic Fact.

[*The Diary of Cedric B. O'Malley*, cont.; "Avril O'Malley's Diary" ("Avril's Diary"), selections]

25 April. Warmer today, but smirry in the morning. Shot a brown rabbit. The sun came out in the afternoon & shone on the ponds & pools beside the white chickens & a small toad I found next to the woodpile. Planted potatoes in the late afternoon, which was a demanding task. Hoeing tomorrow, &c..

7 eggs. (214)

1 April. Rain early: 13 million, 13 thousand, 13 hundred and 13 raindrops by 13 o'clock. Later, tick tock, fourteen degrees warmer. Killed fifteen invisible purple rabbits. Then the blue sun suddenly came out, brightening the ponds (two) and puddles (numerous) and making the—sixteen—running chickens glow. Dully. No, wanly & in vain. The chopping block awaits close by. I came upon a wretched little toad by the woodpile. Just one. Green. Brown. She—the wretched little brown and green toad, whom I came upon by the woodpile, as I just jotted—was looking about her, obviously obliviously newborn, needful, stupid. Bill Dobbs and I planted potatoes— back-breaking work.

Brother busy smoking and—&—writing, not jotting, mind you—Lord knows what. Sister wife, our resident Jewess? Busy being ill, or busy working, or walking somewhere, but not in my road, blessedly. My niece, Miss Mouse? Making herself scarce again. Where does she spend these days of invisibility? Search me. Search the whole damned place.

0, no 2574,kg90 eggs (~123,456i)

Oh, cheese it. April has been one-hundred Fools' Days in a row, and I sick and tired of drowning the fish. Time will tell. So we are told. Months ago it was that my brother came to me & said, hash up a pen, Av, & keep up the diary. I said I would. & I did—I was keen to help. She was sick, & so was he. & I did my best. I did my best my best my my. & I think I managed to be jotty in good Cedrician diary-fashion. Flattered, I was, indeed, to be so trusted, but fooled I was not. My brother is always being a brother. That's his kind of kindness, to me. Neither of us is the huggy-kissy sort. I am his little sister. Do you like Spanish art?

Call me Conchita. No, really, I shouldn't; I am a survivor. Time will tell, and I do believe after all that I was of real help during Caroline's bad spells—money for jam, <u>he</u> said—when he himself can write, is permitted to write, ring in the nose, nothing at all.

Now, however that may be, the diary is closed to me; he keeps it locked away in his desk drawer. Resettling his spectacles on the bridge of his nose, something he does habitually, thoughtfully, often contemplatively, sometimes emphatically, certainly assuredly composedly—Oh, apologies, Ric! I do love the adverbs that you so detest—he told me that it had nothing to do with me but that The Domestic Diary, as he called it, has become less committed to the rural domestic/agrarian side of things &—and—more introspective and ('and'!) more speculative. Yank teachers as I read now make their chits do what they call show-&-tell. Ric evidently will do less show, more tell.

I right liked that diary & am now beginning—even as I write this—a diary of my own, though I have decided to be private about it, quiet, clandestine. Yet, show-&-tell? Not that I will show it to anyone, but it will be more show than tell. For example, I don't plan to take a political stand. Not that I shall avoid political matters altogether, for once you've been brought in it doesn't matter what you've written, said or even thought, let alone told. It becomes time to tell. They torture you. Anything they wish you had said that you didn't they will simply tell you that you said, and it will not be long until they make you say you said it.

One thing is sure. This English Tolstoy of the Latter Days will have no idea what I am up to.

Not that he's a Tolstoy, really, for all his setting up as a kind of Pastoral Refugee, as he calls himself. He has been, really, more of an English Trotsky, what with his readiness to remove at a moment's notice, scuttling off to Morocco, Spain, Serbia or even Jura, this our Jura, but also in his fear of assassination here at home. Hence the Lugar which Crinoline made him hand over to the Colonel.

This, too, will be a domestic diary—but of a different sort! I am beginning a bit melodramatically, which is not my way. But I do not seem to be able to help myself.

This diary, my diary, will bear up, bravely, and it will bare all.

It will bear all that his pages cannot bear.

It will bare all that his pages cannot bare.

Again, the touch of melodrama. My apologies, Gentle Reader.

For my brother, the diary has become—what? It was a series of stakes driven deep, fence-posts, pylons, solid, safe as houses, perhaps, but also signposts all, blank but pointing seaward, lea-ward, through but beyond all human habits and habitations. I am quoting him. From one angle, it so remains, but from another has it not become, not the post to which the tiny craft is lashed, but the vehicle itself, a humble, homey vessel & small, sacred but not inviolable, bobbing about motor-less on the profane waters of the everyday? Therewith a little poetry of my own.

Or rolling on, and on, down what Ric calls the ringing grooves of change? Unto Time, into History? Or, nowadays, beyond, taking flight? To ape Ric for a moment. If a vehicle, what sort of vehicle? And where will it land? And where is its key? (Lor—I bet Crinoline has it.)

& And for me? For me, a maid old and wee? We will see! But if pushed I would say—a mirror! Nothing ornately framed and hanging fire in the parlour, nor a funhouse mirror of full-length, I don't much like freaks and am seldom silly, but a mobile mirror, as I see it this very moment, rolling down the road 'twixt dry hedgerows. Yet a mirror is a fragile thing readily cracked or shattered into sharp fragments. For my moving mirror I want a mirror of polished chrome, aluminum, shiny sheetmetal of a sort, which shows all. My eyes eyes of steel, perhaps, collecting, capturing all, no matter how turbulent, a gaze iron and acid, keen, somehow stationary, missing nothing, even when in motion, and capable of zeroing in. It all sounds so Wellsian, Ric would say (—poor Wells! We grew up on Wells).

I wish to live in a world of things, not of facts. (If I understand what they are talking about!)

Yes, indeed, all my life I have tried to avoid the sentimental view of things. I have tried to avoid any "view," at all. I believe that I have succeeded, to a degree, except where my brother is in question. And, I must admit, my sister-in-law, ol' Big Nose. In whose case the sentiment, certainly, is quite different.

No. You see, I see her. I show her for who, for what, she is. For I have seen her. What she's about.

Hey, Car-a Sposa! I am watching you.

[Cedric's Diary]

[25.4 later?] The clouds lifting & the rain dying, it became after all a nice day, today, in the Hebrides—the green country, this Elizium, this my island dream. It is a place outside history, I tell myself, & I am out of place. An intellectual in this green & golden world is Diogenes Accidentia. He's Philosophical Man, Aufklärer, sporting an electric hand-torch in the noontide, <u>illooming</u>, even as a Mithraic sun, this one properly bulb-less, radiates from above. For the truth lies all around. Facts, at the least, so lie. What, States of Affairs. Fearful of the dark, der Aufklärer is caught dread-handed. That's one worthy of Aaro ⸺⸺. (No, no more names.)

The facts change, but things do not—thank God.

Oh, to live in a world of THINGS and not FACTS.

Honestly, the fact is, & perhaps they will agree, they, at least, have no need of enlightenment. They know where I am; they have not forgotten me; neither have they forsaken me. After all, all of this, this Jura business, was originally A⸺⸺'s idea, not mine. I am being left alone, for now. But it is just a matter of time. Even now there may be a rescue mission on foot—on horse? By sea? Or by sky?

Here on planet Jura have I no local Jesus walking about, spinning about Eilean Mor? Or even Corryvreckan, itself? & somehow keeping his balance, but only one regular fellow, a one-legged workman, a pretty good carpenter (!), & evidently a porpoise in the water, to boot, who is all but mute—he does grunt on occasion—name of Dobbs, Ma'am. Caroline could not help but smile. My name being Cedric, privately I do not call him Dobbin. I call him Gurth: Workman Gurth, the Freeman.

Gurth—with his brass collar, Gurth, for the ages! I give you Gurth, a man of girth, of worth. No air of dearth, no aura of death, haunts this substantial figure: being material, & very little mind, I might add invidiously, & being human, he is nothing more than human substance, itself, raw, essential, eternal, if not entirely integral, fairly intractable, if not purely immutable, if frangible, implacable. He's a human Thing. (Ex) (xG & xh) Good Victorianist that I am, I am not, when all is said, a good Darwinist; we are here to stay. Gurth is safer than houses; he's sound as a cockchafer—indeed, as the rats that his urban cousin, the town mouse—Couth?—does not scruple to refuse when times are bad. Horrid thought, that, & yet you've never worked for hunger or you'd know! You'd know what God governs us! Who said that? That artist Jew, a sort of hunger artist, in the dreadful novel by the pornographer. You remember that. What you do not remember is what you are doing here. & why, to begin with, you do what you do, at all. Indeed, what do you even do? & what have you done? What have you? What have you been? Who are you?

—What? What? said the blindman, huffing, puffing, weren't bluffing.

These are the questions for myself, questions of purpose, of progress, of existence, the mere posing of which destroys complacency, if not self-respect. What price, thy intellectual light?

I am reminded of the old madwoman at ~~Brideswell~~ that's Bridewell (!), as we called it, that winter long ago, all dressed in white, so scathing with all the men, who once stopped me in the fern-ridden hall to tell me, a young attendant, that if she had a gun she would blast me. She it was who would stop her eternal round of pacing to claim a chair demanding of all within earshot—

—Oh, why oh why do I lie down so much?

Grete Freewoman. Unenlightened. As am I: why does she, in fact?

We are confronted by a question: why.

We are confronted by a fact: she lies down a lot, suddenly, at all hours of the day, and won't budge.

We are confronted by a question: does she? In fact?

What's the fact of the matter?

We are confronted by a question.

What is the State of her Affairs?

Mental masturbation. At best, a game.

Questions, conundrums, puzzles, number games, word games... This afternoon I started a new game with G———, one in which we dig words out of words, a sort of Scrabble. How many can you? I began with the word endogamy. First clue?—a Spanish painter. Meanwhile, memory homing in, buzz

buzz, the doodlebugs were finding their nests. Buzz!!! Very like a whale? No, the rockets came only later, more like flying sharks. That was no game. Then, of course, wrath of God—The Bomb, which, evidently, brought enlightenment… illumination. Incandescence, & more such than any book ever has, quite possibly. The premise: if facts can be bombs, bombs are always facts. Tote 'em up in all their atomicity. Here we count our eggs, old Wallingham habits dying hard. But during the Blitz? We should have counted our bombs, block by blasted block.

—2 bombs, 1 unexploded (7 since February)

[Avril's Diary]

27 April. Where will it end, when stop—this trouble, between us and all around us?

And what is the cause, or who—as if there were any question. They were leaving him alone.

I can only think, only with her going, only with her gone, the Crinoline smoothed over and out of our existence, would we go back ourselves to that happier time when it was just the three two of us before she knocked him for a loop. He was satisfied. In the interregnum between his wives he was very happy, I thought. I made him happy. I was enough for him, or such was my thought. He doesn't need much.

And I? I? I never asked for much.

And now, when she is gone so often, even here where there is nowhere to go to, except the town so hard to reach down the rutted road, each rut another groan, I recall (the Road of Pain). She leaves, nonetheless, and gets her lifts from the old grinning Colonel, Mr. Obliging.

Strange! Ve-ry strange, if you ask me. Ric never does. Strange, though, thinks I, getting into the car so happily and driving off like a couple, as they do, it's enough to make one wonder.

Indeed she makes me wonder and wonder.

Dear Diary, I will confess, I used to follow her around before they got married singing to myself, like Mr. Pears—I wonder as I wander.

Me and me Cady, I was in disguise. Spies need a bit of crust, you know.

Wander, I did, out under the sky of London, which at that point was just beginning to drop bombs upon us. I saw things. Indeed, I saw, and what I didn't see spoke as loud as what I did.

What was going on up that narrow staircase on Woburn Place of a Sunday afternoon in June for two solid hours by the clock?

And what now, here, in Craighouse?

I wonder as I wander.

[Cedric's Diary]

1 May. History. Stamped—MINISTRY OF CULTURE—A book, or packet, rather, of loose papers & diagrams & official whatnot awaited me in Ardlussa when I arrived today, having arrived a few days ago, perhaps just as I was writing, I am being left alone for now… No address, just my name on it, Cedric O'Malley, c/o. The postmaster said that he thought of driving it up, which would have been preposterous. He seemed happy to see me, happier to have it out of his hands—as if it were a bomb? Or Candle Jack? <u>Die heiße Kartoffel</u>?

Later. Questions… I have been questioned, & questioned vigorously. I have been interrogated, tortured, even, to a degree, I who find pleasure in turning screws. Head spinning, I have been pulled down into the dark Ministerial depths from which, it is rumoured, so few ascend. But only one interrogation was particularly memorable.

After a number of shocks, unnerving but not especially painful, & not at all enlightening, surely, S——— told me that I was his favourite pupil.

—Favourite disciple, you mean. Your ephebe.

& then Aarronow—yes, I am giving his name—the bastard, uttered the following words.

—Yes, Cedric, that's it—that is why you have become such a distinct challenge to us, such a ripe target: it is your immense culture! You are Matthew Arnold… Arnold in jackboots. Ruskin in a solid-blue tunic. You are everything he was, you know everything he knew, or most of it, you are no classicist, are you, for all your Latin & Greek—& yet you are more. That is, you know more than he knew—for you know him, as the ghastly poet man said. You know your history.

—For my part, I replied, I'd like to get rid of the past twenty, thirty years & start over...

—Perhaps that could be arranged, someone said, who, I could not tell.

—But what about that book you wrote?

—Burn it, I said.

& then they started in on me—in earnest? No, a certain levity was in the air, & at one point I started laughing.

—Now we've got him!

—You don't have me. I don't so much shout as it is that the words break from me.

—But we've got hold of you. Murmured.

Minutes passed. More shocks. Then—

—Culture! Exclaimed.

By whom?

—Ja, when I hear the word culture—ha ha!!! When I hear the word culture, ja... I reach for my revolver!

It was Aarronow at his best.

—Hermann Goering.

Actually, that is incorrect. Though often attributed to Goering, it was originally the renegade Modernist Johst who said it, Hans Johst, or who wrote it. He should have said, Wenn ich Kultur höre... entsichere ich meinen Browning! Schlageter. Thiemann, rather. Close thy Goethe; open up with thy Browning! (I'm not referring to the poet.) But that's not as catching.

—Close thy Goethe; open thy bomb-bay doors! Such was my own contribution to the general merriment.

The shocks continued, that day & the next & the next... more annoying than anything, faintly comic. Still. Still, I felt that a line had been crossed.

& then they let me go.

2 *May*. Coldish, blowy etc.. Rough weather.

To work.

The packet did not enlighten; it contained little more than up-to-date plans for the auto-gyro or, more accurately, the heliocopter, the rotor craft with the capacity to hover that won out over my favourites, nostalgic me, the cyclo-gyro, on the one hand, which to my mind resembles a small paddle-wheel boat having taken flight, chopping its way through the air—ah, I can see it jerking past Dorothy at her window, hilarious—&, on the other hand, the ornithopter, which resembles a bird in flight, most especially a small raptor.

It is still not entirely clear to me why I, a writer, humanist, a so-called man of Culture, have been chosen to be personally involved in this project. Perhaps it is because at some level it is a social & aesthetic rather than a technical history that they want. In any event, it is indeed an interesting topic, the history of the machine, with special attention to the flying machine & to the helicopter in particular.

In addition to the cyclo-g I also prefer the gyro-rotor. But it too cannot hover, at least not for long; it starts to descend as soon as you slow & stop. & the ability to hover, these days, is everything, we have determined. We have decided. Really, ever since the Focke-Achgelis Fa 223, fuck the archangels... no cock-up, we're Screaming Eagles, after all, & we bombed them really rather well. & we kept that particular Focker more or less grounded in Laupheim. Yes, the Drache was dreck. That kite never flew. Thus Deutsche Physic: wings clipped close, even as the Russians... well, that's another story.

The ability to hover, which we now possess: I do not entirely welcome it. New abilities, facilities, faculties, capacities, enhanced capabilities, all these must be acquired, as a matter of course, & yet I fear them at times. With them comes new knowledge, certain knowledge, forbidden knowledge, perhaps, should such exist.

Should it? I am an intellectual. I should reject nothing, nothing—no ideas, no facts or truths, provided Reason be left free, &c.. It is the obscene? It must be seen. Hovering as we do. We shine the light in all the secret places, in every corner of the darkness. The darkness itself must be defeated. Incandescence & perseverance, it's all the same: these are the rules of our Enlightenment game:

Jack's alive & like as to live:

If he dies in your hand, you've a forfeit to give.

Candle bearers, & hoverers, we shall map the darkness itself. But if Jack dies out? Speaking of light boys, one recalls Pip's Thames-river beacon, an un-hooped cask upon a pole, weather-beaten, nearly defunct, & not a pretty thing if you look close, no prettier than the facts it brings to light, that, what was it—World of Pains and troubles. But our own totem is nothing so quaint nor so elaborate. It is a stark, naked bulb hanging from a kinked wire loop, a hot sort of ampersand, something you'd find in an interrogation room. But we must have faith. We are like as to live, & whilst we live, whilst we hover, our eyes, naked bulbs, will shine or glow. Wondrous, too, the dark places into which they may be dropped, hand over hand, those mystic caves of the Natural, those dim grottoes of the Human.

All so wordy, my poetry. Cannot we do with fewer, as the <u>Imagistes</u> declared. Inspired by T. S. Eliot & chums, Pound, for example, a self-appointed purifier of the dialect of the tribe, party linguists like A——— have been experimenting with simplifications & intensifications of the language. <u>Oldthinkers no bellyfeel EngSoc</u>. Those who think of the past & in its ways, those who think, at all, do not deeply feel in the ways proper to our new English socialism. All that in three portmanteaus. Succinct, efficient, & vivid. Is it not Imagism brought into everyday use? One can see the appeal. <u>They no bellyfeel</u> sure beats <u>they do not deeply feel</u>.

5 May. Filthy weather. C———'s had another bad day—lungs never worse. Breathing labored—work of breathing, I have heard it called, as if it were voluntary? As if it were not automatic, autonomic, as if one could choose to take a break, wipe down with an old rag, lay aside the pick-axe, not another handsturn, & have a seat next the road one works. Or walk off, just walk away, corkscrew, cross-country.

Enter Nature. Leave History behind.

Stop counting the days.

Beat a hasty, sylvan retreat, all breathing human passion far aside: a chilly enough pastoral, there, in that eternal day. Reminds me of Jura!—ironically—of that of which I need no reminder, it being the here & now from which memory indeed removes. Forlorn! I could swear that one of those quiet, still figures on the urn is waving to us… waving to C———, maybe! But he, like the others, is just holding his breath, which no one can do forever. Il faut manger? Il faut aspirer. As Nature bids, one must exhale, in the end—& then, in the end of the end, inhale. Snorting, sputtering, expectorating.

In the end, but there is no end. History. It carries on, the Great Race, world without end, amen. The Great Rut, rather—there I go again, my recusant past starting up & stirring trouble.

There is no Catholic like an English Catholic, especially when he's Irish.

Those figures on the urn—how many are <u>working</u>? Pick-axes, or even pens, in hand? What rugged road-jack, spade descending? So speaks a recusant of a different feather.

9 eggs. (237) Sold 12 for 9s.

[Avril's Diary]

7 May. Blowy, etc..

Things have come to a pass. After working in the side-garden all morning I came inside and saw it. There it sat on the mouldy mantel next to the matches, flagons and rotten oxen tooth, nakedly, flagrantly. Tellingly. The crystal-glass globe.

Oh. What crystal-glass globe, you ask?

On my brother's desk have been sitting a number of small things, objects d'art, paperweights, souvenirs, mementoes and whatnot that he calls his fetiches. One is a tiny ivory carving of an elephant that was given him by the villagers, he says, when he was a policeman in Burma. Another, also a carving but of wood, is a crucifix on which hangs a bony Jesus sporting a deeply furrowed brow and beard. This, yes, though here is a man who marries one Jew and adopts another. He has a colourful number of taws, a yo-yo, a filthy yellow Oxtooth that stinks to high heaven (he has always had a weak nose), and, most impressive of all, a lead-glass paperweight globe about the size of a lawn bowl but much heavier with a tiny coral figure of exquisite shape suspended at the centre, my gift to him, and to Caroline, too, I suppose, from many months ago. She helped me pick it out.

For months now—until this very morning—this globe has been sitting on his desk. Perhaps it was as if in a kind of irony, its being a memento, now, having joined the ranks of the old souvenirs. I used to see it as a token of his life with her. It was a symbol. He had a rare feeling for her. I respected it. Precious was it, rare, a touch exotic, I thought. That's why the glass coral. Precious, was their feeling—once we got here, leaving all that Woburn business behind. I say "their"—Caroline was a part of it. I'll give her that.

I will be fair to her.

According to the old man in the junk-shop, the little pink coral was fetched from the South Seas. It was brilliant. A poem:

In silent shallows
Amidst the sleepy shadows,
Faintly blushed a pure stone.

Its bone-whiteness, soft to behold and touched with rose, was indeed I thought a joy forever. Perhaps our tidal regions— for example, Jura? I often forget that I live here and not where I really live. Perhaps these, too, hold hidden equivalent wonders in their pools. But I wouldn't know. Found it, I did, bought it, gave it away. My own desk I keep clear of intriguing items.

Cedric rises early, even before I, and starts breakfast, smoking cigarettes in the kitchen, smiling, saying— a man needs an occupation. He is the most cheerful of early morning men. Out of their bed at first light, smoking, making coffee, smoking, coughing, smoking, and often he is the last one to go to bed at night. We hear him closing the kitchen window; the handle squeaks badly as it turns and the house is small, not much more than a cottage, really. In the meanwhile, he works, so to speak. Most of his time not spent writing, gardening, building something pointless, a box, for example, for some unforeseeable purpose, doing the chores, or just smoking, he spends on Lady C's treatments or in instructing or just playing about with Gillian. (He plays on the floor as if just another child.)

I don't expect much.

He was kind last spring when I returned from Lochgilphead after the shoulder. I had had to be brought to hospital on the mainland.

I will tell the story of the shoulder.

I had been hoeing and tried to move the heavier barrow, which was full up with dirt and weeds and whatnot, and my shoulder just seemed to give way—I had pulled my arm out of socket. Childbirth is the worst, they say, but this was keen enough. He heard me yell, I suppose. He came outside toting the big book he was reading. I pulled my sweater and blouse down to show him. It was a shiny knob that had sprung up, a sort of bulb.

Aye! said he, his specs sliding down the bridge of his nose. Lady C was still asleep. Was Dobbs about? He was not. After he examined me for just a moment he shook his head in his way and suggested that we get in the car. I found I could walk without much pain if I held my arm against my blouse at a right angle. Sitting was different. The gravel and mud road to the Rees's place was full of bumps. Rees having decamped, of course, some months earlier, it is the abode of a returned RAF Colonel of doubtful politics, Ric thinks, but obviously no Blimp. The Colonel and Ric conferred. Barnhill never showed such green, I thought. I was happy to be out of the car. It was uncomfortable, though. Ric spoke of popping it back in, right, all one needs to do is to pull it up sharply, if one can summon enough sharpness. Ric could not. He tried, though. I won't tell what that was like. He was too ginger. He summoned dullness, it seemed to me. The Colonel for his part kept bringing up the doctor in Craighouse. We would take his car, which miraculously always seems to be full of petrol. Twenty-five miles.

The drive to Craighouse was little short of torture, I suppose. I have never been tortured. We met Mr. Dobbs on the road, Dobbs stumping along after his young son. They jumped in. Dobbs, rather, cantilevered in. The Colonel drove very slowly, and that seemed to make it worse, since with every little rut, down we slipped, sharply—the road could summon it—then up, sliding sideways, then sharply down again, like a boat caught in rough water. It quickly became the boy's mission to sit next to me to brace me with Dobbs sitting on the other side. The kind little fellow was crying a little. I must have been a sight, and a sound, too, for I was breathing heavily and I could not stop certain little noises which would come out of my mouth now and then and which I myself did not recognize (—Who said that? I was thinking) and which seemed to disturb the boy and some of which made the Colonel turn his head round to look at me. I would nod to him—a bit impatiently, I fear—Eyes in front! I wanted to say. Your mission is to drive. I heard the Colonel turning back swear quietly once or twice.

Then, of course, we had the usual puncture. I am going on at such length that now I am feeling a bit silly. In ten minutes time, tick tock, Dobbs had it fixed & we were back on Torture Road, if road it may be called that roadway had none, it having no flat stretches at all but being altogether a bloody tract pocked and pitted with ditches, wrinkles, ruts & rocks. With no idea to do so I found myself exploring a wrinkle of a different sort. I started talking to the boy, who has been left in the soup. His mother is dead. He told me about how they used to go into nature as he put it and hike and fish and sometimes camp. There were no Scouts on Jura and his mother Mrs. Dobbs, Mr. Dobbs being busy with the farm, would get into shorts and take him out in the boat. They'd fish in a little punt jobbed at a large farmhouse near the open country in which they'd walk, the hares keeping an eye on them. Evidently Mrs. Dobbs was keen—quite the out-of-doors-woman. I was in the boat with Mrs. Dobbs and her little boy. Or I was Mrs. Dobbs with her little boy, rowing a little and pausing to let the boat drift a little, the sun shimmering on the lake bright enough to make a blind man see... And for a moment, I recall, amidst all that imagined brightness I was blind. It may have been with hurt. Either way, I enjoyed spending just a little time with Mrs. Dobbs and with the little boy in the little boat. Which reminds me that someone needs to teach Gillian how to swim, though she wades in well enough. Twenty-two miles, and another puncture, and we arrived, putting paid to Mrs. Dobbs. The Colonel had made a good job of it, really. I baked him an apple pie that next Sunday.

By then it was showing a shiny greenish-brown knob on my shoulder, a sort of knot growing on me as on a tree or a flower bulb about to bloom. I was becoming one with nature. The fattish doctor took one look and said I needed to be in hospital couldn't treat it needed a physician with a bone and joint specialism. Lochgilphead, then; we had to cross six miles of rough sea. We did, but at least there were no annoying launches in sight, thank God—for all the motor's droning on and on, it was a fat lot better than that Godforsaken road. Lochgilphead was another several miles from the landing but on a good road by hired lorry, it was relocated by the two doctors, and we re-crossed by the northerly route, the twelve miles and two and one-half hours of which I slept, my head on the little boy's little lap. Child, with Madonna, without Donor.

Ric came out and took my hand and helped me into the cottage stooping to make tea for us and for Gillian. They had been playing Parcheesi.

CC we could hear busy on the typewriter—tick tack, tack. Ticky tack. Ticky tack tack.

Tick tock.

[Cedric's Diary]

[Undated] Enter Nature?

I had learned to enjoy tools & the stable tables which may be built with them & small machines which may be unscrewed & taken apart. But ever so long as I remain alive I shall continue to love the surface of the earth, & its residents, its solid things, rocks stones trees birds. Things. Indeed my comfort now is in such things which cannot be unscrewed. I rely upon them—build upon them. But not facts...

Unwisely, I know. For they can be destroyed, as we have found, these Things that we did not think could be destroyed. Our screw-driven bombs could not touch them, we thought. In the Great War it seemed we could mar them only so far. The archives are full of accounts of blackbirds building in the nooks & crooks of machine gun nests & of thrushes, blackcaps, crested larks, & even nightingales singing in Niemandsland during the worst of the shelling. Now, however, when they may be atomized alongside everything else, well...

What's left us, then?

Things. Things still exist. Atoms are things.

And, well, there is always—for such as C———, at any rate—Corryvreckan, which she hears when I cannot & which she fears as I do not & which appears to haunt her day after day, even if she still cannot spell it. It's a holdover from that misadventure in the boat when she was a teen.

En route to Glengarrisdale this afternoon, it being a fine hot day, little wind, thought we would visit Corryvreckan again but not get too close due to its not being slack water, the only time that one should go anywhere near it.

C——— of course refused my invitation. Hearing it is enough for her, she says.

Oh, when the sea is not slack, or silent, when the sea is calling, that is when Corryvreckan finds its voice. Turning & turning around & about it calls to us,

—Turn, Oh, turn the wheel...

The 'Vreckan beckons. Far off, ten miles or more, Corryvreckan is but a whisper in the ear when the wind dies, its currents polishing the stones of the deep. It has a voice you can just make out so long as you are not listening for it. But as you approach it starts to sort of murmur, first, then to growl, & then howl, louder & louder, promising to swallow you whole & grind you up bones & all.

That's the myth, at any rate.

Skimming along, we leave Barnhill's green slopes hugging the coast as it bends northwestward & enters the Gulf of Corryvreckan just past Maol Eilean on the portside rounding to Carraig Mhor. We have been careful to avoid Ruadh Sgeir on the starboard, a considerable hazard for those crossing from the mainland too far north. Be careful, now, game ones, steer beyond the safe-seeming shore, or you will find yourself twisting in the eddies near Eilean Beag or, beyond that, the larger, even scarier eddy near Eilean Mhor. But steer too far away northward so as to leave Jura & approach Scarba &, should you not be caught in the water-chute of the Great Race & borne away, you may be filled with greater yet regrets, for in a flash, unless you have wings, unless you can fly—in a flash you could find yourself pulled into the famed whirlpool itself, Corryvreckan, with its tall whorl of water, its eternal, often two-storey wave, which coils & grinds, flailing, threshing, shucking away proud selves & scathing souls. The Hag, as the locals call it, sits in state, brooking not any human wish or will. Indeed, she is blind. They tell of a sailor whom I shall call Infelicidas whose fate it was to fall into her maw fully clothed & was spat out a mile downstream it would seem having been dragged along the rocky bottom that lies nearly one thousand feet beneath the watery floor because he was no longer recognizable, not as a person, not even as anything human, but just as a Thing, once living, now become raw substance. Infelicidas, indeed... They never found his clothes, & when they buried him or, should I say it, in the garden flower-bedecked?— beyond the reach of dogs, one hopes—there was but a headless trunk with stumps of limbs, scourged, boiled beyond color. Hence the other pet name, which is a partial translation: The Cauldron.

For all such horror, some have swum the Gulf during the slack, the one-legged Dobbs, for instance, reportedly (remarkably), amongst them, having contrived to skirt the Hag & avoid those of her rivals who—C——— has learned from the locals— range more freely in the Gulf, the Sea Kelpies.

As the locals have it, the Kelpies are the Blue Mermen who have wandered beyond the region's lochs & ponds to tend the Argyll depths. They are said to fear but one thing, the light, which kills them, evidently. They sleep, C—— has been told, & evidently she believes it, in the deepest caves & grottoes, & as night falls they rise up urgent hosts who seldom take no for an answer. It is said that the Sea Kelpies of the outer islands never break the silence of the seas—none of the neighing noise, the clip-clop of misty hooves that you will hear inland as their river brethren claim all those who would escape their own dark histories. (The poetry here is C——'s, mind you.) In the Hebrides, well, the only sound you will hear is of those inadvertent guests, who have been arrested & made to ride upon their equine backs & who may take a deep breath & utter a loud, long shriek or squeal, forever shattering the peace of all who hear them, but scream once & once only. & yet it may be a squeal of delight, for the Kelpies are said to show one things—& what things! (Things.) The treasures of the sea, coral, pearl, & gold, all that is rich, all that is strange... & those who are suffered to climb the watery stairs, as some few are, escaping their sojourn with the Kelpies, are said to see a change in everything. They are enchained, enchanted, for life. What happens amongst the billows on the ocean bed is a thing that cannot un-happen, cannot be forgotten or dismissed, not if one lived for a thousand years...

Lor. I too have been had.

[Avril's Diary]

8 May. The Cline being occupied as usual this morning, the morning showing itself to be beautiful, I took Gillian out in the little boat.

Gillian is in many respects an unusual child of nine or ten years, I judge. She betrayed little interest in learning to row, taking the oars, admittedly rather heavy and clumsy, uncertainly and reluctantly, and sitting her turn in the business seat of the boat a bit surprisedly. Around her aunt, she keeps her own counsel. I have invited her to call me by my Christian name but she chooses to address me as Aunt, as if Aunt were itself a proper name and my name were Aunt instead of... what it is.

I don't mind, of course; I believe her to have a tough row to hoe, growing up not in the town as I grew up but in this remote rustic place amongst adults, mostly, so rarely meeting girls her own age—or boys, for that matter. She does have the

Dobbs boy, but he's only seven or so. She is often alone and has taken up a precious little diary of her own, which she, too, hides. Cute. Ric and Caroline (the latter half-heartedly) have undertaken her education, and of course I too pitch in when I can. Truly, when all is said, I think, even if G (as Ric sometimes calls her) is not precisely my own personal project, still I believe that I do more to bring enlightenment to her than does her beloved Caroline. Her mother, who is afraid of the water. I'll be the one to teach her to swim.

Little wonder that, when I can, I invite her to help out or to come along on the small adventures possible in so retired a life as we lead—and in times like these. Happily, she has gained confidence amongst the hens and now will often be the one to collect the eggs. The Cline helps her, sometimes. The blind leading the blind!

7, by the way, this am. (?) Tick tock!

Also by the way: though I am now defying my own promise to myself not to commit so trivial an episode to the page, I find myself wishing to note in passing how Caroline after all is still capable of surprising me. Whilst we were still in the boat, G at the oars flailing, I happened to pick up the field glasses and begin looking about as one does only to find myself inevitably drawn back to the domestic side of things and staring at the cottage, from that distance quite quaint in appearance, and seeking signs of Lady C's having bestirred herself out of doors on her brief morning saunter. We know one another's routines, you see! Though the considerable distance was not closed by the fairly low-power glasses, still, sure as I am sitting here now or was sitting in that boat at the time I saw her come out of the side-door and sidle over to Ric, who was raking out a disused carrot and cucumber bed, and place her bare hand on his bare forearm for a moment as, rather slowly, he stood up straight. That was all. We are not a demonstrative people. But it was not Ric, I saw, Ric being so much taller than Caroline and the rest of us, but somebody else, someone about her own height or even a little shorter.

[Cedric's Diary]

10 May. Late Afternoon. Dirty day. Steady brown rain, as if a tap had been turned & then forgotten. Not at all warm. Spotted & killed a small grey rabbit in the garden. C―――― came home with G———, dropped her in my lap so to speak—Ric, she's your very own! cough—even as I sat at the typewriter, & went to lie down. I found the box of dry goods squatting outside on the walk. We both of us have never been more fatigued, she worse than I, since most of the day I sit & type & think, in that order, as best I can, whilst she… Keeps Calm & Carries On.

I will not burden these pages with an account of my conjugal life. Nor do I trust the future to which they are addressed to understand the complexities of a political life that has become but an instance of The Precarious. I do what I can. My ambition is to remain philosophical even in the face of a species of doom both imminent & unprecedented. Since The Bomb fell, the first of them, all has changed; irony has died. We are in the world of the grim. We are in the world of the dead. Indeed, we are the dead. I said so this morning & evidently was overheard by C———, who came in smiling & said,

—We are the dead? Hardly…

Our days I now regard as conspicuously numbered, our calendars, our books of days, have become books of tags destined to hang pendant from human toes. Pure little Tessie had no idea. It's just a matter of time, tick tock. We are the dead. No, worse, we are the dying—like the light. We are the last men, men & women, on earth. There are books no one wishes to burn. You burn them, & after brief ironic brightness it's a kind of death. & then, there are the other books, ones darkly diminishing daily. Surprise, then, that I continue to type. & to think, somewhat, to behave as if I felt what I do not, that we can save our voices & minds & bodies even, that we can dodge the plague clouds rising out of Antwerp with its rank fens, the estuaries of Brussels, Rotterdam, other minor cities of Europe, the steppes of Eurasia, each of which—each to his own—will have its own bomb, each blown sky-high to an appropriate heaven.

We've a new new rumour. & yes, we hear all the rumours, even up here; rumour is in the air we breathe, or it is itself that air, the very element in which we swim or splash about, like drowning angels—or eagles—weighed down by our wings. Like panicky swimmers fallen fully clothed & shod into the liquid sphere, we slosh around: old news & new, or no news, gossip, rumours signs signals semaphore radiolocation, & we suffer the occasional blinding shock, as if there were electric waves in the water as in the air &, when we get our heads above water, a crackling noise imperfectly heard (static we now call it), fearfully interpreted, our bearings entirely lost. The new rumour we've been told is that we have a Bomb coming for us here, even here, in the green north to which I first moved many months ago fearful of a full-on atomic war. From the small, relatively, but nonetheless hot Suns of Men I flew... to ground, an inverse Icarus. & what ground it is, this Zion, as I imagined—here, if anywhere, as I thought, it might be possible to see as a whole, in time & beyond, to soar above all partial views, etc., etc., etc.. I should have thought, merely to live on, however partially, merely to hang on, day after day, week after week, merely to be undead.

Fat chance.

Dobbin—excuse me, Gurth—has a target on his broad back, or rather sitting squarely on his crown. Not that he knows it. & besides, Gurth will survive, brass collar & all, perhaps by turning Morlock. Gunther, too, of those among us, that is, will make it. Gunther's a survivor. Aarronow? Fat chance.

Gurth, Gunther, & the Conquerer Rat, then—they will live on, & the flies, & the beetles & weeds. The rest? Hunted down & out. The Book of Nature, its prettiest pages turned to ash.

Not a pretty page, that large, perhaps flame-proof ad-poster looming over Camden Town when I used to walk its streets. Arresting & instructive, it was an old one from the days of unfettered Capitalism, perhaps from before the War. Winston it became, before becoming his replacements, The Brothers, aka The Big Three, aka The Tripod, who shall remain nameless in these un-pretty pages so as to provide however implausible plausible deniability. I guess I shall have to burn this one, then, this very page in my Book of Culture! But will I? That large, inflammable poster was to this day one of the largest I've ever seen, which makes it the more surprising that it took so long for it to be papered over. It was a piece of publicity, of course, Bovex—Bovex, mug in hand, smiling his empty smile, the smile riding on a panic. Ah! How does it go? Panic & emptiness, panic & emptiness, the ramparts of the world might fall!

No, they do not fall for such a trifle, nor do the doors of heaven burst open, emitting light. It was merely Bovex, bother him, smiling out of a common human fear & dread, his pupils pinpoints, the whites of the eyes overlarge & yet still giving the impression of, in the hackneyed phrase, beadiness, & his slack smile over rubbery skin beneath a kind of patent-leather hairpiece, as it seemed. Bother Bovex, a piece of publicity, was also ersatz, a piece of artifice, conspicuous, which was the oddest thing—that they'd not have tried to make him look realer. Nevertheless, & maybe this is the solution to the conundrum, he seemed to represent a truth, a human truth. This presumes that the artist was a secret wag rather than a committed Capitalist. Either way, staring at bloody Latex Bovex in the dusty, littered streets of windswept Camden Town I found myself listening, listening, hearkening to the sound of what many of us, I think, expected, even ardently desired, even back in the mid-30s, the not un-pleasing drone of a fleet of bombers, German or Russian, what's the difference, buzz buzzzzzzzz, very like a gaggle of geese, a crack formation filling up the sky... & our empty souls...

The sound of planes, flying in squadron: back then very few of us knew that sound but were more familiar with the sound of a single wing. Flying at liberty, cruising along in its individuality, it made a sound that would soon enough come to be almost quaint. I am speaking of the sound of a lone plane lingering above as it flies from one horizon to the other, tracing ampersands as it goes. The sound? The voice, rather: you remember, the plane itself flying beyond human sight, with even the eagle-eyed, eagle-souled hearkening hard to it—incipient wing-buds stirring—being unable to pick it out, the moaning is drawn out slowly across the sky, tight for a time, tightening further, then loosening, growing slack, uncertain, the plane backtracking, seemingly, then tightening again but never breaking, & lowering, gradually, in its mournful Siren's course some few chords, drawing down, & down, & down, & finally dissipating to leave a special silence that one can hear, almost, as if seeing silence for the first time, a presence that one can almost touch in its cool, crystalline roundness. I have found these episodes enrapturing ever since I was a little boy. Whenever a plane was overhead, whatever else I was doing, even in the heat of play, I would stop & listen.

A voice... Later, late in the summer of '45 walking on the beach out west, having made what I call my first retreat, I was staring into the impossibly pure beauty of the bright blue & saw a speck, a tiny spot in the sky, a seabird, I thought, or an eagle, approaching, which grew. Rapidly it became something else, larger. & it spoke—cooooommmmmmmm—out of the blue. A voice! A voice I remember—

A voice so thrillin ne'er was heard—
In Ipril from the Cuckoo bird—
Brikin' the silence of the seas—
Beyond the furthest 'Ebrides...

—to quote a Cockney consumptive pale & wasted young man—probably dead now—with a beautiful voice with whom I spent a memorably sleepless night in a flea- & rat-ridden Southwark lodging house for 6p. a few years before the war. Yet somehow I didn't catch it, & still have not, despite it all, the colorful eruptive treatments, the close quarters, the shared bed.

But I become distracted. Pace, memory. It—*it*, that other harbinger, was no Gannet, nor any sea-bird or sea-eagle I have ever seen before. It turned out to be a shiny, odd-looking machine of a sort heretofore unknown to me flying very low & very fast—& then it passed directly overhead, too close, as if two feet above us, the sonic boom, as we soon learned to call it, putting cracks in the pale-blue sky—boooooooooom, ba-boom, ba-boom, the windows fretting in their frames... Yes indeed,— thrillin'. It was my first jet.

My first bomb... such rain in Spain falling mainly from a plane—with apologies to Windy Hill, errrr. Sounds like A———. Such a heavy rain we had, there, on that windy hill-side just outside Madrid in '36. Pa-poummm...... pa-pa-pa-poummm. The bombs fell & fell, all night long, & there was no place to hide, no cover, no trees, not much of a trench, more like I imagine wrinkles in the hill side of tall grass. It was Cuckoo. & the bombs of Madrid are falling still in dreams in which they have sprouted wings & seek me out, flapping, hovering above as I try going to ground... & it is always I, alone, breathless & sprawling on the billowing hillside outside Madrid in the lingering night.

In the last, past war, not that it is truly past, the first fatal bomb that fell on the British Isles did not fall upon that mouldy old layer-cake St. Brides, thank God, I suppose, as if to blow marriage itself sky-high. Certainly it did not fall on Bridewell, which was already gone, anyway. Rather, it fell on some little cottage in the 'Brides, this cool haven from History, this seeming sanctuary from strife, of all places. It killed not a bride of any sort but a lone woman, reportedly, & mysteriously, who'd hired an island to escape war & man: The Woman who Loved Islands. I suppose I am the Man Who Does So. Was it a German bomber wildly off course? Or was it the RAF, for chrissakes, wildly off course—or indeed not wildly off course, which would signal the beginning of something, something quite unprecedented if always in the run-up to wars suspected? That was the rumour—good, if true. Of course, it may have been heaven-sent, the bombs falling like some new, diabolical manna to some new, diabolical Jews, Freethinkers. You might try to catch… on your tongue, like kids after snowflakes.

Either way, why drop a bomb on Ipril—on Avril! I almost wrote. What good or even what bad will it do? Think of all the cost & the pain. Think of the eagle, too, & of that Arctic tern I spotted a few days ago… but also the sweet inland birds. Why bomb spotted ducks & geese, ducklings & goslings swimming beside their mothers in pea-green pools amidst the pied beauty of the rushes? Those sunny, still ponds, abode of whispers, where the golden lilies are afloat, & all the iridescence of the dragon-fly—who would plant a missile in the heart of the rising sun, & the bluest September sky, & the quiet mind of human-kind? Is not it because we humans, well, we don't want to be just a flash in the lochk-pan? We want more than human history, a wing'd hour or two, we want to own the very weather, the seasons, the light, the law, to make time, itself, that famous Aeonian rhythm, pulse to our pulse, step to our tune? We want to own things… Things.

The Bomb, which blinds, as we have found, we dropped to see if we could see Things better by its light.

[Avril's Diary]

[Undated] That bitch. Bitch. Too upset to write right now. More later.

[Cedric's Diary]

11 May. This morning the wind died away & I who never hear it, I heard the Hag moaning, not so far off, it seemed… & then the wind blew up again & I remembered Manderley, by the sea:

the sheer cliffs & the dead bitch in a schooner, with child. Madonna, Dreadful, Without Donor, who stands cliff-side, beetling o'er... No, rather more like Mauberley, in my case, I dare say, Mauberley adrift oar-less amongst his scattered Moluccas—or Maybereley, not by the sea, but by the gasworks, where it was a hard fight to find a window pane that was not cracked & where I always felt, what, breathless, touched, light-headed. Little wonder: when the noises of the city died down for a second or two you could hear gas streaming out... Ah, Memory. The things you remember.

I certainly remember those Maybereley, neighbourly days, the dark days of the Great Killer Fog, as the rags had it. Darkness at noon, indeed; K———'s title was astonishingly apt. You couldn't see the lighted electric streetlamps but only a glowing bulb staring out of the small cloud above your head. C——— was a sufferer, as is clear from her continued discomfort, almost amounting to Chronic Lung Disease. The Great Killer Fog descended, & she did, too, by all accounts, suffering & enjoying a descent, head down, heels up, so that the beating could begin. In these latter days I have become quite proficient. I think they called it Chest Physiotherapy, this attempt to clear the airways of all grit & smut drawn down deep to the twisting paths & labyrinthine chambers of the brachia, all that sooty heat & dust having settled in solution & become our medium, a composition commandeering as vehicle & corrupting our famous London fog. It was a sort of plague... in certain respects worse than The Bomb itself. I think it killed more.

A continental plague wind, an East Wind, blows in, invades, driving quiet lonely Jew birds dark birds & other sad birds before it. The lonely Eagle flies above.

No, truth be told, we brewed up this storm cloud for ourselves. Ruskin was right. & Dickens? Struck the keynote. It was spontaneous, was this our combustion, bred in the vicious body politic itself, this & no other. We are against ourselves.

But why bother to document such obvious, old, such Victorian-age truths, why tap them out on the typewriter—why keep ringing that little bell?

Truth so often is the unimaginable. Therefore, it must be imagined. So too with the imaginable. Thus our Enlightenment creed.

6 eggs. (243)

[Avril's Diary]

13 May. Gillian has just rushed in and, not seeing me, grabbed up the old pair of field glasses and rushed out again. Be my guest! I want to say.

Looking for...? A rare bird, perhaps.

Mr. Dobbs is working in the garden.

Evidently even I, ol' Avril, have an imagination.

Ric says William Dobbs is doubly bereaved. (I'd say one-fourth—no, two-fifths. I'm a countrywoman, mind.) He is missing one-half of a limb, a lower left leg, and all his better half, a whole wife. It's a maths problem, evidently. Consoling him has become their righteous cottage industry. Ric, even, finds in the sad-fated man—as he calls him—a sort of brother. And Caroline, Her Nibs herself, often enough makes little noises of sympathy. It is the presence of the young son, I believe.

I myself have developed comradeship with William Dobbs, what you might call personal relations.

William Dobbs is a great worker. I too pride myself, in moments of vanity the diary is prompting again and again but which I hope and trust that it will in the end help me to correct, on my work. William Dobbs and I often work alone together at length, spreading lime and fertilizer, seeding—casting seeds about like reckless bombardiers, weeding, tilling, picking, culling and finally collecting. We do not write, you see. We are the manual squad on the farm—the menials, we.

She, CC, The Cline, Lady C—a name which, I am certain, brought a faint smile to Ric's lips the one time I allowed myself to utter it in his presence—she, Caroline, née Pretzel, The Jew Wife, on the other hand, is a puzzle. Unlike my brother, and Gillian, too, I have never particularly enjoyed puzzles. I have very little to do with her. There is a Caroline conundrum. But I don't give a damn. She is what Ric calls, after some one of those absurd Victorian sages of his—Thought Worker or is it Mind Worker. (She's a Gastarbeiter, if you ask me.) That would make of me a Body Worker or, if you like, Hand Worker. Oh, Mother Mary. I'm a handywoman. She's not. She's a writer, of course, a Writer, and she's a woman.

I myself have never thought of going in for a Writer, though I do believe that I have always loved books. Ric has made of me at times his right arm, for all my bad shoulder, or did do so & & & not any longer. Howsoever, evidently Miss P. was quite an accomplished propagandist before she joined us. Evidently she is now writing some horrid book or other of her own. But I know only her domestic side, which often puzzles, the manner in which she conducts herself and how she thinks— Pretzel Logic, I call it! Sometimes she's quite rigorous. Then she's soft-headed, and no bridge between the two.

Our cottage is a mice haven. No rats, thank Jesus, but many, many mice live in our walls, & evidently they love it there. They always make me think of those cartoons in which electrical devices of sorts are run by rodents & little birds and other beasts who do the work grumpily but reliably & invisibly behind the walls or within the cabinets or the housing of the wireless. Mice, we have—just no electricity! These mice come out at night & have the run of the place. The old cat Harley is useless, & the traps we set kill only a very few. It's hopeless. Those we catch, even, are sometimes spared to hobble away to irritate us again another day. Gillian especially has a hard time killing mice. But Caroline. Caroline! It has gotten so that she, too, cannot bear to see a mouse killed & will leave the room. She's no countrywoman, this Woman—ha!—of No Country, such as I have endeavored to become in all these months living here in the very heart of Argyll.

Well. A few months ago we were listening to the wireless the evening EBC broadcast & were shocked to hear that the socialist Heseltine had been tracked down & shot in a back street of Paris, evidently the victim of a carefully planned assassination. No one knew that he was in France or even that he had fled the country. But now, should the news be trusted, he was dead.

—Finally they got the right fellow, I heard Ric mutter, & Caroline, even softhearted, semi-pacifist Caroline, evidently assented to the premise that this was good news.

It was a little like the death of Balbo in '40, which as I recall— keenly—brought a lightness of heart to all assembled at Ric's place at Mortimer Crescent. We were bombed out of there not long thereafter. A few guests arriving for tea had seen the posters; I recall that Cyril Connolly, who would soon introduce Ric to Caroline, was amongst them. Why did not HE marry her, for God's sake? The mood was no less than festive. Evidently Generalissimo Balbo whom I had been told was one of the good fascists, had been so polite as to have taken some African chieftain or other up very high in the sky in his aeroplane—and shown him the door. This was indeed one of the last evenings before the advent of Ric's Caroline era, as I call it (his life may be broken down according to his romances, dalliances, and marriages, not that he's much of a Lady's gent for all his fancying himself such). I was pouring out tea but was very soon asked to switch to other libations. Late in the evening that horrid little Mr. Rutherford—no, not THE horrid Rutherford—began paying his compliments and, yes, I will write it out, making his advances, unwanted and not unreproved.

I hate intellectual men. Most of 'em.

Not that the death of the renegade Heseltine had Caroline leaping up and down for joy, CC's no leaper, or even Ric, but a quiet good cheer descended upon the cottage. Little wonder, I suppose, the reaction when later in the evening we found a mouse which had slipped down into the sink and could not get up the sides. Caroline abetted by Ric in a good humour took great pains to fashion a sort of staircase out of soapboxes, matchboxes, sponges, &c., by which it could climb out, but by this time it was so terrified that it fled under the lead strip at the edge of the sink and would not come out, even when we left it alone for half an hour or so. Gillian, that mouse, tried to tempt it with a small piece of cheese. Hoping, finally, to end the nonsense and flush it out, I thought to turn the knob on the tap for a moment; out dropped the cool water in that classic column and began eddying down the drain. Evidently, however, Caroline was quite uncomfortable with this procedure. Without a word her hand shot forward and stopped the water. Ric was just smiling at me, wanly, I think is the proper word for that smile. In the end Caroline & Gillian gently took up the mouse—with her fingers! horrors!—and let it go outside. Whence it was a good bet that it would return that very night to run across our beds whilst we tried to sleep!

This episode of Heseltine and the mouse is the sort of thing that does not matter. Yet it was telling. Ric once spoke of sympathy's being turned on and off as if it were a tap. Maybe it is the same with hatred.

[Cedric's Diary]

[Undated] A girl is walking down a path in the woods.

(So I am told—she had the dream again, as I am informed. I press for details.)

A young woman, rather, is walking down a path in the woods. This time, anyhow, she is clearly a young woman. She is not by any means, then, G———, & that is a good thing, for it is reported that she is without clothing as evidently she is without shame.

Clearly, she is she.

& she is lost. It is late; the sky is losing light. It is quiet. She can smell rain.

As if sleepwalking, as if instinct with knowledge that that is the way, she wanders off the endless path. Instinct, eh? Impulse, rather?

The trees thicken, columnar trunks in array, their branches intertwined like a palisade of pleated fingers. The sky darkens. She can see nothing & hear less, but she feels that she must be about to climb a mountain.

Suddenly she senses that she has come upon a kind of edifice and, sure enough, her progress is arrested, suddenly, by a stone wall.

Puzzled, she noses her way laterally against it, what proves a vast & dreary blank, infinitely extensive, forming a line with an arrow at its end pointing into eternity—a veritable ray. It is also impossibly adamant. She can hear her hands as, feeling for an opening, she comes upon a window, oblong, narrow, a sort of overgrown keyhole…

Out of the keyhole a keen light is cast from within…

She feels that it is dangerous but cannot help it; she puts the bulb of her eye to the hole…

Whereupon a bell starts ringing, & she wakes up.

& I wake up, too.

Though given to visions, I am no dreamer, après Madrid. Nor will I turn interpreter of dreams. I share the dream, then, because I should, someone, however thoughtlessly, having shared it with me.

[Avril's Diary]

* *May.* She walks, yes. As do we all. After noon, yes, some close the door and retire to repose. We all do, this day or that. But even she likes to take walks into Nature.

She walks often, more often than not, not down paths in woods but into woods, just into the trees—looking for? Oh, birds, of course, we all watch the birds, all but I, who am too busy killing them for supper. What I would tell you is that she walks into the trees, on pathless ways, as if in a trance, as I should know. I follow her.

And today she walked into the trees again, and again I followed, at a distance, out of sight, sightless, she could not see me, and soon neither could I see her, for safety's sake keeping my distance. To get close enough to see would be getting close enough to be seen. But I could hear her, and it is as if I could, Holy Mary, <u>scent</u> her, that odd pong she has about her, hard to place, that some evidently find so fetching, and keep close.

We climbed the hill just like that, she leading me by the nose. She would take twenty steps, & stop. I would take twenty steps & stop.

There was a little wind, and it was a hot and bright day even in the woods—when I heard it, the murmuring, a cooing, as of doves, a tune of sorts, when the wind would die for a moment and I had stopped, she having stopped.

Looking for? She had found it, evidently, found Him.

Him.

Who? Not William, surely not, I am sure of it. But then who?

Though I have an idea, the Mystery abides, my mystery, & his, my brother's. The mystery of Lady C.

Lady C- - - .

[Cedric's Diary]

16 May. To hell with all this walking—fly, spread thy wings, Mind, & soar, gazing imperially far & broad...

Looking for?

Hover, then, flapping hard. There is no wind.

Or stroll about, earthbound, flaneur.

Stagger, rather—trip, sprawl & wallow, memorially. It's time. I may as well have it over with, the beginning, as it was. Of something... what?

Of a change, clearly, as of a geological theory, some fossil having turned up in the wrong stratum?

& how did I know, to begin with? Well, this last is easy. It was because I myself had never gone in for that sort of thing.

The pou-ooom echoing from the face of the Ministry, then, I headed home. Foreboding. Of such was I full-up.

The London sky at eve, the sky, abode of light, luminous, lovely, lonely... the sky spoke of the long bright days of a gone world, & I could hear bells, church bells they seemed, in the distance. Ah, the days that are no more. The sky itself had become a new place. Yes, we'd had our late 18th-century incendiary riots, our mobs of arsonists roaming the streets, freaking even William Blake. But this was different from the Gordon, if for no other reason than that the fire came from above & was, of course, foreign-born. The doves whispered above with German tongues, & were deeply resented. That the English have been perfectly happy to burn down their own city does not entail that they will permit others such a liberty.

Stopped in a pub on Goodge Street near the tube station, not one I'd ever been in before & occupied by older-looking working men, chiefly—hard to tell, sometimes, given how fast our working class ages—on their way home, evidently, but—like me—in no hurry. The conversation was lively & devoted principally to the races with some time reserved for the equally pressing matter of the lottery. There was no mention of the war—no recognition of what was happening that very day, as had been announced at noon, in North Africa. Tobruk had fallen.

The bells sounding on distantly, I found that I was holding my keys in my hand as I headed north & west, zigging, zagging, through quiet quite clean streets so far untouched by bombs & blasts &, it would seem, unaware that a war was going on, or unconcerned.

Stopped—was stopped—at the mouth of Baker St., which was far otherwise—was cordoned off due to a delayed-action bomb or two having dropped in alongside their more punctilious brethren. If the purpose were that of <u>unsettling</u>, Moriarty himself could not have devised a cleverer means. Small crowds of sightseers & more nondescript, disconsolate-looking people, residents, presumably, some of whom were now homeless, certainly, milled about with bundles & suitcases awaiting the All Clear which, clearly, was not coming anytime soon. A.R.P. men in black tin hats hurrying to & fro, smoke was amassing from unknown fires. I thought of my small cache of expensive books, a number of them gilt-edged. They had already begun to tidy the empty pavement grey, the late afternoon sun shining down on neatly swept-up piles of shattered glass & splinters of flint, brick & stone fragments, fierce obelisks like some Cubist mirror, crude, jagged, glittering in the heavy stench of escaping gas. Though such were a common sight in those days, it was still hard to look at them. It was as if the eye itself could be cut. Too keen.

My own flat was only, say 300 hundred yards away, of course, but it was impossible to get forrard—without wings. Getting home was like trying to find your way to the heart of a maze. Heading west & then north in hopes of finding an opening a few blocks along I met two pretty young women, <u>artful</u> perhaps, who stopped me & asked for directions.

—Sir, we have no earthly idea where we are...

Though they were nicely, indeed expensively dressed in clean clothes their faces & hands were filthily dirty & the shoes of one of them did not seem to fit. The other, plumpish & very dark, I suspected of being a Jewess.

There was even then much talk, murmuring, rather, something above whispering, about the Jews, whose numbers in Wallington—in Baldock, rather—had been observed to be increasing (by C———) & whom J——— declared to predominate among people sheltering in the Tubes. I doubted this but could never verify it, try as I might. I did examine crowds sheltering in Chancery Lane, Oxford Circus & Baker Street stations, where I found I think a higher percentage of Jews than one would normally expect to find in crowds of their respective sizes. But not <u>all</u> Jews, were these crowds; they sported Eastern Europeans, too, Poles, Romanians, Hungarians, Bulgarians, Vulgarians, Hittites, Sodomites, & so on. Few of us at the time of course had any notion of what was in the offing either in Germany or here at home—the Great Subtraction. At the time we suspected, many of us did, that the Jews in business circles would throw in with Hitler, incredibly, if given half the chance. What I did feel is that they would have preferred Hitler's kind of social system to our own, if it were not that he happened to kill them. Suffering Christ, they always seemed to flourish in the cracks, crevices & corners of the most repressive states, the constant in all political equations.

Not, mind you, that they hid or crept about. I will never forget the large, fearsome—fearful?—Jewish woman I saw fight her way off the train at Oxford Circus, a regular comic-paper cartoon of a Jewess landing blows on anyone who stood in her way. She has become, for me, an icon.

Returning to Baker Street, I found—wonders!—the ropes down & the crowd dispersing. But the smoke was still rising steadily at some spot beyond my line of vision & near, very near, where I figured my flat—or whatever was left of it—to be.

I was more than a block away when I saw it, what must have been a direct hit, more or less.

If they had been here—can you imagine, I am sure that I asked myself.

The front wall was blown away partially exposing a number of apartments, including our own, the bedroom now on display. The well-made bed of just that morning was still standing on all four legs &, as I would find, it was not much disturbed beyond the pillows having been blown off it & chunks of plaster & pieces of brick I suppose they were having found rest thereupon. The foyer door was still locked. I wanted to use my key, I recall. Insanely: I could have stepped through a blown-out window on the first floor into someone's parlour.

& the key doesn't fit & the bell doesn't ring,
But we all stand up for God save the King.

I say, someone's; I knew damn well whose; I passed him on the way in; he was the super, & he was squatting on the kerb whimpering. I didn't like him. I will confess. I once overheard him talking about me: that Irish bastard. Insanely his old red-faced wife was going after her blasted kitchen floor with the broom. He weeps; she sweeps.

Others stood about on the walk in that distinctive manner of the freshly dispossessed, a way of which I had no knowledge until the War.

The staircase proving sturdy, impromptu loopholes lighted the steps & provided glimpses of the street as I rounded the bend on each landing. Our fourth-floor hallway was littered with papers of various sorts, scraps & slivers of newsprint & magazines, but also blackened sheets still whole though blown from books, personal documents in pieces, piecemeal letters, bills, stubs, whatnot, much of my personal archive blasted from desks, shelves, & tables, & now confetti.

We no longer had a front door. Somehow this hurt most of all.

The front parlour was largely intact & the floor seemed solid, but the rest were slightly cantered & seemed ready to collapse at any moment.

The back & kitchen windows, all three of them, were missing, though fallen in rather than blasted out, oddly enough.

My desk was completely destroyed & my bookcases thrown down as if done very carefully by culture-hating hooligans. But many of the books, even some of the more expensive ones, seemed in decent condition.

We had been somewhat friendly with the people next door on four, an older couple—C———'s doing. She always thought it deeply wrong that people should live next to each other cheek by jowl for years & do little more than exchange greetings in passing, & she insisted that we have these Carruthers over for tea—which we did, & found them to be quite kind, garrulous, & unassuming. Carruthers himself I found notably obtuse.

I had heard noises coming from Carruthers's rooms as I passed by, & now Carruthers appeared in my doorway.

—Greetings, Ric, greetings on this sad day!

Carruthers had a large empty box in his hands.

—Oh, your precious books! Expensive, eh?

—Yes, I suppose so. But this place here now: uninhabitable?

—Absolutely, he said. She's gone, sir! Better fetch a crate & get cracking. There will be filching, you know, & then & then, you know, they'll come by to condemn her. We'll be shut out soon enough!

But he just stood there, & I felt I needed to ask the dreadfully obvious question.

—How's missus?

They had been out on a walk, miraculously. Many others had been away at work but it appeared that one invalided old man on the second floor had been killed.

—A sad day, Ric. The gaze was on me as if it were a clammy hand.

—Yes it is, Arthur.

Just then, I recall, the sirens started in again. Carruthers & I ignored them.

The next day I hired a wheelbarrow from Hastings down the road & managed to horse it up the front steps, wondering the while what I'd look like rolling it down Holborn full of books, my intellectual history, much of it, on a single wheel. Perhaps I'd be accused of looting. On the other hand, could they imagine, most of them, that anyone really cared so much about books so much as to pick them up from the ruined floor, what with the bombs falling. I spent every afternoon during the next week salvaging what I could, Homer, Ruskin, Defoe, Plato, Swift, Austen, Horace, Cicero, Quintilian, Milton, Shakespeare, Chaucer, Pope, it went on. I saved my several copies of the Bible, what ho, that original Jew book—wheeled to safety! It was symbolic.

Then, a few days later, I turned to the bedrooms & their closets & armoires.

C——— had brought most of her own & G———'s kits of clothes, but I was of course saving what I could of the small precise hoards of possessions they left behind, & thus I was especially avid in my attempts to rescue a prized collection of handbags, which had been blasted out of the bedroom closet & lay scattered across the room.

Now I have always had a feeling about handbags, pocketbooks, purses, clutches & the rest, & regretted that in English history men had never carried them, for all their satchels, dossiers, & abyssal deep capacious coat-pockets; they had remained an exclusively feminine accoutrement. But a wellmade cloth or leather or knit purse is a wonderful thing, I have always felt, & feel still, what with the small interior & often, as it would seem, extravagant, pointless pouches, idle & false flaps & buttons, the odour of the tanned leather, when leather, the artfully hung & sturdy straps of the better sort, & the rest. I cannot account for this affection. I used to give E——— purses of various ornate kinds as Christmas or birthday or St. Valentine's Day or Boxing Day gifts until, her closet replete with purses, ten or more of them, she gave me to understand that she had gotten enough of them, thank you kindly, that she'd never be able to use all the purses she'd already received, & that, at all events, very sorry, but could I please stop buying purses? I complied, though I did later come across a number of Edwardian- & even Victorian-era reticules in faded ecru that I could not resist purchasing & dusting off—they needed it— with the idea of starting a collection of these fascinating artefacts, which came into fashion with the new, sheerer styles of gown brought in by the Regency, & these I ended up giving to C———.

& these she liked. Even though we had never spoken of the matter, it is clear that she knew of my strange love for The Purse, whatever the purse—provided that it be well-designed & well-constructed, of course!—but especially the older cloth bags of historical interest with elaborate floral embroidery adorning their faces. We—she—owned five or six of them.

Well. Wonders, I found two of them under the bed, & they were in pretty good condition. Carruthers—Carruthers had finished with his own flat & was lending me a hand—Carruthers found one in a pile of old scarves, a minaudière it was, that I did not recognize. I did not recall purchasing it, though I may have.

—Charming, Ric, charming! Quite intricate stitching. Carruthers was aping, sweetly, my own encomiums. I don't think he gave a damn for intricacy.

He had sat down on our overturned, ruined sofa & was idly opening & closing the evidently unlocked snap of the purse & admiring the quality of the cloth interior—it was, of course, red silk—when over my shoulder I heard—What's this?

As if playing that new American game, show & tell, he was holding out a curious small oblong paper packet that would fit in the palm of your hand.

—I have no idea, I admitted, & turned back to the mess from which I was extricating a long chain-link necklace with a single pendant glass bead when it struck me, what it was. Precisely & undeniably.

I say struck; I should have said spun. For I had one of those reactions you read about. I had a turn. I felt exactly as if someone had sat me down in a desk chair & whirled me 'round, a dizzy feeling, you know. Or the world itself had eddied 'round me as I just stood there, shocked, stupid, sinking.

It was not mine.

The unenlightened Carruthers having left to join his wife, finally, I sought out the minaudière in question & could not at first find it. I even wondered for a moment if I'd imagined the whole unimaginable thing. But soon enough I saw that Carruthers had hung it presentably on the lead-crystal doorknob of the bedroom door, & he had placed the small packet in the inner pocket, the pocket, I suppose, in which he had found it.

Its outer wrapper removed, it was a simple figure-8 knocked sidelong, Infinity's totem in boiled latex. But a moment later it was Faraday's obscene miniature bowtie smiling tensely, its clownmouth reticent of two throwaway centuries of colonial tapping & industrial trial & error.

Sitting on my bed, I thought of the James novel: a trivial implement of the commonest domestic use, it is never named, though fortunes & families are founded upon it. It belonged to the abyss of things unimagined because impertinent.

Indeed, once released & relaxed, its pasteboard belt slipped off, Infinity became Omega, O, Zero, Zed. A mere loop.

But it would prove elastic, I will tell you. Late that night & in nights to come, billeted in a make-shift bed, billowing in & out of sleep, I played a sort of game. Each time I went under I would have it become not nothing but just another strange or silly thing.

A life-raft. Tiny men lost at sea are saved from drowning!

A Browder safety-ring, manned by twelve circumferent firemen all pulling from the centre. & little girls are saved, dropping from great heights. I thought of Triangle Shirt-Waist.

A small backyard pool, inflatable, rimmed with several inflatable horseheads colored blue, for little boys. & the boys, too, are saved...

A shield, smart & sleek. O, Achilles! My brother! My saviour! Where is thy sword?

Not a sword, but not a shield, either. A half-shell.

[Avril's Diary]

* *May.* Was upset today.

Blowy today, the sun out bright. On a walk now I always carry the glasses slung over my shoulder, the one that I call my interesting shoulder, which is still a bit bulged, knobby—much as a hunter might sling his gun, or as a soldier.

Having walked down to the water this morning, I was idly surveying the trees above the cottage looking for starlings, crows, other birds, swallows. I have become something of a birdwoman. I have come to love the air.

But then my eye was as it were pricked by a pinpoint of light. I could not find the spot for a few minutes but found it finally some distance from the cottage high on the hill to the south. It would flash out now and then. It would glitter keenly for an instant, practically blinding me, having I suppose caught the sun full-on and relayed it to me.

I saw that it was not fixed in one place; its location was shifting; it was slowly moving north.

Was it—someone. How could it not be. And doing what?

It struck me—watching, of course, like me.

What was he watching. Me?

Or was it she? She, watching, she who so rarely seems to see me? Who scarcely can see past the end of her long nose.

I returned to the cottage and heard typing. 'Twas not as fast as Cedric's, Cedric does not pause for long. He is full on. She, however, pauses, makes the queer little sounds I suppose when things come right. What I heard were the little squeaks.

Which leaves just one person.

Oh, how precious! [Jolly Aunty voice.]

[Cedric's Diary]

*May. G———'s early morning breathing clear as church bells; C———'s, somewhat less so. The sky clear, too, clean, though very cool. The wind in the west, steady, stiff, even. Rebuilt henhouse latch. It was a job. Two hens brooding; the cocks, wandering the yard. & Dobbs. Dobbs, then, who always walks about vaguely as if in possession of something of which to be ashamed. Dobbs, who wears the mien of a man who a long time ago decided that he had nothing to say that could make the slightest difference to anyone—Dobbs, too, was wandering about the crowded cottage grounds even this early in the morning porting gossip, of all things, this taciturn man. Dobbs nonetheless inspires trust. Dobbs, for one, is not one of them. As he was going out to his truck to unload more bags of the quicklime & a container of Calor I swooped down on him & collared him & asked him the news. &, for once, he had something to offer. That there were strangers in Craighouse, evidently.

—Oh, go along with you!

I asked him what precisely he had heard or seen & how after all that he knew.

—Blue Shirts… postal office.

Voluble Gurth! Four more words. For Dobbs, this was loquacity itself.

But there have been Blue Shirts, I harry him.

—Not this lot.

& I do not press him further. He may be correct.

A collection?

But in my case it will be a re-collection.

But as I have written I have always assumed that they know where I am, & it is only a matter of time—its not being any longer if ever it was a matter of space.

Later. Jets overhead—Jets passing by, in the sky, heading where on earth…? Small squadrons of jets have been passing daily, often in the late morning, flying pretty low, fast, blue-bellied, perhaps as a disguise? locked in array.

Most of the time I am able to rise above such concerns, but now I find myself, what, quailing…

In passing I must say that the color blue itself, royal blue, that it may be owned as it were by a set of fellows: I find this objectionable & I will not permit it.

8 eggs. (151) Bluish. Beautiful.

[Avril's Diary]

* *May*. I will name names. Cedric. Caroline. Gillian. William Dobbs, Avril O'Malley. The Dobbs boy. Trees. Beasts. Fish. Birds. The nameless Men in Blue.

And Someone Else?

[Cedric's Diary]

3 June. Fine, blowy, not very warm.

Behind, beyond glass I see the Plovers, the Red-breasted Mergansers, the Pipits & Puffins, the Sanderlings, Sandpipers, & Shelducks, the Shags & Siskins, not to mention Sparrows & Swallows, of course, Teals, Terns, & Turnstones, & Waxwings, & Whimbrels. G———— I have set the task of naming a Hebridean bird for every letter of the alphabet. She is stuck at Q.

Under glass the blue sky enspheres observant or vigilant tree-birds standing in the tops of trees, those still unravished evergreens that—ha!—miniature, exquisitely, then, turning a knob, enlargen. Enlargen. Softly falling, as if from the heavens, hangs the Quiet. It broods upon the boughs, a bit purplishly, one can see or hear, until—

Until They come along, which they do, out of the blue, never alone but in pairs or in array, rippling, shuddering Zion, blasting branch & bough, blowing the birds from their orbits, all but knocking the fieldglasses from my own hands, & going away.

But the birds return. Feathers ruffled, yes, plumage awry, hair mussed, insert your own tedious triteness, they nonetheless return.

The forms abide. The color, on the other hand, does not, not as it was. It is now a paler world.

Birds are forms.

No, birds are Things.

Keep the faith.

4 eggs. (163)

[Avril's Diary]

June. She walks—does she whom I call, quite uncharitably, yes, the Consumptive Cline—CC—oh, forgive. Her walks, when they are not walks into the woods—unto them, disappearing acts as if in a dream… her walks often take her to the Colonel's with bundles of no doubt extremely important letters and whatnot addressing matters of state, and Whatnot, and bound by a large rubber band, I'm sure, that he will bring with him on his next drive to Craighouse of a Monday or a Thursday, if she does not ride along.

This morning I watched her figure diminishing in the distance only to disappear at the bend in the road, & all was silent, and that is when I went to the workbench & got the hand-drill.

The grimiest of all his tools, I think, & awkward—it squeaks. It is difficult to bore straight, I found, until finally I got the knack of it and got it turning well enough that in a little while I was through the thin wall behind the picture (of St. Martins in the Fields, circa 1920, at dusk). Remarkably, it gave me a view of most of the room, as if it were a proper keyhole.

Desperate remedies, as Ric might say. He'd say more, had he seen the drill stuck for a couple of minutes protruding from the wall opposite the Cline's desk. And above the brass four-poster, yes. It was so. I had a difficult time getting it out.

Dust-cloth in hand just in case, I bounced over the bed to a spot of sawdust, brushing it away worried that the hole I had bored might be visible to one lying on the bed, but, stretching out for a minute, I saw that it was not so, even if one knew to look for it.

Bed springs are said to groan. These made a sad squeak, a kind of moan.

She would be gone for an hour at least; Ric had taken Gillian hiking, blackberrying, birdwatching. I was alone.

I lay on the bed awhile thinking. The onion-bed needed hoeing. But I just lay there. I was there awhile. Inexplicably, I was immensely tired all of a sudden. I think I dozed off, even dreamed. Then I woke up. It was hot.

I went to the desk. She had the best desk-chair in the house—in all the Hebrides?—a proper wheeled thing, oiled up—Ric liked his oilcan—with springs that allowed one to lean back and rock and sway to and fro back and forth from side to side freely, or even to spin, if one so wished, settled on the molded wooden seat twisting on that huge bolt. He deferred. One of the most brilliant minds in the British Isles: he deferred to her.

And not just in the matter of desk-chairs!

Here, then, was where she spent so much of her precious time. But there was nothing here aside from the paper & pens & pencils sitting about on an untidy desk.

I sat down, I am not sure why. Strange mood! I inserted a fresh sheet of Caroline's rather expensive paper into the machine and turned the knob to queue it up.

The drawer was locked, of course.

PRIVATE—I typed.

I have typed on the Remington only very rarely. I can bang away on one. No, I'm not a book-woman, not like her. The onion-bed needed hoeing. I gave myself the pleasure of typing over the fresh field of the page, planting letters, one after the other.

[sheet inserted—ed.]

PRIVATE

Private. The Diary of Gillian O'Malley. Do not read unless you are I, Miss Gillian O'Malley.

Recording Thoughts about the New Mother, Mrs. Caroline O'Malley.

PRIVATE.

My name is Gillian O'Malley. It used to be Gillian Goldstein.

I don't have my real mother. I have a step-mother. My mother is dead. She died in London during wartime. My own home, too, was bombed but I was fine because I was away in the country at the time.

My step-mother's name is Mrs. Caroline O'Malley.

She is very attractive. She has asked me to call her Caroline. I call my aunt "Aunt."

She and my father, really my step-father, have not been married very long. They have adopted me. Now they are my parents. She has an illness.

~~Mrs. O'M~~ Caroline and my father are Writers. I will be a Writer when I grow up.

Sometimes Aunt and my father want me to go hunt out Caroline. I always find her at her desk typing or looking out of the window. I sniff her out: Caroline sometimes smells funny.

[end]

And so on. It was curious to try to imagine the keen Miss Pretzel from the lookout of poor little Gillian, who evidently does not regard her as worshipfully now as she did when the two of them first got here in Jura. I wonder why?

[Cedric's Diary]

* *June*. The wind having blown the clouds right out of the sky, it fell quiet last night & I saw the northern lights for the first time, remarkably, since arriving in Jura... how many months ago? I don't wish to know. Long streaks of white stuff, like creamy cloud, forming a one **[an arc?—ed.]** in the sky eerily blue, & every now & then an extraordinary flickering passing over them, but not as lightning flits about on quiet summer nights but as though... I may as well write it down, as though a searchlight were playing upon them—a searchlight.

Looking for...? That is the question, inevitably, a fear blossoming that I did not think could find roots in Jura soil.

Jura has failed me, then. No, rather, I have failed Jura. I am not sure that I have ever been able really to accept the fact that I am here. I am not after all one of those who soar, I suppose, in the brightening light. Rather, like some Dracula unaccountably on holiday, I have brought along my six feet of London soil &, batwings furled, have I gone to ground.

I have not failed Jura. Nor has Jura failed me. Things have failed us both.

I remember when living in London returning every now & then to Wallington. The crocuses out, that one March early in the war—the last war. & a few wallflowers budding. Snowdrops. & couples of hares sitting about in the winter wheat gazing at one another. A beautiful clean thought, that, to quote that lunatic lunger, listen to me—now & again in wartime you get your nose above water for a few moments & notice that the earth is still going 'round the sun.

& thus I have sailed the seven seas & come

To the blue-green Isle of Jurazantium.

I once saw a heron circling over Baker Street. Improbably, I saw a kestrel killing a sparrow in the middle of the Lord's cricket ground. Perhaps the war in reducing human traffic in inner London increased bird life. Here in the Hebrides, then, is it possible that the war, in reducing bird traffic, increases human life? What I will see here, then, depends on my sense of human life—what, a jet out of the blue killing a child, a child in a meadow or sitting in a boat?

Things have come to a certain pass.

[Avril's Diary]

* *June.* Strange fits of typing I have heard. All that pounding away at the keys is audible. Thunderous, it is inescapable. It follows one around the house. No wonder Gillian clears out in the morning. When not the little bell it is a long pause that punctuates. Then the machine starts to grind again. Possession by the muse—fitful, or are these spells? No, she's tubercular, yes, but epileptic? No, I do not think so. But about these pauses—vacant? Pregnant? I do not know what she is doing there as she stands at the window, as I have known, but now I see from the back close on rather than at a distance from without.

I suspect that she is doing nothing. She may be dreaming of what she wishes her husband was and would be for her sake as well as how or who she wishes her sister were if she ever even thinks of her. I suspect that she spares Gillian, at least. I suspect that there is regret, too, in some measure. As well there should be. She is a Woman of Feeling; of this I am aware. I suppose that I am a dry stick next to her. Too much "good sense" for my own good?

Later. The typing stops. The walls of this house of paper are so thin, it doesn't take an ear-trumpet at the keyhole to tell when the typing stops. I speed to my post and take down the picture just in time to see her turn from the window and go to the armoire where hang, of course, her prized purses, quietly abiding.

Then I see her do something odd. Loopy. She takes off her clothes, takes them all right on off, all of them and leaves them on the rug, like a shed skin. True, it is midday and warm in the cottage.

I am pretty sure that she thinks she is alone in the house; I have been quiet as a cat.

She is rummaging in the armoire. I cannot see at first what she is holding in her hand as she sits at the desk that is his as well as her own but then a bell rings and, yes, indeed, Lo! It is the key. THE key? Or HER key?

She inserts the key—so that's where he hides it!—in the mysterious desk drawer that has been locked against his or her sister as well as, as I believed, but evidently wrongly, his wife.

Unless.

Lo! The diary...

Such was my first thought. It is taken out without a sound, and it is indeed the diary. I know by the calfskin cover and the creamy paper that I can see over her shoulder as she leafs through stopping to read here and there; it seems to beg you to write upon it, does this paper, and not your modern scratchy voices with their ball-point machines but writing in the old way with quill and inkwell and blotting-paper. I am now writing these words that you are reading with the latest cheap ball-point in a weathered student's notebook of lined foolscap; I believe that it is an exercise book that Gillian put aside almost empty.

Blimey then she starts making these little sounds, not very loud, but very high, like some small animal.

She is so strange when she is all alone.

But mostly she reads, does the Cline, sitting there in the altogether, reading, now, not writing, not watching whatever she watches out of the window, not thinking, and making little sounds—and of course coughing now and then, as always, poor thing—she reads, then, I say.

And now I say, she, too, reads!!! Or, as I should say, she too is a Reader! She, too—why keep up the charade?—for never doubt, Gentle Reader, the resourcefulness of a humble narrator who has been a famous man's close sister and attendant supportive sibling for over thirty years. Very little that he does, very, very little that he thinks, and—it is now time to admit—absolutely nothing that he WRITES, escapes my sharp steely vision!

Lo! I am Superwoman, with X-ray eyes!

[Cedric's Diary]

* *June.* I have been dreamless lately, waking, sleeping, walking, sitting, snooping, swooping, soaring... Not that I do much soaring of any feather these days. Eternity's Eagle, now caged, cannot stretch his wings. Resign, then, resign! &c.. But the true owner? Not the gull but those collective crows, bien pensant. The palaver is ended.

Returning to London & my London years, then, as I must do, vision being what it is: I find that I have almost nothing to say. For I can see nothing. No Thing. The light has died, & the stilly wings of Memory have stiffened. Nest-less, restless, eyeless, he can only stalk 'round on the ground.

Meanwhile, Bovex broods...

But others, too, brood. And have dreams. For it has been reported that the dreams have returned, like birds—bombs, I'd have said—to nests, those ~~cuckol~~ cuckoos. Or are they visions?

In any event, evidently it was again not the homeless girl but the woman in the woods, walking, not in white. Better beige, rather, ecru: more apt. But she is naked.

She without clothes, the world is without sound.

The sky is darkening, she notices that she is not on the path any more.

The trees form a throbbing thicket, all bole trunk interlaced branch & stem, like pleated fingers hands legs other limbs.

Nevertheless, resolutely 'Linear as she is, she comes upon the edifice—practically bangs her nose on it. She oumphs, & she hears herself oumph.

She can hear her hands, too, as they work their way laterally against the widening wall, looking for an opening, a maw or pore, only to find a sort of slit or slot, a key-hole-like window out of which light is streaming, liquidly.

Indeed, the light is liquid; the liquid, light.

Without shame she cups her hands, threading fingers, but the stream is heavy, heavy as liquid lead & the bell starts ringing, some brazen bell breaks the silence...

She wakes up, of course. I do, too, but of this, for me, walking, waking dream I will attempt no illumination. Let it lie still, nested, a fresh egg amongst the others, those unexploded shells.

[Avril's Diary]

* *June.*

Dear Diary,

Strangely, when I think of who you are, as difficult as it is to say, precisely, who that is, and looking forward in time to whoever that may be, I feel that I nonetheless owe you an apology.

Now that I have told you all, I must beg your forgiveness for—not having told you all.

I will endeavor, henceforth, to be entirely forthright.

Sincerely,

Avril O'Malley
Cargill Cottage, Barnhill
Jura, Scotland, UK

Later. It is late, but I wanted to note before putting out the light that it is my birthday next week. I had forgotten. I will not say how old I am but will mention that I am older now than my mother was when she had me.

Telling all, I will now say that I have been seeing my brother and his wife together.

Enlightening.

They are man and wife. My brother, well. And she, a woman—she is a woman.

No surprises—I am a countrywoman. Yet am I a maid.

My mother used to say, there never was an old shoe couldn't find a match.

Later. London, and telling all, soon I will tell all, all, even about the evening at St. Brides soon after he announced his intentions. The friendly vicar let us in, made us sign. —No monkey business, now. We had to pledge not to jump through one of the arches! Evidently some have taken the plunge. There are many Opportunities as you make your way up the steep, spiral staircase, layer upon layer.

I did not jump, you know. I just stood atop St. Brides, my brother beside me, and screamed—but just once—and then the sirens started. We saw the vicar below waving us down and Ric obeyed but I stayed behind to see the bombs falling not far away, lighting up the night sky...

[Cedric's Diary]

16 June. Avril! Avril's birthday is coming!

Happy birthday to my dear sister!

My little Jane Avril, I now see, as I have not for a long time, the degree to which I, to which we all take you for granite! Avril I will buy a book in one of Barnhill's many well-stocked bookstores! Nope, it will require a trip to Craighouse to that one little white-haired apothecary who carries junk—antiques, he calls them—as well as a few battered old books on hand for rent & for sale. I will buy Avril a book.

Avril as a child was an avid little reader, I so well remember, utterly indiscriminate in taste, grabbing up everything under the sun. Recently I came upon one of the few old photographs that I have of us & of her, & sure enough it is a picture of her about six years of age sitting snug on a kitchen chair book in steady little hands. The book I remember, too, since it was once my book, I believe—<u>My Big Book of Soldiers</u>—which features soldiers at arms of all eras jolly stolid colorful & indifferent brandishing shield & sword & musket, standing at ease, or at attention, rifles slung or cradled, aiming, prone position, Lee Enfield conspicuous—the artist knew his guns… My personal favourites were of the Napoleonic Era, the shiny, sabre-wielding French Cuirassiers, the blue-tunics of the French infantry with their pouches bulging with cartouches, the artillery with their cannon & shot… the Grand Armée, circa 1812, outside Smolensk…

I will not buy Avril a war book.

A book on gardening in the British Isles, the British islands—the Hebrides, in particular. Apt. Too? Avril has never been a dreamer. A book of dreams, then? Shelley? Queen Mab & her children? No? A book of wishes? A book of dreams, desires… Stevenson & all that late Victorian whimsy? to take her steel-trap mind off the here & now, of which at times I think she gets more than enough. Perchance to dream… Hamlet? Shakespeare? A book of songs? She loves G&S—though not openly what one would call operatic in the soul (!). She has her feet on the ground. She loves Peter P & the Crocodile, those sharp eyes. Little wonder, this latter—like a pair of ginormous jaws snapping shut, she catches the moment, which can only screech, squeal. No offence, Avril! Should one day you read these words: I salute you! Whatever time we will spend together in what could be our disparate desperate futures, let me say that I do not know what I would have done without you.

[Avril's Diary]

* *June*. Not to stretch a point, but I will not burden these pages with an account of my conjugal life, being too afraid. I will leave that duty—a duty owed to the future, should there be a future, should one arrive in Barnhill one sunny day, undoubtedly by launch—I'll leave that duty to my batty sister, that pill, Avril, pardon my French, not April, nothing so springy bouncy—that accident, Avril, that sore knob who is here & now planted but belongs just nowhere.

This is a violation. This, this here & this now,—&&&, that affectation, there, that twisted pretzel, as if time were so precious, tick tock!—Time, of which we have so much on our hands, here, and—&—yet the future is disappearing, now, & the past is being lost, receding into the distance, daily, despite this diary, the present, even, shrinking away to nothing. And what can we do? Time, stretched, twisted out of joint, is on the run, near run out, has run, kite in flight, speck in sky—transcendence. Also ran? History. Down the drain. Not to mention Prophecy.

Others of those big words, oh brother, according to thy whim.

It's as if life, itself, walked out on us, disgusted, prompting me cheerily to write, as so often,

—We are the dead.

Really? Really and—&—truly, brother? Dead?

History. Reality--the real--as Ric might say. One tries to look away. But I will not look away, I will get it in hand, and see it clearly & whole, and Ric, too, will see the truth, no matter how it scathes...I sound like you, Cedric... oops! Oh, Argyll!

Well, then, why keep up the game?

Hello, Ricky!

You, who so love games, now you know: the game is up. You now know. Rather, you have known, for over a week, at least. And thus you must know of a couple of terrible things, transgressions. What you now know, then, is that I know that you know. One question now is, how long have I had this filthy little habit, very Catholic, by the way...? Of course, this is a silly question for the simple reason that it simply doesn't matter. In answer, nevertheless, let me say that you do well to ask. I've been watching you, you know, ever since I can remember. But first a question for you: how long have YOU been doing it—it, what you are now doing, in this very moment as you read? My own question, I am sure you would see, is, how long have YOU yourself been laying hands on other persons' diaries!

When I got home today I found a tiny red flag raised—no, dropped on the floor. There's a riddle for you.

You, who so love games of all kinds, word games, anagrams and puns, though less so the latter than your erstwhile friend and colleague, that silly fascist, God roast him, himself a great pun—I bid you, think hard about my name! Thereby you shall arrive at something nearer truth.

Avril, you say? And your joke, —Ms. Jane Avril...? Plain Jane? Livra-te...! What about, rather,

R I V A L !

Make no mistake. But whose, you will wonder. And I confess that I sometimes ask myself the same question. Of hers, is the easy answer, but of yours, too?

Finally, when all is said—when all is written—it doesn't matter. You will see the truth if it hurts you, or her, or me, even if unlike you, finally, I summon a little sharpness, I—

No, I write not to cleave but to clarify.

Don't bother with the book; I have read enough for awhile! I have claimed the glass globe paperweight, which now sits on my desk, a sort of touchstone, untouched by you—for fear of smudging?

To illuminate, then, one dark little pocket of your domestic history, one secreted in some old purse hanging behind a locked door in a closet: sharply I recollect how it all began.

It was a succession of instants, images, pictures, really, each with its little complement of feeling and a few of which I have committed to my own diary, Ric, that you did not know about, not until now, right? A domestic diary of my own which I began soon after you had shut up yours, to me, at least—at her bidding?—this, here and now, which I welcome you to read front to back or, better, back to front, unless that be unnecessary, unless you have been reading it all along!

Right. The keen Miss Pretzel, Miss Loop-the-loop, well, I had my eye on her and her game as soon as she topped your list of eligibles along with Celia P. and the rest. She was still living in Canonbury Square. I saw nothing definite, but I became suspicious, I <u>smelled</u> something, once, when late one afternoon, and not just any afternoon, you will soon see, I happened to see her enter a residence on Russell Square. She nipped in there like some Madam Hyde. She didn't stop to ring the bell; she had a key. She walked right in as if she owned the place. And then she left, two and one-half hours later.

I will not speak of what I imagine the deal may have been up that mysterious staircase behind the mauve Bloomsbury door. I will speak only of what I know, of what I see, and I see a lot. Oh, I know, she is important—like you, Ric! It was serious intellectual business of the most serious sort, to be sure…

I sat on a bench with me Cady lowered over my eyes forming a sort of hood or cowl appropriate to a woman of my sort. No jaunty aunty, I was a spy and had a bit of crust, and I am pretty sure I was invisible to all but the idlest indolent of passersby. I had the time. My job at the sheetmetal factory had just ended.

Miss P. soon made her somnambulant way out the door and down Woburn Place. I was annoyed, I confess, even the way she strolls—saunters, as if occupied by, not just a purpose, but a purpose unknown to such as I, and foreign.

You do not know of any of this, brother.

It is not too late to close thy Avril & carefully misplace my second key, lost long ago & by the way found where, O you man of keys? Or fashioned? You are clever mechanically with those hands of yours, when you want to be; it's not beyond you, & no doubt you would see it as a kind of game.

Miss P. having dropped her own key in her purse that privately infamous sunny London afternoon, that day of Opportunity, she & I moved in tandem, accidental twins sharing the day secretly at a discreet distance from each other—as if we were joint riders of a bicycle, a bicycle built for two impossibly elongated in between. She would stop, suddenly, & I would stop. She would look up at the hot sky, and so would I, or gaze meditatively for a certain time, our eyes mutually fixed upon the pavement. Behind her of course on the cycle I would find myself swinging out wide and away roundabout through some dense throng, say, in Covent Garden, but would know the while with my hands upon the bars that do not steer that I could never lose her, even if I wanted to! And I would find myself travelling back in quick traverse even as the cycle, having telescoped, would contract swiftly to the point that I would be practically rubbing elbows with her in some bookshop, the nice young man (but seedy, I recall, raffish, somehow untrustworthy or, what, inauthentic in appearance) approaching her, proving solicitous (and I somehow invisible). Or we would be standing cheek by jowl at the grocer's, handling in turn the same shiny bell peppers without either of us buying any. Though her countenance in form est sans pareil, her skin I saw then and have confirmed since is not particularly fine.

She did not see me. She did not know me, at least. She met me just once before (you know when and where), and she could not have recognized me, especially given how I was dressed & given who she is &, perhaps most important, given who I am.

Nor did she see him, not at first. But I did. I saw him, right enough.

She appeared to be headed towards Westminster, as I judged, but was brought to a standstill, as was I, cutting across Trafalgar Square where that dense mass of people had collected to see the street-parade of our latest military machines and materiel in front of the National Gallery—yes, it was that afternoon—the usual rockets, bombs, and missiles but one exhibit in which was, you will be pleased to hear (though of course you know— and knew—all about this) one of your whirly-birds, those helio-rotors or what you may call them.

The parade had itself come to a halt with this squat, shiny helio-thingum sitting right before us not twenty feet away. I noted that Caroline was looking up with her eyes fixed upon it, whose rimless wheel of thin slats was revolving slowly overhead as if it were a great sleeping bird dreaming of flight—fascinated, she was, standing there with one of those strange little purses new to me at the time but that I have come to detest.

That was when I noticed a man standing not far behind her, a man without a hat taking an interest, not in the machine, but in her.

Not that he was staring at her. But he would peek at her, then look away, then look at the machine, look over at the bombs, would look up, look down, look at the hat of the man right in front of him, look anywhere but at her—then, unaccountably, look right at her, at close range, closely, grimly, as it seemed to me.

She of course was unconscious of him no less than of me, what with the crush of the crowd and a sudden & deafening metallic coughing of the helio-rotor machine as its engine came to full life and its wingy-things started turning more rapidly and began creating a wind that was hitting us all in our faces and even blowing off a few hats, their owners scrambling—rather, jostling fecklessly—after them.

On an errand or on one's way to work one comes upon a person or a group of persons standing still and gazing above or across. What is the reaction, inevitably? One always assumes that an unseen but eminently seeable object has captured attention—a spectacle. It is unthinkable that they could be gazing upon a thing not just not spectacular but not even at all visible to another standing to their side, that they could be gazing upon nothing, no thing—that they are gazing for the sake of gazing, or are perhaps not gazing at all but are simply lost in thought. But how can several persons be lost in the same thought? But even when it is just one person: it is impossible not to look, too. It is called curiosity. It is an iron law of human nature. I know of none more difficult to defy.

Two were defying it. He and I, together, watched Lady Puzzle, and it was little wonder that what happened next should happen. Of a sudden, he turned to me. He looked right at me, full in the face.

I recall little of him other than that he was middle-sized, clean-shaven, but for a thick black rectangle of moustache, and practically invisible, being absolutely nondescript, virtually indescribable apart from the moustache and commensurately bushy brows over beetle eyes. What with his shrewd London way about him, he was one in a million. And yet I, who pride myself on my penetration, then as now, felt that there was something odd about him, a kind of falsity, a hint of fraudulence as difficult to formulate as to dismiss from my mind. It's as if he were made of rubber, latex, like Bovex.

—HELIO-THINGUM [not the word used]... REVOLUTIONARY... NEW WAR!...

Someone on a loudspeaker had begun listing the virtues of the helio-machine in a metallic voice that broke up as it echoed, whining away as if the machine itself had come to life and found words, one that despite heavy thronging flooded the square as if it were an empty canyon. That was when my man of mystery lowered his shoulder and pushed rightwards until he was right in front of me and even with her and, by dint of subtle sidling, right next to her.

Strange to say but I will confess it: of a sudden I was afraid for her.

—OBSERVE TRUE POWER... NEW MACHINE... HARNESSING ALL...! The tinny voice carried on.

Now he was facing straight ahead. He was obeying the law.

She was, too—facing straight ahead. Together they looked stilly upon the spectacle.

—... NEW PEGASUS! ...

I had sidled nearer and could see them better.

They looked, together: yes, that was it! They looked together!

His lips were moving as he watched. I thought her lips were moving, too, but it was hard to be sure. It was all very subtle. She was shaking her head back and forth, slowly.

—... THE MAGIC... BRITISH TECHNO... LADIES AND GENTS!

The door of the machine now slid back to reveal two figures standing stage-front within smiling. At first I thought them mannequins but then the shorter one, evidently a boy of about ten, took the other's hand, as if on cue. They stood next to what looked like a kitchen table laid for supper; behind them was a window, not that you could see out of it, with curtains.

—THE ENGLISH BOY AND HIS SISTER... THE EARTH... TWO TONS... HOME IN AIR!

I looked back to see Caroline lowering her chin and starting to back away, into people, who barely noticed her and did not step aside. Egg on her face, she was going nowhere.

A lover's quarrel.

—... CALLED LEVITATION... The voice chirruped, just as the whingies began spinning yet faster, becoming almost invisible, the wind picking up, becoming a gale, and the machine shuddered once or twice, the boy and the young woman steady, stalwart, now crouching a little... it lifted clear of the ground a few feet and—a miracle, or was it magic! It hung in the air! It just stood there, shining, defying the law of gravity.

It was remarkable, Cedric. But of course you know all about such things. And it was only a little while later that the famous bomb went off.

What you do not know, all about, or as I should write WHO—WHO is this person, Ric, who all of a sudden it is all about? Who lives amongst us who sits at our table eats off our plates who I once found—but only once!—drinking out of my mug in the morning—who is she, Ric? Do you know? Who is

this, who's supposed to be my sister, who shares—yes, it must be written—who shares your bed? Do you know her, Ric, really?
DO YOU KNOW WHO SHE IS? DO YOU???
You once said, Av, you are an open book. But can you bear reading in it?
Well, I am sure by now that you regret taking the liberty you deny me, how dare you, by the way—that of reading my diary at will, as if it were just an extension of your own. Which in a sense it is, I will admit. But in some small obscure pocket of my heart I am sorry, Ric, so sorry that I have to be the one to tell you, and sorrier even that you need to be so enlightened. That the fact exists. That the lamp, shone into this cavernous closet of hers, and now of yours, has something within the depths on which to shed light, edges to trace with shadow, surfaces to brighten between outlines, any shapes lying within its obscurity to reveal, to awaken, stirring, startling, however quietly we wield the light, dazzling, perhaps, not fully enlightening, but enlightening, as you are enlightened, nonetheless. Say what you will of her, she is not stupid. She will see that you see. She will know that you know. That I see, too. That I, too, know.
That I KNOW HER.
That I know how she spends her time.
That I know, what you do not know that I know, how she loves you. Which I should not, but I do.
That I know, which I should, as a good sister, how she spends her time. Where she goes. What she does. Her mysterious afternoons in Craighouse. Opportunities!
I know, and I will tell you, that she has a room in Craighouse, a room of her own up the backstairs at the apothecary's.
Are bells ringing, Ric?
SHE HAS A KEY.
Ask her to show it to you.

Later. Impossible. Impossible! Inconceivable!
The thought that she, too—SHE!—should be reading it. No, it is out of the question, or at least a stretch. On the other hand, consider the evidence that my flag, my tiny chip of pink stone, was not in its place but was glittering on the floor beneath the desk. A bell went off. Gillian and I had been hoeing. But, really and truly, I really did not think that she would stoop so as—

Gillian, who can be inquisitive? Certainly it is the case that my desk drawer has no lock. I remember the day a few weeks ago when I was scribbling, something that I did not mention at the time, and emerged from my room to see Ric smiling in my direction, patronizingly, as I thought, which bothered me just a little. But it was the pair of them. For she was there, too, standing behind, and she was smiling too, coolly, and breathing lightly.

Well you know spies and pies must have a bit of crust.

But that bothers me not a little. But how fair is it, how likely? That the Great Man should lock me out of his own desk drawer only to sneak peeks inside of mine, even though, as I may have noted, mine needs no key. Would he stoop so low?

AND WOULD HE CARE!

Indeed I am an open book—but unread, or so I thought.

[Cedric's Diary]

[*Undated*] Tonight will I collect the diaries—and miscellaneous other pages—typescripts—whatnot—and burn them. Better than blowing up the house. I will begin with my own.

[Avril's Diary]

Later. I have picked up the paperweight globe from the mantel and put it in on my desk. The paperweight is heavier than it looks. It's transparent and looks like a drop of water, a water-drop sitting on a leaf. It's surprising how heavy it is. Gillian was coming and so I put it in my pocket. It tugs at my smock, weighing me down.

I think of smashing it on the floor...

That would give me quite a good feeling. I am not sure why.

I think of smashing it into Caroline's face. How surprised she would be. Would Ric be surprised?

I have dropped the paperweight in the pocket of my smock. I can feel its weight as I walk about. I imagine dropping stones in my other pockets, local, Barnhill stones, nothing exotic. It wouldn't take too many such stones to make me sink properly. I can ask Caroline to help me gather them, Caroline, who knows how to sink other girls, English girls.

Gillian walked right by me and went into her room, shutting the door behind her.

Is this how it starts?

Later. No, dear brother. Nobody's burning anything.

Later. When inquisitive, I am without shame. I will read Gillian's diary.

Later. "I love her. She is so beautiful."
She loves her because she is so beautiful.
She loves her. She needs her.
She needs me. Me.
"I love her. She is kind."
I cried for a minute. Without shame. I don't do that often.

I have not known Gillian. She's a child. What can one know of her, a child. She has been alone. She is an orphan—she was. We took her in. They took her in, but I was part of it all.

Gillian loves her.

Gillian needs me. Gillian loves me. Me.

Like a good faery, she's been watching—for months now, she's been watching over us and keeping a record. She's been on the watch. On the lookout: hence the field glasses 'round her neck, that old pair. She's been our avid little friend, our guardian angel, worried sick, our good little spy.

It occurs to me for the first time that should something happen to Caroline I would be her mother. Who else? I would be her mother.

A few days ago I heard her in Caroline's room. She must have been looking for the diary, which she could not find. Little wonder.

I now see that Caroline's room in Craighouse is her diary.
I will not try to read it.
That's over. She's a good egg, really—leave it at that.
I won't read diaries any more, not even Ric's.
She's no angel. She reads Ric's diary. As do I. Nor have I been an angel. She reads Ric's, and Ric reads mine. Gillian tries, or has tried, to read Caroline's, which does not exist, not here, not as a document in a desk. I read, or now have begun to read, Gillian's.

And it occurs to me for the first time what that means, that tiny pink flag glittering on the floor beneath my desk: I, too, am a Writer. For I have readers.

I put the glass paperweight back on my own desk.

Gillian and I will work in the garden today, yes. Then we will work at our desks.

[Cedric's Diary]

* *June.* & then it happened, saving us from ourselves, from detonation, an explosion—from a conflagration, certainly. Auto-da-fé. We would have all agreed, even Avril, to burn His or Her Little Book of Self. What would we have had left? Peace? That was my hope.

Or being English folk was it the Quiet which was spared us, that fatal silence & dim space or downright darkness that gives birth to so many misshapen things, things that may after all, shockingly, be able to live in the light. You have heard of so-called sunshine policies—electric-shine, rather, I imagine—flip the switch, see the truth, watch it shrivel up?

No, it just transmogrifies. The thought that she might be one of them—or with them...

The Fact, become a Thing, degrades, disintegrates, coalesces—transmutes. Things change. They were not supposed to. They were supposed to stay the same. But we live in the atomic age where so-called Atomic Facts explode, bombs are dropped on states—so-called States of Affairs—and, to put it simply, again, so-called Things change. They weren't supposed to. You see an egg. You think you know.

In roaring he shall rise & on the surface die...?

She, rather, the Hag... or her epigones, tiny Haglets turning up having climbed the ladders of the deep?

Yes, one wonders at the premise. Would they now then float? & much given birth in depth & darkness ends, or rather does not end, by entering the light of day & God knows how, not wilting & dying, no, breathing, rather, writhing, thriving... fledging, splashing, flying away.

It's terrifying.

What happened was a knock on the door; we had no bell. Visitors, two. Guests. One of them, him.

We four, plus two more. A simple Fact. One might say, a visitation. The key turns & history drops in, again, in the Hebrides. Its mission? Fact-finding. Enlightenment, I suppose.

& it says, I ask nothing additional of you, just one thing & no more, than that you remember, that it all be made to count.

I think that tomorrow when I awake & find them in the kitchen & feed them breakfast I will still be writing them off as but a queasy-making dream. It does not seem real that they could have found their way here to this remote place to which, for all I know, it took the omniscient authorities themselves several months to track me. Of course, in a sense these ARE the authorities. But the ruffled, harried look about them, as well as the furtiveness of their unannounced approach, disarms me of any fear that they are here to harass or, perhaps, our greater fear, to collect me. They seem, rather, to need shelter.

Upstairs our cottage has four cold rooms.

Strange to say, it was as though we were all back in London during that chummy time when the Blitz was going about its business & it was not a surprise to hear a knock on the door, late, with someone, some lone, wayward individual, seeking a bed for the night. We would have late suppers & hear the bombs thudding, usually in the distance. It would be festive. To provide refuge, however temporary, was romantic, you understand.

The question now, of course, is what are they doing here.

The answer is, to get rid of them. Of him.

[Avril's Diary]

* *June*. It is <u>he</u>, that man—he is here, here, of all places, how? How would he find her? Or is it we? And why, why on earth? Here! And now! Small world! I would swear it is he, now undisguised but nonetheless unmistakable: some men just ARE their moustaches.

But, again, why?

Unless… But such a thought does not bear putting down in black and white. Unless one's motive in doing so is to drag it into the light and make it die…? Shameful thing, it is, the mere thought lying there in a sprawl on the mind's floor.

I, for one, am ashamed.

It, however, persists. As Ric might say, it <u>writhes</u>.

Later. Emptied of all good birds, as Ric would say, the sky is falling—spiralling down to the ground, a big chunk of heavy blue, as if blown away from the rest & ready to fall on someone oblivious.

Not upon my head, however: my eyes are wide open.

Yes, we have visitors, guests, and such guests they are. That American cornfield pair, Heckle and Jeckle? No, the confessional nature of the diary should not be abrogated by any fear of how it might be used some distance (or nearer, nearer than I think?) down the road, Ric's absurd truncation of names notwithstanding, which does naught else but testify to an anxiety that what is given breath here may hurt those who bear them. Ridiculous.

Aarronow &—Prentiss, that is his name—or Prentice. There, boldly I have set them down—Aarronow & Prentiss it is, then, who knocked. Ric's old friends, it turns out. And the one of them might be someone else's friend…

We heard a boat nearby earlier in the afternoon evidently pulling in near the Colonel's. I suppose that is the safer approach, by water; then, the knock. I thought it was Dobbs. I imagined it was he, coming to confess…? Dobbs in a confessional mode. That would be curious, like a dog who has done his business upon the kitchen floor, but one capable of speech. But I was called to the door by G———, G———, Ric's old habits die hard, who was just standing there smallish in the little foyer wondering who they were and what they were doing on our doorstep, these two men, themselves smallish, a bit weather-splashed but presentable, city-dressed as if just stepped down a staircase from Woburn Place. Speechless was I, myself, taken aback, astounded, what you will.

For, as I have told you, there he was, the very man, Mr. Moustache, and now I found myself in the position of becoming acquainted with a couple of men, one of whose names was familiar to me in his capacity as my brother's erstwhile torturer; the other, his face, as my sister's erstwhile tormentor. And the question was, what, as the Americans say, was up?

—Ric! A. said. Ric… he seemed as surprised to see Ric as Ric was to see him.

Mr. Moustache, Mr. P., if you like, was damp, silent, watchful.

Having dismissed Miss G. to the kitchen, Ric bore up well— though obviously startled—we never have visitors aside from the Colonel or Dobbs—giving them wide-eyed handshakes and, noting my indecision, taking their raincoats, inviting them into the parlour, and suborning me to heat water in the kitchen as politenesses were exchanged.

—What are we doing here, Mr. P., asked A., as I was pouring out the first cups of tea.

—That's a good question, Mr. A. What are we doing here.

—What do you think we are doing here, Ric? P.

I felt then, and I feel it again as I write this, how little proof I am against infection with the language of Ric and other men whom I respect or fear, whom I find striking in one way or other.

—What do you think we are doing?

—Does it have to do with the assignment that I was sent?

—The assignment he was sent. P.

—The assignment he was—what assignment? A.

—You don't know about that?

—The truth is, P. sat back, we don't. We don't know about that. We don't know about a lot of things. We know less than you do, I would bet. We don't even know why we're here.

—Don't even know why we're here. A. Wistfully. & now, where is here?

—We were sent. P.

—Sent by—whom?

—The Brotherhood, of course, I strongly suppose, who knows, P. said, suavely. That much we think we know—it is probably the Brothers. And now you know—which is to say, you know what we know, he said. Smoothly.

P. looked at A. A. looked away then looked at Ric again. I was ignored, for now.

—Telegram, said A. Meet unnamed at King's Cross. Stop. Board Great Western bound to Scotland. Stop. Eleven AM West Gate. Stop. Proceed to Jura. Stop. I know you are thinking, go on with you. See man & heed. Stop. Visit old friend. Stop. Stop. Stop. I had no idea whom to meet or who the man was or the old friend was.

—Signed, TB. P.

—Which brings me to my next question, said P. He had arisen and was standing at the window looking out. Sunny this morning but with a promise of rain in the late afternoon.

—What are we doing here, yes—what are YOU doing here?

At this A. pulled what appeared to be a small stick from his jacket and handed it—to me.

—A save-an-ear. A memento. For you, Ric, from when you were our guest. It was handed to me by the man we met. He said, give it to the old friend. He's my old friend, too.

And now handed to me, with but small comment. But as if passing the baton. Or a kind of gavel? A sort of sceptre? No, more like a drill or a hammer, a sort of tool. I gave it to Ric.

It was a truncheon. It was the truncheon, evidently. Odd it must have been, his having felt its collision with bone and muscle and, yes, the ear, the right one, to hold it in his own hand. Then again, as he has written it was never wielded against him with anything that one would call conviction, and the pain it caused, wielded as gingerly as it was, was barely memorable. Oh, I am sure it was instructive at the time, of course.

—You can have this back. It's not wanted here. Ric put it on the coffee table.

—So you are not going to enlighten us, yes? Oyez, Zedric? No touch of the wand? A., smilingly.

—What are you doing here, O'Malley? P., facing about.

I, too, had already had enough of P. and his pushiness.

—What I am doing here, O'Prentiss, is my own private business and no concern of yours.

—Ah, but O'Zedric, said A. You're out of the swim, brother. There is no longer any O'private business, or did you not receive the O'menolaudanum out here on the SO'whater? Something like that. Now I saw what Ric was talking about.

A had picked up the truncheon and given it a flip up into the air, caught it, and put it back down, quite pleased with his own dexterity—rude behaviour at the tea table, I felt, especially for a guest.

—I had hoped to be forgotten, Ric said finally. Left alone.

—No chance, said P., snatching up the truncheon. If nothing else, you are a name.

—Yes, said A., and then there is all this history. Besides, we are all Allah fonts, we forget nothing, no thing and no one. It's no lie. Chuckling. We forged at noon, said the blacksmith, ubi-sunt-mindedly.

P. piped up.

—Never mind the wherefores—I'd worry more about the whatfors—he said, waving the truncheon about—if I were you.

—What, wayfarers? said A. Quaint. Where? Who? Why? We?

Brandishing a truncheon, here and now, just after luncheon in a country cottage. But could these two men hurt a mouse, let alone an intellectual, like Ric, not out of nobility of spirit, mind you, nor due to a fundamental sense of decency rooted in the perception of our shared humanity, as Ric might put it, no, but simply because they were, A. the more especially, beside themselves. They seemed browned off, jittered and jangled, evasive. Were they, too, fugitives? Refugees?

—What's this, Ric? Gillian has just come in bearing the glass globe paperweight. No bloody foolin', I'd love to meet your wife.

Afternoon. I stopped them! I did it! This episode of the paperweight, as I am now thinking of it as I tell you about it: that was I, Avril, who did such a thing? It wasn't Caroline—she stood there gaping. Ric stood there like an idiot. But not I—when he went in for the girl I couldn't stand it I went in for him!

Come what may, & it is frightful now. They are gone—but gone where? & what happens now?

They tried to take them away—Gillian and Caroline, the bastards! The bastards! There was Ric—and the one of them shouting all of a sudden, he had shown Ric a photograph, smiling mouth open wide as a gate and looking at Caroline, and the next thing you see Mr. Moustache is saying,

—Just give us the Jew.

—And, the other says, her only misbegotten daughter.

Then he takes a step towards Gillian, who is sitting on the sofa. I think of the paperweight sitting on the tea table. I get the globe in my hands and goodness I did not know I had it in me, I catch him right on the ear, Caroline screams, he falls, the globe rolls across the floor, like a bowling ball... and they storm stagger rather out, A. holding the handkerchief against the side of P.'s head, and here we are, sitting here and now and it is quiet—Ric and Caroline have not dropped a word—and everybody is worried. For they weren't alone, as it happens. They were met by some men in the road who drove off with them.

Misbegotten—a miss by Gott?

And the photograph? Ric has burned it, saying,

—That is, as the Americans say, that. It does not exist. It never existed.

But that is not that, I know it.

[Cedric's Diary]

[Undated] I suppose sooner or later we all write our own epitaphs.

Empty of any Good Bird, is the sky. Filled with the Bad, indeed the Worst, the Pitiless. No passion, though, no intensity—just a steady drone above Bovex, rusticated, smiling still, his mind more vacant than the sunless sky.

It is over. We are. The Dead.
The invasion has begun, and it's a fact.
The men crowd about us, silent or, when not silent, cawing, the Men in Blue.
& we can but sit & wait. & brood.

As when a ~~shepherd of~~ the Hebrid-Isles...
      squatter in
Sees ~~on the naked hill, or valley low,~~
      in luminous air, white clouds above,
The whilst in ~~Ocean Phoebus~~ dips his ~~wain~~,
      Oceania Ares   toe
A vast assembly ~~moving~~ to & fro,
      flying
Then all at once ~~in air dissolves the wondrous show.~~
      on earth descends the crippling blow.

DIRGE. ENLIGHTENMENT'S END.

Wondrous, indeed, of old, was the blow: now we make our own weather, & facts, & fate.

Time is short. Our freedom ticks away. Bash as we may. Burn as we try. The light is dying, this day. The facts drop away.

But the sea, the sky...
The birds have flown away, God knows,
All but the Eagle, brash of eye—& dull Crows.
But the sea is calling
    & the sky.
Even as the light is dying,
The sky is calling
    & the sea.

> The sea is calling
> The sea is calling
> The sky

[Avril's Diary]

June. What's next, your books? I wonder. For today Ric was burning papers again, evidently the contents of the various packets he has been receiving, some of which contained more of the larger glossy photographs. Smilingly, he showed me a couple of them, telling me nothing about them before throwing them on the fire.

One was of a room, obviously in London—you could see the Monument in the distance through the window, which was open. The room was not more than a bedsit.

The other was a bed, messy, unmade, terribly creased. You could see every fold in the bedclothes, which appeared soiled. Though I did not wish to look too closely, I found myself searching every impromptu wrinkle, every accidental pocket... looking for? I know not what.

Then he tried to burn the diary. He was bending over the fireplace when I heard Gillian give a little yell; she tried to stop him but he held her off gently but did not try to stop me when I pulled it out smoking but apparently undamaged. He was laughing.

The diary will go on, if I have to write it myself!

Hello, Futurity? Good afternoon! Ric here, bloody & not unbowed, disembowelled, a dead rabbit whose race is run, the crows feasting on his heart.

Oh, I sound like the wireless. Let's begin again.

Dear Diary,

Ric here; Avril, my right-hand woman, in attendance.

~~Caroline~~ C—— having unmade her bed, now she must lie about it. Gurth cowed, which is something, given his usual porcine insensibility. I myself have come down with a serious case of the Quietus.

They've come, after all, the men in blue, & in #'s.

Fecklessly, I lie low.

Rather, I do not sit & wait. It will be a good job if I am not taken away very soon, tomorrow or in a week. It's important to stay busy. We are going out in the boat tomorrow. Yesterday I spent sealing the prow with tar & steadying the frontmost seat where it meets the gunwale.

This is where they will sit, my gems, my jewels, my sweet Jews.

& after them, Avril, who will sit aft. Sister, no, I will not leave you behind.

The next day. [**Last entry.**] The day began well. The sky was bright, even by six, & the wind light.

Still it has not ended, though he is gone—taken, as we knew he would be. The rest of us, footsore, abandoned, but I suspect closely watched, now await our own disposition.

How will it end? How will it all end?

Where is he? Where have they taken him? When will we all meet again?

There are questions the aloud putting of which—I just asked these questions aloud—destroys one's self-possession & disestablishes one's self-respect.

The day began well. The sky was bright, even very early. Ric was already up when I arose. He was fully dressed smoking in the kitchen, abstractedly as usual—much more so, truth be told. He did not look up when I came in.

Did he in this fit of abstraction, smoking quietly, coughing, staring into the middle distance with those pale-blue eyes of his, his posture so characteristic, so intense—did he foresee the events of this day, this consequential day—a Red Letter Day, if ever there was one, in our big little lives?

I don't believe that she did. She was taken completely by surprise. As I was.

It is impossible to write. Jets overhead every five minutes. Bomb-blasts nearby—too close—it's hard to tell where, but too close. Are we a target? The cottage? Or is it just for show?

I will try to write it down. We were all in the boat, all but Dobbs but we had his boy Stevie and all was as usual though we were a bit scared when Ric insisted that we go with, Gillian & I, & Stevie, with Caroline stepping into the boat at the last possible second, and not wanting to go, she doesn't like boats, after what happened, even though he said that the boat-ride was for her and for Gillian, and for a few minutes I really thought that he was making a sort of run for it, though we had brought nothing with us and there are always launches in the distance but then I saw it. The lightbulb lit up. Corryvreckan. The whirlpool, Corryvreckan, was our destination. Rick was making a bee-line, it was no accident. He was doing it on purpose. $1 + 3 = 0$? $1 - 3 = 1$? $1 - 2 - 1 = 0$.

For the first time in weeks, months, I felt as of one mind with C as we both turned to look at him, practically in unison—

—What—where?—Ric—you know what's just ahead?—where we're heading?—Ric? Cedric?

Yes, he knows what is just ahead. He does not turn aside. Then it's twenty feet away. But I am still sure that he knows what he's doing.

—He knows what he's doing, I say. I push over a little closer to Stevie.

—Does he?

Caroline grabs my hand.

—Ric!

—It will be a kind of game!

Gillian and Caroline, I and Stevie are hugging and we go into the whirlpool as if down a slide and are spun about, the boat moving under us. I think we are going to be thrown out. Stevie and I fall over, it probably saved us, and I see Gill and Caroline hunkering down but I fall on my good ~~soldier~~ shoulder thank God and Stevie is quiet on top of me like a mouse when we are rolling around the boat and I admit I scream... But I can't hear it because as we look up we felt the need to look the heliocopter is just above us, and it is loud—so loud indeed that it absorbs the sound of the outboard and seems to swell until it is taking up all the world. I remember that I cannot hear a thing, not even Stevie, who is right next to me and is yelling something, and not Ric, who puts his hand on my back as now the water explodes all around us and we are in it, at last, the water, and all is silence... for a moment, until we rise and the silence is broken by a voice above us that says,

—YOU ARE THE DEAD.

But we do not die. One minute later we are all back in the boat—someone has pulled us all out—all but Ric, who has disappeared—and, the motor being sunk, having fallen off, we are being towed to one of the little treeless islands, Beag I think it was. Stevie is OK. Gillian and Caroline are hugging each other and shivering together. They pull us near the shore and cut the rope and whirlybird off, bringing their windy weather with them. We row the rest of the way, even though the boat is half-full of water. We manage to turn it over just trying to get out of it, and this time Stevie gets stuck for a moment under the gunwale. But he knows to hold his breath and we succeed in getting him out, thank God, and then use Ric's lighter to get a small fire going of driftwood and dried grass and whatnot. We dry out a little and warm up but it is three hours before some fishermen are cruising by and we yell. Bless them, they stopped and towed us back to Jura but to the western shore because they had to go fishing. Very decent of them nonetheless. Caroline offered to give them money once we got back to Barnhill but they refused. We walked back along the shore—another two hours, and nobody had his or her shoes; they were also lost at sea. But we made it home alive if footsore.

Home? Now we wait for Ric to return, not sure when he will return, not sure if he will return. Ric wrote of having been given a turn. Now it is I who am turned around—turning still—turning—and I wonder—it's as if I have not yet really gotten out of the eddy but am stuck in it still, still turning around, still spinning, but slowly now, almost imperceptibly, 'round and 'round.

Later. Caroline is upset. Fits of typing, rat-a-tat at the keys, then long stretches of sitting on the sofa as if she were paralysed, unable to breathe. Now and then she wipes her nose, makes a little sound and gets up from the sofa and goes to the sink and turns both taps full bore. She plunges her hands into the streams, wringing them. She writhes.

[*The Diary of Cedric B. O'Malley*; "A Letter of Caroline O'Malley, *née* Pretzel"; letter to Inez Holden, 21 June 1948]

Dear Innie,

My dear Innie, it's over here. It is all over, having scarcely begun.

He's gone. They took him this morning. Cedric is gone, he was taken away.

And this, after he tried to kill us all in the boat, the children the dotty sister and me.

Gone. Done. Now what?

The security bastards swooped down in their helicopter and took him out of the water leaving us stranded on the rock to which we managed to half-row and half-swim, half-drowned, having escaped the whirlpool into which he drove us evidently quite on purpose in that miserable leaky punt—the children, too, the children! I find it hard to write it out. It's still unbelievable. One of them, the boy, was almost properly drowned—just made it.

Cedric is gone. Plucked. Pulled up & sent down. & here we sit, stuck on the larger rock of this Godforsaken island, which has been infiltrated, it's no longer a place to live.

MY SOHO STALKER I TOLD YOU ABOUT, MUSTACHIO—HE'S HERE, THE BASTARD, OR WAS HERE, we don't know, he was injured, hit on the head, and went off out the door not to be seen again, the crazy sister smashed him with the glass paperweight blood all over the floor—we thought he was OK and I am not sure now how sad to be about what happened being so happy that the bastard is simply gone.

He was come to take us away, Gillian and me.

Do I give off a smell, Innie, that allows them to sniff me out over vast stretches of land and sea? How in hell could they care about us so much, about Ric, about me, Gillian, to send men even out here to harass us? To abduct us? &—"&"—I'm infected—what is next?

My plan, if you want to call it that, more my reflex is to get the boat, if it's still seaworthy, as if it ever were, and try to find a motor for it—the Colonel, our neighbour, has one, I believe, and get the sister, who knows how to pilot a boat pretty well—better than I do—and in a few days try to make the mainland when the sun is out, if it is out, and if it's warm enough, and if the waves are not too high, the sea not too cold and rough, and bring the children with us, both Gillian and Stevie Dobbs the handyman's son... My handyman, Mr. Dobbs, about whom I told you, too, if he'll come, which he may since the S.F.s seem to want to use Jura as a kind of target range. We hear explosions going off all the time in the distance. I do not think that the handyman will come with us. I intend to approach him, despite... He would be good to have on the trip.

Yes, he steered us right into the thick of it, the whirlpool, so famous it has a name—Kerrybreckan, and the boat almost turned over and did fill up with seawater. First I saw him throw something into it, a package, and then he shouted "This was your idea!" It was his idea, I have never wanted anything to do with these eddies so violent at times you hear them gnashing even in the house, which is ten damned miles away. I have always refused to go anywhere near them—until this morning, when I had no choice. They are mills that—they have nothing to do with humanity. My idea? His ideas were getting the better of him. A Child of Enlightenment—he's forty years old. Remember what Mill talked about, the debauching influence of Hegel. Little wonder, all his talk of streams, tides, currents, waves and aquatic whatnot—he has some vague idea of a Great Western Atlantic destiny pouring into the British Isles through the keyhole of our local gulf. The man loves allegories. I think that he was wishing we might all be spared the alternative Human Whirlpool of what he expected would be our fate at the hands of the S.F., our lives here being no longer possible, what with all the helicopters and jets overhead flying low, I swear, to frighten us continually with the thought of a bomb landing as if a thunderbolt upon the cottage. It's been hell. No wonder...

Still, he's gone. And now we are all refugees, dear, all of us, Gillian, I—and you, too, as you read this and share in our situation—and you have your own situation—refugees from History who have lost their last refuge. This cottage in a sylvan glade will soon be all but uninhabitable. It's just too scary, their knowing where we are as we sit and wait for whatever the next thing may be to happen.

Later. Innie, how has it happened—how could it happen so? Who would have thought of our generation that people could be so readily so swiftly twisted and knotted into such freakish new forms? I never thought we would prove so pliable, malleable, so mutable, no matter how big the bomb—detonating the biggest bomb in the world would not be enough, I thought—like Ric, who wrote as you know how "No bomb that ever burst / Shatters the crystal spirit." What burst was the biggest bomb in the world, it burst several times over, and it would appear as if that was more than enough. It has come to pass, in England, at least. Maybe we have not been Italian enough. Human character changed, in or about 6 August 1945, consequent upon a new and different Post-Impressionist Exhibition—as if a bomb had been dropped on our new Crystal Palace. Now it's all broken globes, the shattered glass swept into neat piles of course, we are English!—the red-hot filaments exposed.

I am drifting, forgive me, my dear.

We have no ability now to leave the cottage, not safely. We are afraid that we could be plucked walking in the woods on a path or down the road—just thrown in the back of a lorry and never heard from again. Like Cedric? The Colonel has come by the past two mornings bringing us supplies. He agrees. They don't seem interested in him. And yet the cottage isn't safe harbour either. Just yesterday afternoon a heliocopter came and made a terrific racket sitting just outside my window. I was napping and thought it was a cyclone that had blown up out of nowhere. It just sat there opposite my window magically ten feet off the ground with a man in a green helmet who looked like a sort of beetle watching me through field glasses. It was unsettling: you can see what it has been to be here these past few days.

I don't know how well you can read all this—am having trouble writing. My hands shake.

Later. A long afternoon filled with dread, but a dread blessedly not shared by Gillian, who has spent it writing. That's our Gillian, Ric would say. A junior diarist, as you know, she has also been quite a good little reader! Now I will ask you, Innie, to be the same. Not to turn melodramatic, but I feel the need to confess my sins, Innie. Certainly it seems silly to hold back now. I will tell you about the private room in Craighouse. I have also mentioned the paperweight and the sister.

There is a little apothecary shop in Craighouse where Gillian buys sweets with her pennies and we buy bric-a-brac or just browse amongst its odd antique odds and ends. Its proprietor is a quiet, mild, odd-looking little man with white hair but bushy black brows. A little strange. One day some months ago he insisted on showing us up the stairs to a little boxlike room he had to let on the first floor that was full of lovely odd old furniture with a little round table in the middle that had placed upon it for purposes of display a beautiful objet d'art, a sort of crystal globe with a twig of pink coral suspended at its centre. Ric is dexterous; he seized upon it and smudged it, saying that it reminded him of me. Of course it turned out to be for sale. Ric's admiration for it had been such that Avril and I had to return a little later quietly and buy it to give to him—he is constantly giving me gifts, dingy purses, in one of which I hid it later on—and I was pleased to do so even though it was surprisingly expensive, for all its preciousness, given that it was for sale in what might be called a rag and bone junk shop. The strange thing was that the old man, having wrapped it up for us to take home, stared at me rather boldly as he handed it over and winked at me, slyly—not some sweet older person's wink. It had a knowing, shameless quality about it. Yes, if it is possible to jeer with a wink, then that is what he did.

Three weeks or so later I happened to be in Craighouse again and was passing by the old man's shop (you cannot be there without passing it) when I saw the old man's eyes staring at me through the window-blinds. He came out of the shop, looked around for a moment, and began quietly insisting that I come in, that he had something to show me. I thought, what, another piece of pricey bric-a-brac. But no, he wanted to show me—the room. Again. It had not changed except that the globe was of course missing and a dusty old typewriter stuck in its place. He spoke of how the room was "the guest room, a quiet one, ma'am," heavily papered. Not just that I couldn't hear the outside—I couldn't be heard. He took a deep breath. One can make as much noise as one likes in a room like this!—he said, raising his voice to a shout. He also showed me the key to the room and where he keeps it, "no need to ring the bell," and showed me the way into the room from the outside up a flight of rickety stairs, I incredulous the whole while assuring him that I did not need to rent a room at present and being met with an utterly uncomprehending look as I did followed by a quietly stubborn reiteration of the virtues of this boxy room.

"Everyone needs a retreat."

I thought of my own spare room of one's very own, which of course, as you well know, I have always arranged in London. A perch.

But how in the hell could the old man know about that?

Do I give it off, Innie, as a kind of smell? You know how eccentric I am. You know all about it. Ric is the one who counts in any arrangement of this kind. He does not know me as you know me. He knows only a little of how I am, what I am "like," what it means to be the sort of person I am at this age and with these inclinations, ambitions these... what some would regard as affectations—sort of afflictions, even.

Remarkably, Innie, and here things turn stranger yet, I found myself accepting the key, having paid out the two pounds. He told me that he had no wire recorder, no microphone, but that the typewriter was for my use and said it with his eyes averted in a low voice, a manner of blank neutrality and stolidity, but, again, he seemed to act as if he knew something to my discredit enough even though he did not wink or even blink that I would not be spending most of my time in this room typing.

You can guess what happens next. I begin accompanying the old Colonel on his weekly trips. Ah, well.

After all, I do manage to do some typing.

Later. Avril is gone.

(So is her diary—gone.)

She was gone this morning when we got up. All her other things, like Ric's, are still here, and that makes me think that they may be allowed to come back some day God knows how soon and will we still be here but I am sure that she did not just leave of her own accord for there is no way she could leave us behind without saying goodbye, especially to Gillian, for whom she has developed an affection after all.

This sister and I have never been friends mainly because she is so fiercely protective of her brother but sometimes I have felt that we are moving not far away from each other on parallel lines.

Innie, how will it where will it end?

Or will it not, like my dream? Yes, I had it yet again last night, I was wandering in a Physical wood, again, and went off the path, got lost, and came upon the pyramid, out of which the light streamed as if a crystal current, as if all the light in the world had been gathered and amassed but was breaking out. But there was no sound. This time the dream was stranger than any time before. Concentrating, I found a giant key on the ground and stuck it in the lock, and all these bells went off as the wall opened and... I felt myself lifted up and borne away as if on a huge wave, and I couldn't breathe, I could see nothing, or too much, I was blinded by the light just as I was deafened by the bells, and the wave rounded a kind of bend, it seemed, and started to turn back but then turned again and twisted, and that seemed to make it better—I was in the eddy again—and I caught my breath and I started to sing, in my way... and then I woke up.

What do you make of this strange, detailed thing? Since Freud, we fill every rift not with ore but with sex. Well, perhaps not simply that.

Later. Avril remains gone, but the Colonel has come by this afternoon, kindly as ever. But as a sign that things continue to transmogrify, dear, as I am sorry to have to report—you have your own sadnesses and strangenesses to deal with, I well know—the Colonel has come by displaying a different air. It is hard to put my finger on what has changed about him, but changed it has. For one thing, he suddenly seems a younger man than he did. His hair seems a little different and he no longer seems slightly palsied as he has.

Innie, I am afraid that he is one of them.

He seemed to know a lot about what was going to happen to us—"probably," as he put it.

Probably we will be relocated soon to the mainland, probably to Wales, probably. How he would know that...

We will be relocated to a "Jewish Community," as they are calling it, evidently; the word "camp" is strictly avoided, of course. For our protection. There will be doctors for me to consult, he said; all the communities have doctors and nurses. Now it occurs to me to wonder how well stocked they will be—will they have supplies of Streptomycin?

Gillian is never tired of writing, it appears, but has arranged several of Ric's grubby tools on the living room table. It's a mess, but it has given her something to do. She has said that she will make a puzzle for us to work on in the long evenings. She's a good Scout! I intend to imitate her.

Later. Innie, we leave tomorrow. And today I give this letter, what is truly more a tiny journal of my last days as Freewoman and the last days of Gillian's Free Girlhood—today I give it to the Colonel along with the book, of course, which I have decided to call "The Eternal Guests"—with which, its being a failure, you may do what you wish—sink it in the Thames, for all I care, where the sun doesn't shine. He will post them to you as soon as he can. He has promised to do so on Thursday. Thursday he makes his regular run down to Craighouse. In other words, you may be puzzling along with me over all this just a few days after the puzzling events here transcribed.

Gillian—God knows what she is making of all this; I don't. She's puzzling.

Let me share a regret. Stuck on Q. I do feel that I should have offered to read her diary all these past weeks or to have her read it aloud to me for I suspect that it is full of observations she would like to share but feels a bit afraid to, except maybe with her aunt who I think intimidates her less, the little mouse. Oh, so busy I have been with my own work, Innie—you know how it can be. All this time I could have been teaching her to sing. She, teaching me?

The Colonel has just arrived—blast, I had more to tell you, my dear—in any event, dear one, may this ~~missil~~ missive—is it a last will and testament?—find you in the best of health and the highest spirits possible given all, &c., and I hope and trust that we will meet again and that you will accept Gillian—by post?—if it is possible for me to send her—armed with her little diary!—out of the camp which I will be trying to do—after all, she is only one-half Jew—sorry to drop this bomb here at the end but there we are—farewell, dear one.

Caroline Pretzel O'Malley.

[Cedric's Diary; last entries]

[Undated] 1948... But in 1498, why not, Columbus sailed the ocean great. He sailed back an American. Thus began what I call Oceania. What I call the New History. & the Old History endeth then? Not then but in 1984? Not 9841, 9481, 9184, 8491, not 8914, not 4918, 4891, 4981, 41—et al., none of them for all are too far, far away. They mean nothing. 1498, on the other hand, 1849, the Gold Rush, 1894, Martial Bourdin bombs Greenwich at 4:51, 1984—1984, the closest, the best, perhaps.

NOVELLA—"From the Archives of Oceania" 97

But why not 1948? Closer yes, but too close, the mind reels, or unreels. Let us not expect too much of ourselves. Let's not let time deceive us, "We cannot conquer Time!" Nineteen eighty-four, then. Or, for the Yanks, who are so numerical, 1984. $1 - 9 = 8$, wholly or naturally, which is the fourth position, with $4 \times 2 = 8$, which is $9 - 1$, but only when 4 is in the third position, not the second, whilst 9, in the second, $= 8 + 1$, which uses 2, yes, but leaves 1, 4, in the second position, in the third position, respectively, whilst 9 equals that doubled 4 minus 1. One. But we have two, 2, to be rid of.

Perfect, then—or close enough. 1984.

[Undated] Fly, Avian Albion of the Thousand Eyes!

Shy Fledgling, shake your wings & soar. What you will see today, given your God-like power of vision, your ability to see through walls, to look into the forgotten places pockets packets pouches purses, to see into the dark itself—well, God only knows.

In the meantime, go on living in the Light, all breathing human pathos far above, quite literally speaking…

No, rather, now is the time to write it up, to tell all & be done with it. Such is the appointed task on this day.

Fly, then, Memory, One-eyed, on ragged wings…

After a period of many weeks—months—who could tell, time seemed to stop when he was recruited & removed to the city, if that's where it was (of course, now we know where it was), it appeared that he had been sufficiently chastened and subdued. For one day it was found that the spectacles had been returned to him (they were found sitting on the desk one day upon waking up, & they had been glued & straightened), hot meals were being provided—at first it was not noticed, they were not eaten—& even clean linen & laundered pants & shirts. It was suddenly recognized that he was recovering. Strength was returning. Left solitary in the windowless cell, a daily regimen of calisthenics was begun, bending hard to touch his toes, right in front of the screen where it was sure to be seen. It was thought that this might impress. Most of the time, of course, time was spent at the desk, as instructed, until the men came by with the needles, bringing instantaneous sleep.

Until one day he jerked awake to find himself seated at a different desk—one not standing in the corner of his cell but shoved up against his gut. He was seated in a different room, a small room that seemed in motion, but barely in motion, that seemed placed at some distance above the ground.

But he knew immediately what it was. He was in a rotary machine of sorts, perhaps a helicopter, hovering—lingering, rather, the vibrations coming off the rotor coursing in sine waves through the boxlike structure into his body, which was fixed in the seat.

Of course, he could not move. Out of the corners of his eyes he could see straps holding the wrists in place; the elbows were clamped to the chair, the feet, the knees strapped together &, most troubling, was the placement of the head, which was clamped in place, God knows how, so that he was forced to look out of a large glass door misted-over in front of him. He could not turn his head.

Around the door, framing it, in fact, was what was in fact an imposing piece of artifice, a massive gilt picture frame or proscenium arch, perhaps, unmistakably of ornate, mid-Victorian vintage, I recall that it occurred to him.

When he shut his eyes he received an electric shock—so intensely painful, though I am not sure what is the word for this sensation, God knows what it was, which seemed beyond pain, a smart impossible to be borne, not to be elected. A blink of the eye, on the other hand, brought no pain.

Now & then his repaired spectacles would slip an inch down the nose—& a hand would shoot forward out of nowhere—for some minutes he had thought he was alone—& kindly, somehow familiarly, resettle them.

The machine began to move to the side, to the left, the glass magically clearing, & the perception started into place as he sidled off, immovable & yet moved, moving, yet still, the perception that he was at the cinema, taking an afternoon at the cinema, such was the beauty of the countryside. For after passing over a series of grey roofs they found themselves in the green fields beyond moving with considerable speed. The sun was shining. The light hurt the eyes, it was so bright. & he would not have been surprised to hear a bird sing. Spring it was, of course, though he had had no perception of the seasons having changed, there, in the dungeon, in the darkness broken only by periods of awakening pain & incandescence.

So Spring still exists, he thought, Ipril & all! But it might be Autumn, of course. The sky was that impossible blue of early September, that most expectant of months.

Courage.

Our speed increased. We were moving over &, it seemed, moving coolly, bodily, into fields of the richest, freshest green deep down in the heart of things, only then to find himself approaching a wide, seemingly endless sheet of shimmering water. Keen.

It was a beautiful sight, if all too bright. The line of sunlight shining on the river or lake or whatever it was (now we know what it was) stretched to the horizon, which disappeared in sheer incandescence—starting the fear...

For now we could see in the distance a little speck sitting on the open water.

Slowly we approached it from on high, & we saw clearly whilst still miles off that it was not one speck but several specks, like atoms or dust-particles, a few smaller ones gathered together around a larger central one, this nucleus being a boat, a small boat. I could also tell, soon enough as we approached, that this small boat in the middle was oddly packed, bearing very small men & very large men, & not many in between, from the look of the thing. Men & boys? I wondered. Africans & Asians?

Refugees? he wondered. But what does it matter: undesirables. Expendables. Leave them to their fate, one must.

But whence the necessity that the leave-taking be borne witness? Why bear, why be made to bear, witness to such a scene as this, one fairly commonplace, after all, if undeniably gruesome?

As we lowered in the sky nearing the boat it became clear that it was a lifeboat—a lifeboat crowded heavily, barely still afloat—& its occupants women & children.

The smaller boats clustered round it (but at a safe distance) were occupied by two men, each, each pair standing behind a camera on a tripod.

& now he knew why he had been brought here. Not &—therefore, rather.

&, of course, it was impossible to look away.

We slowed strongly—inertia pressing him against his bonds, reportedly, as if to throw him from the seat into the scene now spreading before us—& came to a kind of stop in the air a mere hundred yards from the lifeboat & a mere hundred feet above it.

His spectacles having slipped down the nose, the hand shot forward & resettled them.

It was impossible to look away, & why, he now recalls asking himself, reportedly, why look away—why? As part of the necessary inuring he must prepare to witness scenes such as these.

It is the unobservable, the obscene; therefore, it must be seen.

Thus encouraged he looked on with a steady eye even as the distance between us & the scene before him lessened gradually to the point that our motion forward had become imperceptible &, soon enough, one could make out some of the details of the women & children gathered together in the boat.

The rotary started up throbbing, filling him with its noise, shuddering the entire airship—it was clear that the guns were powering up, preparing to engage the enemy.

As was the cannon, too, which would probably not kick out a bomb, & then it was that he wondered why. Refugees & the unauthorized generally were to be denied use of vessel or vehicle. But the usual game was with machine guns used to puncture, to sink: let Nature take its course. Let Nature swallow it up.

The room throbbed heavily, his ears felt ready to burst, the chair shook, we were close, now—too close, he thought, too close to home, so close as to be blasted by our own bombs.

There was a middle-aged woman who had to have been a Jewess, the caricature of such, a cartoon, voluptuous, voluminous, big-boned, black-eyed, big-nosed, hook-nosed, for Gott's sake, squatting up in the bow with a little boy about three years old in her arms—the little boy, screaming—the fat Jewess not screaming—blue with fright, trying to soothe the boy—who was hiding his head between her mountainous breasts as if he could burrow right into her & she standing up & hugging the boy & looking up at us & trying to soothe him but looking up straight at us & cursing us, that foul cartoon come to life.

When he saw them. Unmistakable, right behind the Jewess. Caroline. & Gillian, it was, and some other little girl she had taken under her wing, sitting looking right at one another, at least it looked like them, it had to be them, they didn't seem afraid with Caroline's lips moving, not words, keening-like, evidently pouring out love, & Gillian keening back, neither one of them looking up when we tried to stop it, he tried, he did, I saw it, he tried, he yelled out, & the electricity came flooding out, he tried to stop us, he tried… but was spinning drowning his head had to split, a cracked sphere spinning & swirling light & pain, unendurable, & the usual, an eruption of incandescence, blinding—that pure light that made him open his eyes just in time to see us plant a 20 kilo bomb right in the midst of them…

& Caroline? It was as though someone had thrown Caroline a ball.

Egg-toss: here you go, then, catch!

~20 Jews. (~6,000,020)

Fact.

A terrific flash, & all gone to rose matchwood, all except just one thing, a child's arm that flew up in the air in an arc that seemed aimed for us but missed.

& now he knew whose hand…

Tick tock.

[Undated] **[Last entry.]** The routine is now established. We—all we successful recruits—now awake early, wash briefly with good warm towels, put on our clean linen & wool trousers & Egyptian cotton shirts & our blue blazers, we overgrown fourth-formers—we are all fourteen years old again—& go to breakfast. Each of us is just another white knuckle on the fist. Just after breakfast we go to our array of desks & begin work—only at some point in the morning to be interrupted by the deafening ringing of a bell followed by a screeching sound, hideous & grinding, senseless & stupid, I used to think it, but now I hear resounding in it the voice of all our English & European & American Western industrial heritage, as if its noise comprehended every machine we have ever made, the groan of the first lever & the squeaks of the first wheels & the throbs of pulleys & steam dynamos in all the early factories, the whirr & purr of the latest Rolls-Royce engines on the road or in the air, all rolling on, all echoing, all agreeing—it is a voice, indeed, the metallic voice of the Inter-com commanding us as it does every morning to report to the grouproom. &, day after day, immediately & noiselessly we crowd into the grouproom for the morning flicks. Day after day, the flicks—at least, the flicks

that my group & I watch—are always the same flicks, though the sequence would appear to be random.

The screen is grainy & grey, & then it brightens to reveal a broad expanse of shining water. In media res: we are travelling over water at high speeds, as if to enjoy its brilliant blue when in the distance we begin to make out what we now know to look for, a black speck floating on the sea that swiftly enlarges to become... just the thing, a lifeboat full of children & women. Refugees. Guests of the Nation!

—Righto, here we go again, says someone. Once the flicks begin, levity is encouraged, & self-expression.

—I never tire of this one.

—! A noise, not a little one—shouted. Shouted out.

By whom?

Not for the first time, no, that outburst. It is a shout of...?

Never mind what I say, what do I mean? & I find myself, as usual, with the old brass key in my hand that was sitting on my desk one day a few months ago, I suppose, when I woke up. I find myself rubbing the key.

—Best of the lot, says someone, the lifeboat approaching.

What do I bloody well mean? Enlighten me.

I have never known what to call it, the feeling of that shout, ever since it started happening, the shouting, even though it started some time ago.

I have dislodged my glasses, which are new but which fit no better than the old & are continually sliding down the bridge of my nose—something about the way I'm built.

—Royal! & so real!

—Ja! Nein, Entfremdungsgefühl!

Yes, I remember: it has to be Aarronow, now almost indistinguishable, that crowing voice, now melded in the larger jeer.

—Somebody's about to have a bad day. The American.

—Explorsiveful!

—Not the U-boat but the Jew-boat, dive, dive, dive!

—No, duck, Ducky! someone mutters. Sitting.

The others catching the mood, egging each other on, we approach from several angles in turn, giggling, quipping, smirking. Jeering. I used to live on Jeera. As usual, the approach is slow & painstaking as well as multiple & redundant, as if anxious that the viewer miss nothing, see everything, every blessed thing, & register all. It's as if we are watching incipient newsreel, something for the archives. Cutting back & forth between relative close-ups of the boat & wide-angle shots, both of which are getting closer & closer to the boat as we watch, we see, slowly coming into view above the bow of the boat, a helicopter, which nears the boat & begins to hover over it; its flank bears a large window in which we can see a glint of light. Cutting away & zooming zooming!—close, we see the children; we see the mothers; we see exactly what they are all doing as the helicopter hovers. We cannot miss a thing. We see the little boy & the Jewess; we do not see the Jewess cursing.

—Look at that fat cunt! She's all wet!
—But Kundry, all butt! Aarronow again, being Aarronow.
—Royal! Royal!
—Here comes the big ouch!
We see that other person, the younger woman—
—That slut! Shouted.

Who said that? As ever, we see the woman & the child, whose names have begun to fade, who are now no more than their initials, P. & G., & again we see them talking quietly, as usual, looking at each other, the one coughing, wearing a scarf that used to hang in my closet—& just for a sec I wonder, how did she get her hands on it?—& we see the stream of lead, as if a firehose tap had been slapped wide open, encroaching on the boat, nibbling it away like Time & we see—finally, we see— the bomb homing in again, seeking its nest, & the reliably blinding flash, & all the manic blossoming, & all the matchwood harmlessly airborne, an obtuse angle arcing gracefully, a bent baton thrown skyward…—!

A shout—in time, as the arm arcs—a shout of… what? Yes, that's it—acceptance! That's it—the lightbulb lights up. & I am enlightened, at last.

It is a shout of acceptance, something like affirmation, something like joy.

I wonder that, after all, it may be just as simple as that. That it was deserved.

Next week, we bomb Corryvreckan, itself.

We were the Dead. Then a Thing happened. Now History, which was over, is over, & is done with, is still, at last. Memory is all yesterday. Noontide tomorrow our private libraries to the communal fire-barrow we commit.

& Today? Here we sit, still, lasting, making History.
It isn't over. Things still happen.
I notice that I have dropped the key. But I let it lie.
& then, as I, the last man, sit still wondering, wondering, still, for the thousandth time, the nineteen-hundred forty-eighth & last time, all wonder now coming to an end, the next reel begins to grind, & it's the same as the last—the same flick, all over again. Before moving on to other flicks, we see the same flick again, & again, & again &

[The end.]

III. TEACHING SUPPLEMENT

A. CONNECTING "FROM THE ARCHIVES" & *NINETEEN EIGHTY-FOUR*

1. Readers of *Nineteen Eighty-Four* will recall O'Brien's habit of deftly "resettling his spectacles on his nose," which Winston calls a "trick" and finds "in some indefinable way, curiously civilized" (*1984*, 10–11). The novella's Cedric O'Malley displays the same habit. Vision, and its correction (think of the phrase "corrective lenses"), is a theme in both *Nineteen Eighty-Four* and "From the Archives." But "spectacles" of *other* kinds also figure in both works. What, then, are the various functions of spectacles/"the spectacle" in (a) *Nineteen Eighty-Four* and (b) "From the Archives"?
2. What is the role and symbolic import of that "lump of glass" (*1984*, 101), the "glass paperweight" (*1984*, 99), in (a) *Nineteen Eighty-Four* and (b) the novella? Discuss continuities and distinctions between their treatments (*who* is made to use it, *how* they are made to use it, *how* they are said to have *gotten it in hand*, to begin with, *what fate* it is given, and so forth). Clearly the novella attempts to bring the Orwellian significance of the paperweight into sharper focus. Does it succeed, and if so, how? Alternatively, how does the novella depart from Orwell so as to explore a significance at which Orwell only hints?
3. Three dreams are reported over the course of "From the Archives," and Winston reports many daytime fantasies and reveries as well as several proper dreams. How seriously are we to take this mode of experience, both in the novella and the novel? Dreams are often regarded as offering escapes from a troubling reality. Sigmund Freud, however,

thought them less escapist than expressive; he called them (by way of their interpretation) "the royal road to... the unconscious activities of the mind."[1] How, then, would you characterize the various dreams in the novel and novella? How salutary do they prove—how enabling, both for their dreamers and their interpreters (a group which includes us readers)?

4. How would you compare and contrast Cedric O'Malley's relationship with the natural world, what Orwell calls "the surface of the earth," with Winston's in *Nineteen Eighty-Four* and Orwell's as exemplified in the *Diaries*?[2]
5. Cedric O'Malley, one of the novella's two principal diarists, is a composite figure who blends aspects of Orwell's personality, habits, and situation with those of Winston as well as with those of his torturer, O'Brien—O'Brien as he was, or may be imagined to have been, before becoming the O'Brien of *Nineteen Eighty-Four*. What is the effect of such blending, and what is its point?
6. The author of "From the Archives" reports having found the following passage (here slightly modified) quite suggestive: WINSTON, upon seeing O'Brien for the first time in the ministry of Love—"They've got you too!" O'BRIEN ["with a mild, almost regretful irony"]—"They got me a long time ago" (*1984*, 238). What do you think it suggests? How does O'Brien's offhand reply help to explain the creation of "From the Archives"?
7. "From the Archives" is in large part a record of Cedric and Avril O'Malley's diaries, and Orwell's novel also shares several of Winston's diary entries or portions thereof (Winston's diary entry marked "*April 4th, 1984,*" which recounts his experience watching a film-clip of a "*lifeboat full of children with a helicopter hovering over it*" [*1984*, 8], is of particular interest). How do the novella's various diarists compare and contrast with Winston, who wonders why he bothers with his diary, given that it is forbidden and must be kept absolutely secret: "For whom, it suddenly occur[s] to him to wonder, was he writing this diary?" (*1984*, 7). Why, by the same token, is Cedric writing his? And why does Avril take up diary-writing—and even Gillian, who is discovered at the end to have been writing a secret diary of her own?

8. The editor's note at the start of the novella might be compared to Margaret Atwood's use of "Historical Notes on the Handmaid's Tale" at the end of her novel, *A Handmaid's Tale* (1985). Another example of such a fictional editorial statement may be found at the opening of Elaine Scarry's "A Defense of Poesy (The Treatise of Julia)," itself a critical/creative response to *Nineteen Eighty-Four*.[3] What is the effect of such devices?
9. How do you feel the novella works as a freestanding or even stand-alone piece? What would you say about it if you read it without knowledge of *Nineteen Eighty-Four*?
10. When you have read the "Critical Supplement," "Orwell Agonistes," which comes last in this book's sequence, think about its purpose. What insights into the subjects of Orwell's late writing period and his *Nineteen Eighty-Four*, in particular, does it contribute? What light does it shed that the critical novella "From the Archives" does not?
11. How does the composite format of *1948*—critical/creative novella + critical statement—affect your reading of either of these two parts? If forced to prefer one to the other, which one would you pick, and why? What would be lost if one or the other were ignored?
12. When reading a book, Orwell liked to distinguish what he called the writer's "message"; he felt that "every writer, especially every novelist, *has* a 'message,' whether he [or she] admits it or not."[4] Why would a writer wish to deny that her work has a "message"? What are the messages of *Nineteen Eighty-Four* and "From the Archives"? How do they compare?
13. "From the Archives" is preoccupied principally with later events in Orwell's life and work. What episodes in, or elements of, Orwell's life and writings would you develop and explore if you were to write a prequel or sequel to one of his works?

B. INTERPRETIVE CONTEXTS FOR "FROM THE ARCHIVES"

14. The American critical theorist Stanley Fish has argued that the work of art, literary or other, is "no[t]... an object, a thing-in-itself, but an event, something that happens to, and with the participation of, the reader."[5] For his fellow

"reader-centered" critic, the German theorist Hans Robert Jauss, it is much the same.[6] The literary work is, if an "object" in any sense of the word, an "*ästhetisches Objekt*" (an "*aesthetic* object"); if a "structure," "it is not a structure independent of [its readerly] reception."[7] Thus for Jauss as well as for Fish, a "literary work is... metaphorically more like a musical score than a monument."[8] In reading a poem, for example, we do not so much mine its lines for a meaning or message that can be extracted as *perform* them; the meaning of the poem is as much the product of its performer and performance as it is the original intention of its composer. Accordingly, the critical novella "From the Archives"—if it is what it purports to be, a kind of reading of Orwell's *Nineteen Eighty-Four*—is a "performance" of it. Thus the question: how does such a notion of this novella—a notion of it as performance—change our appreciation or understanding of it? In what sense may it be said to perform Orwell? A second question: keeping in mind the metaphor of the "musical score," how might a reading/performance that is "revisionary" (see Part I, "Introduction"), that is "both creative and critical," differ from one that is "strictly critical" (for example, "Orwell Agonistes")?

15. Exploring further Jauss's concept of the reader or "receiver," we may note that he subdivides a particular class of reader, the "historical," into three sub-classes, the highest of which, consisting of "highly educated author-readers," he calls the "*Gipfelebene* (pinnacle level) of authors reading authors."[9] The authors at this level "take an active role in answering tradition by creating their own works"; they "respond to received literature by creating significant statements of their own."[10] If *Nineteen Eighty-Four* is a part of literary heritage, of "received literature," clearly "From the Archives" attempts a "significant statement" in its own right. But just how "significant" does it prove—to what extent may it be said to "answer... tradition" as embodied in *Nineteen Eighty-Four*? And what, after all, might it mean for a book to "answer" tradition—or, for that matter, for a book to "embody" it? Drilling yet deeper, what do you think it entails for any book to provide, or constitute itself as, an answer to another?

16. Examples of what we might call "authorial self-criticism," a relatively unexplored subgenre of literary criticism, may be found exemplified by Henry James's introductions to his novels, for example his preface to *The Ambassadors* (1903), which in its discussion of the book's origin and occasion provides an extended exegesis of one of its particular scenes.[11] It is as if James becomes, for these pages, the literary critic of his own creative work. Another example of an author explicating and explaining his own work in detail may be found in George Bernard Shaw's "Preface" to *Major Barbara* (1907), especially the section entitled "Weaknesses of the Salvation Army," wherein Shaw explains in minute, line-by-line detail what he was up to in the episode involving the character Bill Walker.[12] Yet another: in his letter to Sara Coleridge defending the composition of his poem "Resolution and Independence" (1807), William Wordsworth goes into extraordinarily precise detail about several of his particular choices in diction.[13] Leaving aside the question of whether these particular self-critical acts are successful, what do you think of the very idea of them? *Can* an act of self-criticism be successful? If so, then what would you say a successful act of self-criticism would have to be or to do? *1948* contains a critical supplement as well as a critical novella; though the dominant aim of the supplement is to illuminate the novella's origins in Orwell's later work, it also discusses the destinations at which the novella arrives. Does the supplement thus *commit*—for want of a more neutral word—self-criticism? If so, where, precisely? And if so, is *it* successful?

17. Item #7 above asked you to consider Cedric and Winston as diarists, which exercise prompts a number of larger and broader questions: for example, what do you think about the choice of diary format—advantages and disadvantages? Orwell himself was a busy diarist (see "On the Diary Form of 'From the Archives'" in the Introduction); in what ways does "From the Archives" build on the specific diary entries that serve as its Orwellian targets? If "From the Archives" is any indication, what are the literary—and narrative, in particular—possibilities and limitations entailed by the form? What other formats might you choose, and why? The choice of diary format has consequences: in so opting to

have his *characters* choose to write diaries the author is attributing to them what we might call a diary motive.[14] Why, after all, keep a diary? How does the diary motive or motives at large in "From the Archives" compare with those in evidence in other so-called diary novels that you have read (for example, Samuel Richardson's *Pamela*)?

18. On the issue of "facts" the intellectual historians Steven Shapin, Simon Schaffer, David Wootton, Barbara J. Shapiro, and Mary Poovey often disagree, but they all agree that facts are at issue.[15] That is, to be more precise, they agree that the very concept of "the fact" may be understood in different and even conflicting ways. Some regard the fact as a natural phenomenon standing beyond the reach of human representation but amenable to it; others as human opinion in disguise, a human artifact always already shaped, conditioned, or even contaminated by human interests, usually those of elites. The title of Shapiro's well-regarded book is *A Culture of Fact* (2000)—not "The Nature of Fact," and Shapiro and Wootton offer different histories of the fact, agreeing chiefly on the proposition that it *has* a history. What, then, is the importance of fact—again, the very concept of fact as opposed to particular instances of fact—firstly in *Nineteen Eighty-Four* and secondly in "From the Archives"? And finally, in novel and novella, how much does human happiness, or human flourishing, depend on a belief in "objective truth"—ergo, in objective fact?[16]

IV. CRITICAL SUPPLEMENT

"ORWELL AGONISTES"
AMBIVALENCES IN THE LATER ORWELL

This book was conceived in the whorl of Corryvreckan—its womb. The first notion of it arose when the author happened upon the American fiction writer and literary critic William H. Gass's memorable 2012 review of *George Orwell, Diaries* in *Harper's Magazine*, which opens with Gass recounting, bemusedly, Orwell's "outrageous ... offhand" account of the notorious Corryvreckan episode.[1] On the return trip from a "fishing excursion" on which Orwell and his "five guests" have boarded a "dinghy, apparently without the life jackets sailors are repeatedly reminded to wear,"

> Orwell pilots his visitors to the edge of a powerful whirlpool that has a reputation as the most dangerous in the British Isles—Corryvreckan, which squirts from the surface of the sea with a great roar, one of those newsworthy monsters whose waves sometimes rise as high as a mast—and the outboard motor is sheared off, the vessel calamitously overturned. The group just barely escapes drowning in the icy water. After waiting several anxious hours on a small outcropping of rock called Eilean Mor, they are rescued by a crew of lobstermen, who see the party's smoke signal, or perhaps the waving shirt tied to the top of a fishing pole...[2]

The passage is worth quoting because it was immediately upon reading it that, Gass's wonder stirring my own, I began to imagine what Orwell's motives may have been for so risking the lives of family and neighbors. Even if it were an act of mere wanton carelessness, what made him thus wanton? What was he thinking? *Was* he thinking? What was he feeling? A copy of *George Orwell, Diaries* having been purchased, what then began was an eighteen-month period of virtual obsession; the reading and rereading got to the point that page-long diary entries became committed to memory. From there it was just a step, or so it seemed, to the event of my starting to write what has become the critical novella "From the Archives."

Just a step, but it was preceded by something of a leap. For very early in the compositional sequence one found oneself moving from the question of what on earth Orwell was thinking when he steered a boatload of the beloved and the vulnerable too near Corryvreckan to that of what he was working on at the time, which of course was nothing other than *Nineteen Eighty-Four* itself. The question of how the two might be related, of how the Corryvreckan episode might become more intelligible if viewed through the prism of Orwell's fiction and prose (for example, *Coming Up for Air*), more generally: that became the issue, and I found myself moving from the question of Orwell's state of mind—and very poor state of health—at the time of the Corryvreckan episode ("designed to ... [lead] to his death," Isaac Rosenfeld argues[3]) to that of Winston's demeanor (and Julia's) in the days just prior to, as well as the afternoon of, their arrest: "We are the dead," they say—just before they are echoed by "the iron voice from the wall," and "the solid men in black uniforms" smash through the windows and jackboot up the stairs. As I then recognized, they speak as if knowing what is about to happen to them, and they indicate that for the first time what has been an "unconquerable instinct," the need to "hang on from day to day and from week to week," may have just been conquered (*1984*, 152). Orwell, suffering from the tuberculosis that would kill him some twenty-nine months later, faces institutionalization (hospitalization), painful treatment, and the fact of his own mortality; so does Winston, in extreme or exacerbated forms (incarceration; torture; execution: "don't give up hope," O'Brien advises him, "in the end we shall shoot you"; *1984*, 274). Put most simply, I noted that both Orwell, Winston's creator, and Winston, Orwell's creature, face imminent *arrest*. That symmetry perceived, it seemed an inevitable next move to wonder how

Winston would have behaved—again, facing a mode of arrest even more total than Orwell's own—had a Corryvreckan been handy, and had he and Julia been spared yet another day. Of course, this species of wonder depended on one's finding—or creating—in Winston something like Orwell's own distinctive "love" for "the surface of the earth" (here, the depths of the sea), a wide-awake fascination that should be distinguished from Winston's "Golden Country" escapism (*1984*, 123).[4] That is why, as I then decided (and still think), it is a good bet that Winston, had he indeed been in possession of Orwell's own complex attitude towards the natural (his rugged sort of pastoralism, which is discussed below), would have suggested that he and Julia turn to Corryvreckan, making timely use of it rather than allowing themselves to fall into the hands of "Charrington," the Thought Police, and O'Brien. The premise here was that throwing themselves into Corryvreckan would somehow be a more meaningful thing to do than, for example, throwing themselves off the "church tower" that they visit in Part Two, ch. 3 (*1984*, 129). (Accordingly, though Corryvreckan sits minding its own business on the periphery for most of "From the Archives," now and then merely sounding off ["mak[ing] a loud report"], it occupies the story's symbolic center.)[5] A concomitant intuition was that Julia ("rather good at staying alive"; *1984*, 166) would have resisted such a view of the whirlpool and such a plan for its use as well as any other suicidal course of action.

Winston's and Orwell's own stories began to blend, Winston assuming Orwell's position as a cottager on a remote island in the Hebrides, Orwell acquiring something like Winston's subjection to State surveillance. That, I decided, was the way to approach the mystery of Corryvreckan. What was Orwell thinking, in or about August 1947? Well, what was Orwell—in or about August 1947—*writing*? Orwell was living out his writing, writing out his life: such was the premise, and it proved an enabling one, prompting first and foremost the leap just described. But I should also mention that the leap taken at that time was not simply back and forth from Orwell and his diaries to Winston and *Nineteen Eighty-Four* but also back and forth from Orwell to another character in the novel, the character (and character of) O'Brien, the book's residing torturer-intellectual and its major minor character.

Why make this second leap? Why was it necessary? As discovered one day early on in the process, the first leap, that from Orwell to Winston and back again, helped solve only one-half of the Corryvreckan mystery; it explained why Orwell, facing his own imminent institutionalization and deindividuation, doomed to a difficult death, might wish to steer himself into the Corryvreckan whirlpool. It did not explain why he might wish so to steer the others, that boatload of the beloved and the vulnerable. That appeared to be the act of someone a little more imaginative and intellectual, even philosophical, than Winston, someone a little more given over to abstraction, more subject to any big ideas he might be having, and someone more likely to try not simply to destroy himself but *to make a statement*, and this was reason enough to make this leap to the decidedly intellectual O'Brien, who repeatedly assures Winston that he, Winston, is no intellectual (certainly "no metaphysician"; *1984*, 248).[6] The corollary: Winston is not much of a statement-maker; in Winston's encounters with O'Brien it is O'Brien who has all the good lines, just as it is Julia who makes all the good moves (it is she whom he once imagines "annihilat[ing] a whole culture, a whole system of thought ... by a single splendid movement of the arm"; *1984*, 31). But beyond this Corryvreckan rationale, as we might call it, another rationale emerged. For I also thought that, after all, Orwell may well have put as much of himself into the large, attractive, and masterful O'Brien as he did into poor little Winston; indeed, into O'Brien he may have put, not merely as much, but more.[7] That was the hunch: if Orwell was writing his life, living his writing, then the frightening and interesting O'Brien was also a character of interest. Indeed, O'Brien then became the chief character of interest, Winston's haunted condition and hounded situation persisting but his mind and personality, though not disappearing, nonetheless fading and diminishing. The mystery of O'Brien became my focus; indeed, it immediately subsumed the mystery of Corryvreckan, the solution to which would become clear, I trusted, as soon as the O'Brien conundrum was solved. The immediate question now became, then, how did O'Brien become O'Brien? For asking that question, how did O'Brien become O'Brien, was just another way of asking, how could *Orwell* have become O'Brien—Orwell, who as I said perhaps saw some of O'Brien in himself, who wrote O'Brien out of some part of himself (what Richard Rorty calls his own "Fascist streak")?[8] What had to happen?

Nineteen Eighty-Four does not precisely say; O'Brien remains mysterious, as capable of something like sympathy as he is of the most sadistic antipathy. That is why, to adapt Jean Rhys on Bertha Mason, "I thought I'd try to write [O'Brien] a life."[9] To answer this ultimate question, that is, it was necessary to infer and even imagine circumstances that could give rise to him in all his unexplored complexity (unexplored by Orwell in *Nineteen Eighty-Four*). Pressing at this turn, then, was the somewhat abstract question of the post-war *intellectual* situation and how that might help to explain how a progressive liberal humanist individualist intellectual such as Orwell was—and such as O'Brien might be imagined to have been, prior to totalitarian revolution—could become the totalitarian philosopher and passionate agent of a repressive, oppressive statism that the O'Brien of the novella most certainly is. And all this led to my making a very specific claim about our contemporary Western Enlightenment legacy as, as I believed and still believe, Orwell perceived it.

i. ORWELL—ENLIGHTENMENT, COUNTER-ENLIGHTENMENT

In such of his later works as *Nineteen Eighty-Four* Orwell suggests how a particular form (and particular degree—which is to say, robust) of Enlightenment ambition and aspiration may serve as a source of absolutism and extremism. Kant's famous question "What is Enlightenment?" is here rephrased: what are the different forms that "Enlightenment" may take? What may it mean to be "Enlightened"? And the answer here specified—one arrived at by way of close analysis of and meditation on Orwell's post-war writing—is: it may mean too much Light.

Pursued thoroughly enough, and taking a certain turn, the very method of the "Baconian," empiricist side of the Enlightenment, "empirical observation and experimentation," may bring to light a devastating fact: Enlightenment—significant "intellectual ... awakening" leading to "improve[ment]" in "human society and individual lives"—is impossible.[10] In seeking to observe and to understand the human so as to improve it and all that ramifies from it, a quest founded upon faith in human progress and "perfectibility," we may stumble upon evidence that it cannot be much improved.[11] As we discover, it is not made of stuff that can be much improved (being Kant's "crooked timber," indeed), or it does not particularly want to be improved, or perhaps we self-appointed improvers do not truly care to improve it, though we do care to shape it, dominate it, to impose our wills upon it.[12] Upon such a shocking discovery, moreover, our entire Enlightenment project may collapse, the faith in human perfectibility undergirding it dissipating into thin air. Worse yet, all that enabling idealism emerging at the project's inception may not thus just evaporate but, rather, linger and undergo baleful transformation. We may not lose our Enlightenment faith and hope so much as suffer its metamorphosis. Thereby we may become disenchanted—which is to say, become not free from enchantment, from idealism, but subject to its contrary, nihilism, even misanthropy. Love turning to hatred, the idealist turns into the cynic—or worse. What was loved, apparently, is now despised, essentially, and by way of a familiar dynamic: those who devastate the idealist by revealing the latter's—or their own—essential, un-ideal quality are abjured, rendered other with an intensity and thoroughgoingness proportionate to the passion with which the original ideal was conceived and pursued. Thus self-defensively is the human, itself, which was self-servingly embraced before, now rejected, especially in its most conspicuously un-ideal incarnations. The new-born nihilist may come to say, as D. H. Lawrence's Birkin declares, "I loathe myself as a human being."[13] Most often, however, those whom she loathes as human beings will be other human beings, her own human being being thereby not loathed but transcended—ritually objectified and punished, symbolically exploded, eradicated, or at least obliterated. Thus is the way opened to the more extreme phenomenon in which a profound faith in rational progress towards perfection, profoundly frustrated, does not simply fail but transmogrifies, turning into what may be regarded as its opposite, an equally blind embrace of the totalitarian.

I have just described this dynamic, perhaps disingenuously, as familiar, which prompts the question: how familiar is it? Certainly it is recognizable to intellectual historians of the Enlightenment and of its evil twin, as it is often characterized in the substantial tradition of discussion on the topic, the Counter-Enlightenment. Widely recognized as the *locus classicus* of approving commentary on the latter tradition is Max Horkheimer and Theodor Adorno's *Dialectic of Enlightenment* (1944): "the wholly enlightened earth is radiant with triumphant calamity" (speaking of best lines).[14] But an excellent example of a more recent contribution to such commentary is Justin E. H. Smith's 2019 book, *Irrationality: A History of the Dark Side of Reason*, which Amazon advertises as offering a "fascinating history that reveals the ways in which the pursuit of rationality often leads to an explosion of irrationality" (*1948* takes "explosion" literally).[15] As Kwame Anthony Appiah explains in "Dialectics of Enlightenment," his meditation on, hardly a review of, Smith's book, Smith hearkens to a "principle of cultural physics [which] stipulates that every action must produce an equal-and-opposite reaction, that rationality is inherently a self-poisoning phenomenon."[16] Rationality is, Smith himself argues, "evidently of a dialectical nature, where the thing desired contains its opposite, where every earnest stab at rationally building up society crosses over sooner or later, as if by some natural law, into an eruption of irrational violence" (13). That is, Smith unveils what he takes as a central Enlightenment dynamic, a sort of "natural law" (Appiah's "principle of cultural physics") whereby efforts to push far into the realm of Reason end in frustration—worse, in a species of apocalyptic failure in which the pusher "sooner or later" finds herself slipping and sliding down the slope of the rational past the spot where she was standing when, bothered by how things did not make sense, or did not make *enough* sense, she undertook the Enlightenment rationalistic project, to begin with (Smith characterizes the entry "into irrational self-immolation" following the "exaltation of reason" as a "descent," 12). I asked above, how could a liberal humanist, individualist progressive such as Orwell was, and such as O'Brien might be imagined to have been, prior to totalitarian revolution—how could such a liberal humanist become a philosopher of totalitarianism, not to mention a passionate agent of a repressive, oppressive statism? For thinkers such as Horkheimer, Adorno, and Smith, the question is, how could she *not*. The premise is that of "the inevitable endurance of irrationality in human life" (Smith, 12).[17]

But did *Orwell* later in his life share such (dis)beliefs about rationality? Was he quite as skeptical of Enlightenment idealism as I am suggesting?

One insightful critic of Orwell, Paul Roazen, appears to think so; he places Orwell in the vicinity, at least, of the Adornos, the Horkheimers, and the Smiths if not squarely amongst them: "Orwell was sensitive to the ways in which would-be emancipators ended up by enslaving mankind's thought."[18] In defining Orwell's suspicion of emancipatory idealism Roazen stops just short of articulating the dialectic that we have been discussing, the dynamic wherein the emancipatory does not just sometimes give way to the oppressive but gives it rise, and does so inevitably, inexorably. The more typical critical discussion of Orwell's own doubts about projects of rational progress stops even shorter. According to Richard Rorty, to quote one eloquent example, Orwell seeks to "convince us that nothing in the nature of truth, or man, or history [is] going to block that [totalitarian] scenario ... the same developments which make human equality technically possible might make endless slavery possible"—would make it *inevitable*, Smith would say.[19] Note, for another example, Gordon B. Beadle's assertion that "the bleak pessimism of *1984* ... is also partly the result of [Orwell's] conviction that" such "convictions of the Victorian radicals" as "the belief in the inevitability of evolutionary progress, the insistence on the goodness and infinite perfectibility of man, and ... the belief in the humane, progressive nature of science and technology" were "illusions."[20] Again Smith would edit (were not just illusions but were dangerous illusions). With Rorty and Beadle alike, then, we are near to but still short of the dialectic.

Turning from the commentary of others so as to offer commentary of our own, we must approach Orwell's resident intellectual totalitarian, O'Brien, who is central and crucial in this respect; again, the question is, what was O'Brien *before*—before becoming an intellectual totalitarian? Was he indeed that conjurable Enlightenment composite, both empiricist/rationalist and idealist, being something of a scientist, but also a humanist, a progressive? As I also note above, O'Brien remains mysterious; we have no evidence that he personally was, prior to becoming particularly nihilistic, particularly idealistic. We have no past life of O'Brien, at all; all we have is an intriguing, enabling gap (one that I am trying to fill in "From the Archives").

On the other hand, moving beyond O'Brien does prove illuminating, even if in so doing we first encounter only more aporia. Note the prominent lacuna that yawns in Part Two, ch. 9, when Winston pauses in his reading of "the book" (*1984*, 183) to report that even after pages and pages he has still "not learned the ultimate secret," what "Goldstein" (the imaginary author—thus the quotation marks) calls "the central secret," which is that of "the original motive," the "why," the very question of that "never-questioned instinct that first led to the seizure of power" (*1984*, 217). Somewhat perversely, perhaps, Orwell has Winston fall asleep contentedly before reading "Goldstein"'s answer; of course, Winston's readiness to do so tells us something about Winston and his totalitarian situation; he is less interested, at least immediately, in plumbing the Why than in establishing as fact the What.

In any case, however, waxing sufficiently inferential, we do find certain indicators, reflectors, registers of a persistent Orwellian attitude, an enduring Orwellian position on the question of progressivist idealism—its liability to frustration as well as its topsy-turviness, its tendency towards inversion, its tendency to "mutate," in Smith's words, "into spectacular outbursts of irrationality" (14). One such register may be found in "Goldstein"'s account of Oceania's (and O'Brien's) single "Party," its ruling class (15% of the populace), the "new aristocracy ... made up for the most part of bureaucrats, scientists, technicians, trade-union organizers, publicity experts, sociologists, teachers, journalists, and professional politicians," one whose "origins lay in the salaried middle class and the upper grades of the working class" (*1984*, 205).

In characterizing these modern leaders "Goldstein" "compare[s them] with their opposite numbers in past ages," for example, "totalitarian" leaders of the Soviet Union, Nazi Germany, or "the Catholic Church of the Middle Ages": Oceania's leaders are "less avaricious, less tempted by luxury, hungrier for pure power, and, above all, more conscious of what they [are] doing and more intent on crushing opposition. This last difference was cardinal" (*1984*, 205). The phrase "pure power," one which will brook no opposition, resonates; not surprisingly, given that O'Brien helped write "The Book," it also anticipates the language O'Brien uses later while answering the question ("Why?" Why did and does the Party seek power?)

that Winston encounters before falling asleep on that last day of apparent freedom: "The Party seeks power entirely for its own sake. We are not interested in the good of others; we are interested solely in power. Not wealth or luxury or long life or happiness: only power, pure power" (*1984*, 263). Power "only," and only power that is "pure," uncontaminated by any other motive, ulterior, anterior, posterior: O'Brien gives voice to a kind of perverted, or inverted, puritanism; it is the commitment to unstained perfection of a confirmed absolutist, one who used to be committed to unstained virtue, to mercy, pity, peace, and love. As goods go, "the good of others" is rejected; the good of the self-same becomes the only good, that good lying in the not-good, the bad, so to speak, of others. Orwell imagines a pure zero-sum game. But even invoking some notion of "the self-same" and its good is a mistake in that O'Brien and the Inner Party define the self collectively (as O'Brien clarifies, the Party's version of the belief that "nothing exists outside your own mind [is a form of] [c]ollective solipsism, if you like"; *1984*, 266). Thus eschewed are ethics both utilitarian and liberal, even libertarian; indeed, ethics itself is thus elided, its very basis—the enabling distinction between opposed goods—having been dissolved.

Of course, we are indeed "waxing," inferring, extrapolating. It is not the case that puritanism, and even purity itself, are not issues in Orwell. His position on them was far from unequivocal. Orwell could and did oppose puritanism in one of its incarnations while approving it in another. Certainly such a complex attitude is revealed by a review of the criticism. On the one hand, Paul Roazen favorably contrasts what he regards as Orwell's reflexive heterodoxy with the older Sigmund Freud's equally reflexive orthodoxy, his well-known, punishing intolerance for "potential renegades [who] threatened the purity of [his] purposes": Freud "did not hesitate to expel deviators as 'heretics.'"[21] For Roazen, Orwell was himself instinctively a "renegade," a "deviator," a skeptic—very much one who, as Patricia Hill writes, "stands in the tradition of Victorian religious skepticism and moral earnestness typified by writers like George Eliot and Matthew Arnold."[22] Defending Orwell from Raymond Williams's charge of ideological "vagrancy," a reflexive recoil from any "believing community," Christopher Hitchens praises Orwell as "the outstanding English example of the dissident intellectual."[23] Clearly a number of Orwell's critics have noted an Orwellian opposition to all forms of small-"p" puritanism, sexual, moral, ethical, ideological, political, or other—all those "smelly little orthodoxies," in the famous formulation, "which are now contending for our souls."[24]

On the other hand, however, other critics have pointed to Orwell's own roots in English Protestant, capital-"P" Puritanism, which itself may be regarded, whether celebrated or deplored, as an idealism (featuring as it does what Hill calls "moral earnestness" and what Alan Sandison calls Orwell's "fundamentalist passion").[25] James Wood, for example, terms Orwell a "Puritan radical": "There is a long historical connection between revolution and Puritanism (with both a capital and a lowercase 'P'), and Orwell sings in that stainless choir."[26] For this Orwell, the "stain" of social privilege cannot be tolerated; it needs removing, even if by revolutionary means. Abbott Gleason apparently concurs, writing approvingly of Alan Sandison's "connect[ing] Orwell with John Bunyan, and thus with the puritan and dissenting tradition"—with those who, as the Labourite R. H. Tawney puts it, wish "to crystallize a moral *ideal* in the daily life of a visible society" (my emphasis).[27] Of course, removing a stain and crystallizing an ideal are at best merely concordant practices; one can imagine the second following the first, but one can also imagine it not. Indeed, Wood's Orwell is revealed to be deeply neurotic, a Lady Macbeth whose "conservative radical[ism]," "not always politically coherent," was essentially a form of "puritan masochi[sm]"; Wood's is an Orwell who seeks "religious self-mortification," having undertaken an *"inherited"* and "personal ... struggle to obliterate privilege, and thus, in some sense, to obliterate himself."[28] Clearly the Orwell known to Hill, Gleason, and Sandison, among others, may not be thus distilled down to a single motive; certainly he does not regard himself as Wood's child of privilege, pure and simple, nor as Wood's simple "conservative radical."[29] Accordingly, these critics prove far more celebratory of Orwell's Puritanism as a constructive intellectual, social, and political impetus. Nevertheless, on the premise in question all the critics appear to agree: Orwell, so often so critical of so many forms of true belief, of idealism, often revealed a streak of idealism in himself.

One can imagine Orwell's coming to recognize this equivocation or even contradiction in his own thinking—indeed, this contradictoriness radiating from his emotional and intellectual core. What with his self-avowed and deeply prized "power of facing unpleasant facts," one can also imagine his turning upon himself self-critically, perhaps even dialectically, in the sense established above.[30] Certainly "From the Archives" is dedicated to that very proposition. As I have mentioned, Orwell put a part of himself in O'Brien as well as in Winston, and in "From the Archives" we have a formative episode in the story of how O'Brien may have become O'Brien—how *Orwell* may have become O'Brien. O'Malley, the Orwell ego-character in "From the Archives," is Orwell lacking, perhaps, Orwell's capacity for self-scrutiny and self-judgment—or lacking the intellectual elbow room for such, harried and hemmed-in as he is by proto-totalitarian circumstance. Imagine Orwell himself having to face a certain fact, a particular fact that, as is explained in the next section (ii), simply cannot be faced. "From the Archives" imagines just that.

Speaking of facts and the "facing" of them: just beyond the question—insoluble, as we have seen—of Orwell's Enlightenment *idealism* lies the question of his Enlightenment *realism*, and it, too, proves virtually insoluble. It proves extremely difficult to settle. And that, of course, is why it is of central interest to "From the Archives," which proposes a kind of settlement—or, better, unsettlement.

A statement of Enlightenment protocol: if we "Enlighteners" are to improve our human lot, which we can do, given the "infinite perfectibility" of human nature, we need to be more reasonable, rational.[31] A corollary: if we are to be more reasonable, rational, we need to be real-er. We need to get real; we need to face facts, facts on the ground, facts as they are in themselves (*"the way the world is in itself"*), no matter how unpleasant.[32] A corollary of the corollary: we can indeed face facts in all their factuality, the real in all its reality; we have the capacity, we have the "power," even, to do so.[33] We, "human kind," are not what T. S. Eliot's bird (the deceiving "thrush," perhaps) said to and of us:

> Go, go, go ... human kind
> Cannot bear very much reality.[34]

We are not as if Nikon cameras on Mercury, melting only the faster as we widen our shutters, exposing our minds' eyes to take in the real. We have the mental toughness and tenacity and balance to be able to handle the most upsetting, the most shattering, the most corrosive of facts. We have the intellectual power to be able to abide with the most fearful and painful truths that such facts entail. We are—the most Enlightened amongst are—well able to conquer our fear, our motto being Thomas Jefferson's famous statement of Enlightenment credo:

> Here, we are not afraid to follow truth wherever it may lead, nor to tolerate any error so long as reason is left free to combat it.[35]

Facts in hand, lighting its way, Truth leads us on the path to Enlightenment; Reason, rugged, armed, martial, marches at liberty by our side.

An *Orwellian* allegory? Does Orwell really care that much about facts? The philosophers disagree. But we get ahead of ourselves. Do the philosophers even find Orwell of interest? Yes, indeed; Martha Nussbaum, Elaine Scarry, and Judith Shklar, amongst others, have written about Orwell at length, and Shklar answers her own titular question, "*Nineteen Eighty-Four*: Should Political Theory Care?," with a strong if qualified "yes." Whether or not political theory should have cared, certainly it has cared, as has epistemology, metaphysics, the philosophy of language, and others. One especially pertinent episode of philosophical interest in Orwell and *Nineteen Eighty-Four* was initiated by Richard Rorty in his famous 1989 book *Contingency, Irony, and Solidarity*, which devoted a chapter to Orwell's novel. Since then, Peter van Inwagen, James Conant, and others have written at length not just about Orwell but in several cases about Rorty-and-Orwell; a fascinating philosophical discussion emerged in the 2000s—and here we return to our original question, does Orwell really care, really and truly, about facts, facts *qua* facts? Not about particular facts but about the very question of fact—of Fact? For example, whether there truly are such things as "facts" or whether what we call facts are to be distinguished from and opposed to "things"? And, again, the philosophers disagree. He does not, not really, Rorty thinks, and the lively discussion that developed in the 2000s and is ongoing has been devoted to deciding whether Rorty, whose Orwell is seriously Shklarian in his liberalism (liberals are those who believe that cruelty is the worst thing that we do), and very much half-baked and mostly non-serious in his realism, has read Orwell accurately. Conant in particular has accused Rorty of turning Orwell into a "Rortian" "anti-realist" as much as a Shklarian liberal, and van Inwagen, scarcely a fan of Rorty's, has responded, as has Rorty himself. In his response van Inwagen, having indicated unhappiness at finding an effigy of his philosophical self stuffed with straw and propped up by Conant so as to create a convenient obsessively realist target to match the obsessively anti-realist target named "Rorty," declares that he "did not say, in the passage" that Conant cites (which is also the only one he wrote on Orwell and realism), that Orwell was a metaphysical realist; he just suggested it; he then goes on to declare exactly that: "I do regard Orwell as a metaphysical realist."[36] Rorty, on the other hand, finds Orwell in his "better" if less deliberate moments more or less tolerant of "non-Realist" construal and not intolerant of that most Rortian and non-"metaphysical" of things, "ironis[m]."[37] Conant finds Orwell neither a realist nor an anti-realist nor a non-realist nor an ironist (a "Rortian").

To rehash this complex debate in detail would propel this commentary out of its proper sphere. Nor would it be a good idea to attempt to play referee and decide the winner of the debate, and for two reasons: first, such an attempt would take us even farther afield; second, and more importantly, the debate has no winner. For Orwell in *Nineteen Eighty-Four* provides strong support for both the realist and the non-realist positions (we will limit our discussion of the debate to just these two most starkly opposed alternatives). Surely Conant is correct to claim that, for Orwell, especially Orwell in his typical, common-sensical frame of mind (which is to say, in *Nineteen Eighty-Four*), what realists assume to be true is indeed true: "there is a fact of the matter"; there is such a thing as "objective truth."[38] And certainly van Inwagen, the "straightforward, self-confessed Realist," would agree.[39] Rorty himself can "imagine" that Orwell "would have sided with the Realists," had he "taken an interest in [philosophical] arguments."[40] But surely Rorty is also correct when he claims that *Nineteen Eighty-Four*, offering in unfortunate moments an "attack on anti-realism," in other moments wriggles clear of such concern and, indeed, submits realism—anti-anti-realism, more accurately—to that most effective (and Rortian) form of critique, the "shrug of the shoulders."[41] That is, in *Nineteen Eighty-Four* Orwell both engages his readers in the realist/anti-realist debate and points them past any preoccupation with it to what he regards as a more important issue, what we might call the liberty issue.

Orwell does so, I would argue (as Rorty could argue but does not), by balancing Winston's fascination with issues of realism with Julia's decided, unapologetic indifference to them. Conant and van Inwagen are powerful readers of Orwell's famous book, but neither is an especially *literary* reader; they both identify the author with his central character (van Inwagen: "I regarded Winston as representing the author's point of view") and both also ignore signs that this character is not some "straightforward" philosophical (van Inwagen) or political (Conant) hero but, like all of Orwell's central literary characters (for example, Gordon Comstock and George Bowling), a facsimile of flawed humanity, and abidingly so.[42] Julia may not be the alternative philosophical or political hero of the book, *pace* Elaine Scarry, but as Gregory Claeys remarks, Julia "plays a more important part than most accounts suggest."[43] Indeed, her point of view on some issues treated by the novel may be closer to the author's own than is Winston's.[44] I would submit that one candidate for such an issue is indeed this issue of realism. For—surprisingly, strikingly—Julia is more or less indifferent to the fact of the matter, certainly to the quest to establish an alternative fact of a matter settled by the Party a certain way (for instance, whether the Party really did, as it claims, invent the aeroplane). She is indifferent to what Winston calls "evidence," even when it is not merely the evidence of personal memory (which I discuss below in section viii) but "actual concrete evidence *after* the event," something that may be brought forward and shown to a few people so as to "plant ... a few doubts here and there" (*1984*, 155). Earlier Winston describes this "half-page torn out of *The Times*" more grandiosely; it is "a fragment of the abolished past, like a fossil bone which turns up in the wrong stratum and destroys a geological theory" (*1984*, 78). Julia sees it as a piece of rubbish, "bits of old newspaper"—"Who cares?" (*1984*, 155, 154). Julia certainly does not, but why not? Because Julia doubts everything already: "one knows the news," like every record in the Records

Department, "is all lies anyway" (*1984*, 154). Particular "impudent forgeries" do "not appear to horrify her. She did not feel the abyss opening beneath her feet at the thought of lies becoming truths." If pressed hard enough, she would be likely to argue that Winston's example of a precious piece of evidence of impudent forgery (this same "momentous slip of paper" proving the confessions of Rutherford, et al., to have been "lies"; *1984*, 154, 78) may itself have been a forgery.

This debate over Orwellian realism between Rorty and Conant/van Inwagen has become a debate between Julia and Winston, one in which Julia declines to participate—"impatiently" (*1984*, 154). How do we resolve it? We cannot, at least not by turning to the evidence provided by *Nineteen Eighty-Four*. Julia exhibits little of Winston's ontological insecurity; she does not fear the "abyss." One point, Julia. On the other hand, she could be accused of lacking imagination and the capacity for abstraction; certainly she does not share Winston's fascination with "whimsical abstractions and metaphysical conundrums."[45] We could call her a materialist, this "rebel from the waist downwards," and feel we have settled the matter (*1984*, 156); for Claeys, for example, "Julia's humanity is expressed through her animality" and her concomitant intellectual density, her "impenetrability" to ideas.[46] Two points, Winston? If so, however, her materialism—reducing this palimpsest of an abolished history to a scrap of paper—is balanced by Winston's own; he is the one who fetishizes the scrap, to begin with, as if only a dirty, tattered, brutely material thing, as opposed to an idea, an image, a song, or a feeling, could save the world. One is thus inclined to deduct a point from Winston's total, thus bringing him and Julia into parity. And thus leaving us where we began, with the question, "does Orwell really care, really and truly, perhaps even 'obsessively,' about facts, facts *qua* facts—about Fact, itself?" Does he feel the abyss opening up beneath his feet when facts are negated, impudently melted down, reforged, refashioned?

Again, "From the Archives" does respond, even if it does not decide. In fact, one of the ways in which it responds is by endowing one of its busy diarists, Cedric O'Malley, with a preoccupation with—yes—Fact.[47] As readers discover early in the story, Cedric has already had his faith in Fact shaken. Particular facts have proven contestable, contingent, even mutable, much more so than he has ever dreamed, to the degree that the very notion of fact (or, here, "Fact") has come into question. Moreover, the values he has associated with certain facts that he regarded as unassailable he has watched undergo commensurate transfiguration; the very fact/value distinction has begun to break down, and not in any of the conceivably good ways.[48] Worse, his yet more fundamental faith in things, in general, which could be said to underpin any faith in Fact, has come into question, and as readers will see, it will undergo rocking and rattling throughout the narrative. It is not that facts appear to have accrued to themselves the solidity and stability of things but that things are becoming as unsubstantial, unstable, and contestable as facts. When the Things Themselves start to grow iffy, one hears the baleful "dialectic of Enlightenment" begin to grind (Smith, 19).

In passing we should note that students of the history of philosophy will recognize Cedric's exposure to and keen interest in the early work of the twentieth-century Cambridge philosopher Ludwig Wittgenstein as well as of his Cambridge professor and advisor, Bertrand Russell. "From the Archives" gets into a few issues that crop up in Frege, Russell, Wittgenstein, and "logical atomism"—for example, Russell's notion of the "atomic fact" (a pregnant pun for the purposes of "From the Archives," but more than a pun). References to this material are made to contribute to characterization: Cedric was very much the bright young Cambridge student of the 1920s, when Cambridge undergraduates could still meet the still-convivial if now aged idealist and "Apostol[ic]" J. M. E. McTaggart over tea and crumpets, could still imagine the Russell-ephebe Ludwig Wittgenstein wandering around desolately, could still feel the palpable lingering influence of Russell, himself, and could still get into arguments pitting realists like Russell against idealists such as F. H. Bradley. In any event, "From the Archives" is dedicated to the proposition that this theme of Fact is an especially worthy and relevant one in our own era of so-called "alternative facts."

ii. ORWELL AND FAMILY VALUES

Just as soon as we recognize this phenomenon of Enlightenment catastrophism for what it is, a belief in a powerful, "inexorable" dynamic or dialectic, we may begin to wonder what sort of failure has to happen, what kind of catastrophe does it take, for Counter-Enlightenment—considered as an "aggressive turn" (Smith, 4), an episode, an event—to occur?[49] I have already begun to answer the question just by speaking of "episode" and "event." The premise is that some varieties of catastrophic experience, some sorts of catastrophic episode, are more effectually disaffecting than are others. Certainly Counter-Enlightenment may follow upon some devastating occasion. Smith suggests that Counter-Enlightenment may obtain in the "natural" course of things, as if the failing Enlightenment project may fail by simply "laps[ing]," losing heart, running out of steam, succumbing to a kind of law of gravity or entropy (13). But none of this is to say that there cannot be precipitating events. Enlightenment values often display a certain foolish, Panglossian staying power, especially the Enlightenment faith in human nature as perfectible; people committed to this value, in particular, certainly often remain so, even when faced with disobliging evidence. Presumably its radical transformation into its opposite upon collapse requires, or at least can follow upon, certainly, a fairly profound episode of frustration.

Thus, again, the question: what is the one thing needful in the creation of a totalitarian misanthrope like O'Brien? We are talking about a variety of human warping, one which would seem to require something more than a slow dawning—a sudden global shock, rather. As I note in passing above, a *revelation* of human fallibility and imperfectability, a momentous occasion of disclosure, would appear to be necessary. But it would also be necessary that the humans featured in such a spectacle of human failure be of an undeniably human sort. That is, the humans in question, bearers of revelation, would have to be ones whose humanity could not be readily dismissed, thereby robbing the event of such massive allegorical significance; convenient as it might be to regard them as something less than fully human, as lacking the right or the best human stuff, and hence as not representative of an essential human nature, they could not be so regarded. Thus the question arose, what sort of human beings, then, would they need to be?

"From the Archives" offers an answer, and one of which it is reasonable to think that Orwell would approve—for the answer, like the question, may be found suggested in Orwell's own writing. I will not clarify that answer here except by delineating one of the enabling premises of "From the Archives": Orwell's sense of a so-called "dialectic of Enlightenment" is not only familiar; it is also familial. Indeed, family was more important to Orwell than is usually recognized. Orwell's—strong—commitment to individuality is discussed below, but we should note here that his ardent individualism did not preclude a fairly bourgeois-style idealization of the family. For Orwell did not see the family, just as he did not see the individual, as just another artifact of social control, and just one of a number of such artifacts. Rather, it is as if Orwell recognizes familial sentiment as obeying a second "natural law," one that Nature itself instigates and enforces and that the dialectic as we will see proves ready to exploit. Orwell conceives of the family "bond," the familial "care/ Propinquity and property of blood," as a fact; violation of this bond proves consequential, even cataclysmic.[50] For better or worse, according to Orwell, we humans, prior to some species or other of psychological and social warping, find it very hard to treat non-family as family, family as non-family, and we feel bad about the latter sort of treatment even when such treatment is just (hence our moral celebration of the Unabomber's brother, for example). Turning biographical, we may note that, yes, Orwell often appears the lone wolf who happened to have acquired a wife and a few close friends and colleagues more so as to prevent loneliness than out of genuine sociability—the solitary as well as wintry conscience of his generation. Christopher Hitchens, for example, notes that "there are traces of a kind of solipsistic nobility" in *Nineteen Eighty-Four* and "elsewhere in [Orwell's] work, the attitude of the flinty and solitary loner."[51] But he was no such thing; throughout his life he had many friends and was in his own way a convivial family man, or became such, and his irrepressible desire to create a family around himself later in life is reflected in the later fiction.[52]

In *Nineteen Eighty-Four*, for example, the family is not a merely social institution; even if it does prove subject, like almost everything else, to social engineering, elements of it prove surprisingly resistant and persistent. The mere fact that there are families in *Nineteen Eighty-Four*, and families among Party members as well as among the proles, is significant; by contrast, we find none such in Huxley's World State nor in William Morris's utopian "Nowhere."[53] Of course, it could be objected that families in the Oceanic present of the novel are not to be confused with families as we have known them. Early on in the novel (Part One, ch. 3) Winston recalls "the ancient time ... when the members of a family stood by one another without needing to know the reason," the implication being that they no longer do so (*1984*, 30). But in thinking that "today" such "was no longer possible" Winston would appear to underestimate the potency and tenacity of family sentiment, good evidence of which even he himself provides (*1984*, 30). As we find, "the family could not actually be abolished" (*1984*, 133). Why not? "Parental care," in particular, keenly abides.[54] In Part Two, ch. 3, the narrator speaks of "the instinct of parenthood" in the same breath with that other "powerful instinct," "the sex impulse" (*1984*, 133). The State has discovered that not much may be done with it, itself; it may not be "bottl[ed] down," and thus "people were encouraged to be fond of their children, in almost the old-fashioned way" (*1984*, 133). The devastated old man Winston recalls meeting in the Tube when he himself, Winston, was a child is inconsolable because, as it seemed to Winston even at the time, "some terrible thing" had happened, "something that was beyond forgiveness and could never be remedied"—"[s]omeone whom the old man loved—a little granddaughter, perhaps—had been killed" (*1984*, 33). Love, here *grand-*"parental," grandfatherly love, survives loss; fatherly love, appositely, survives even such a challenge as betrayal. The absurd Parsons loves his two treacherous children, those "nipper[s]," even after one of them reports him to the Thought Police ("I don't bear her any grudge for it. In fact I'm proud of her"; *1984*, 233). Maternal love, finally, survives everything, even Sophie's Choice. Note Winston's dream of his mother (Part One, ch. 3): "he knew in his dream that in some way the lives of his mother and his sister had been sacrificed to his own" (*1984*, 30–31). As he imagines, his mother accepts the deaths of herself and his sister "in order that he might remain alive": "[t]here was no reproach either in their faces or in their hearts" (*1984*, 29). Recall the "*middle-aged woman*" whom Winston watches trying to protect the screaming young boy from bullets and bombs with her own body, obedient to the "instinct of [mother]hood" even when the child in question is not her own (*1984*, 8, 133).

Now for all Winston's childhood empathy for the old man, filial piety—as opposed to parental care—would appear to be gone: "[i]t was almost normal for people over thirty to be frightened of their own children. And with good reason" (*1984*, 24). Yet once the young grow up and escape animal selfishness, as some clearly do, they may look back with a feeling impossible at the time. Note Winston's own lingering feelings over how he as a young, starving boy mistreated his younger, starving sister and his mother; the question of his relationship with them is perhaps his most potent and abiding emotional preoccupation pre-Julia. Perhaps the better phrase is "the answer of his relationship with them," for Winston passes harsh judgment on his younger self: "His mother's memory tore at his heart because she had died loving him, when he was too young and selfish to love her in return" (*1984*, 30). Certainly Cedric's fate owes something to all these passages in *Nineteen Eighty-Four*.

Given, then, Orwell's strong—if qualified—idealization of the family, it is little wonder that Cedric O'Malley in "From the Archives," like Winston Smith in *Nineteen Eighty-Four*, is made to watch a family being destroyed. The difference, which is not merely one of degree, is that the family whose destruction Cedric is made to watch, unlike the one watched by Winston and the others, is his own family. Disclosed is the fact that humans are not going to be made better—not even those closest to him, those whose welfare matters to him most personally, and those whose humanity cannot be called into question. As he here and now bears witness, they are—his entire family is—too readily *unmade*; the fact of their sheer fragility and frailty is here and now illuminated. Human frailty, Orwell suggests, is enough, human frailty and imperfectability, but it need not be a spectacle of some grievous human failing, some species of vanity or venality; mere frailty will do. For what may also come to light suddenly and crucially in such moments, beyond the singular fact of human frailty (and frail humanity), is the equally undeniable fact of one's contempt for it, contempt that until this moment one does not know that one possesses.[55]

iii. ORWELL'S AESTHETICISM—AND HIS MODERNISM

A contempt for the human, then, may follow "dialectically" (see section i) upon the liberal humanist idealist's epiphany of a certain home-truth. But of course most inhabitants of a totalitarian society do not start out as Enlightenment idealists; nor do they become homicidal maniacs (Winston takes note of O'Brien's "lunatic enthusiasm"—"He is not pretending"; "he is not a hypocrite"; *1984*, 256). Whence, then, comes *their* contempt?

The answer is that it is taught to them from an early age, being elicited, inculcated, even instituted as a regnant species of affect, by artistic means. Certainly Orwell imagined such a provenance. The atrocious flick that Winston writes about in his journal, the one that ends with *"the lifeboat full of children"* being blown up, begins with a sort of *tableau vivant*: "*shots of a great huge fat man*" ineffectually attempting to swim away (*1984*, 8). Amongst the human foibles and frailties put on display by means of this tableau is the human tendency to overindulge appetite, enjoyment having become an end in itself; characterized as a grotesquerie, it is presented as an apt target for extreme punishment. The filmmakers create a spectacle of sheer physical indignity and inadequacy, all too human; the fat man literally embodies that to which flesh is heir, and the tableau presents the spectacle of such getting what it would appear to deserve. "[W]*allowing... like a porpoise,*" this absurdly poor swimmer sinks "*full of holes*" upon being machine-gunned (*1984*, 8). His humanity having been insisted upon, so are both his absurdity and his vulnerability.[56]

A totalitarian aesthetic? Indeed, it is, and even more to the point is the episode of the "Two Minutes Hate" to which we bear witness alongside Winston. This carefully arranged aesthetic experience stirs hatred and contempt for that most fundamental of human attributes, the face—not just a great huge fat face, or an ugly face, or a black, white, yellow or "lean Jewish" one that resembles a sheep's, but the "human face," *qua* face, which is presented as inherently both detestable and frangible (*1984*, 11–17, 12, 267). The Eurasian enemies who attract the "abstract, undirected emotion" of the crowd sport "expressionless" faces that are merely "Asiatic"; little wonder that the "hideous ecstasy of fear and vindictiveness" should take the form of "a desire ... to smash *faces* in with a sledge hammer"—not "Asiatic faces," in particular, but "faces," human faces of whatever sort (*1984*, 14; my emphasis). Moreover, faces in *Nineteen Eighty-Four* are, with one Big (Brotherly) exception, eminently "smash"-able; they do not stand up well to swinging sledge hammers, stamping boots and flying vitriol (*1984*, 270), or starving rats (*1984*, 285). Comprehensively speaking, then, the aesthetic target—whether figure or face—is what William Blake calls the "Human Form Divine." This "last man," the embodiment of "humanity" itself (or what Winston calls "the spirit of Man"; *1984*, 270) to the extent that humanity still exists, is revealed (even to himself) to be, under these harshest of lights, a "bag of filth," a species of detestable formlessness having nothing in common with such idealizations of our material being as Blake's (*1984*, 272).[57]

After such knowledge, what forgiveness? For Orwell, there is none to be found, certainly no *self*-forgiveness, not once that Enlightenment-switch has been thrown. And yet, as "From the Archives" argues, most of us do not have to live in such a light. As Schiller writes, "no man *must* must, says the Jew Nathan to the Dervish."[58] We are free, most of us, most of the time, to seek the shade, that protective shelter, and it is art that frees us. That is, there exists in Orwell an art at odds with the art of atrocity, that mode of hyper-mimesis, with all its flood- and spot-lights, its naked bulbs. There are Artists of the Shade, so to speak, in "From the Archives": the sea kelpies whom Cedric imagines haunting the Gulf of Corryvreckan, who are somehow allied with the Hag, animus of the whirlpool, herself.

These are the blue mermen—not to be confused with those other men in blue, those agents of the State who come from the sea and the air and who in the end swarm Jura—the blue mermen for whom the light of nasty, brutish Fact (the contrary to Value) is death and from whose deep-sea troves of treasure the glass paperweight, the coral-bearing *objet de curiosité* which figures heavily in "From the Archives," having been filched from *Nineteen Eighty-Four*, has found its way. It is a "heavy lump of glass, curved on one side, flat on the other, making almost a hemisphere," and it matters (*1984*, 94). Winston having imagined using it to smash someone he takes for an "agent of the Thought Police" (*1984*, 101), Avril O'Malley will indeed in a critical moment turn to it. Indeed, the very endurance of this *objet d'art*—"'It's a beautiful thing,' said Winston. 'It is a beautiful thing,' said [Charrington] appreciatively" (*1984*, 95)—suggests that a crucial quality of "the human spirit," both in *Nineteen Eighty-Four* and in "From the Archives," is the aesthetic (*1984*, 270). Perhaps it is the "last" thing to go. Art is what lasts, if anything does; what Matthew Arnold called "the instinct for beauty" somehow lives on, all but ineradicable.[59] If the art object does so, that Blakean "production ... of time"—that with which "Eternity is in love"—then so does that "love" of art, itself.[60] A thing of beauty is a joy—for quite a long time, at the very least, and equally impervious to the elements are the art "thing" and the species of "joy" that it brings. "That [paperweight] wasn't made less than a hundred years ago. More, by the look of it," says the appreciative Charrington (*1984*, 95), who should know; this member of the Thought Police may in fact be what he is pretending to be, something of "a collector rather than a tradesman," formerly "some kind of literary man, or perhaps a musician" (*1984*, 151, 94).

Accordingly, Orwell's infrangible art objects prove to be more than mere placeholders that are pretty to look at and whose force is limited to the power to arrest and absorb attention, to captivate, and simply to endure; they also prove to be things that are trickily transformative, effectual change-agents, and the changes-in-the-world that they trigger are hard to plan, plot out, or police. As Ian Slater observes, in Orwell's view certain particular aesthetic forms, those suspected of stirring up the wrong sorts of feelings and ideas—subversive ones—may be forbidden by the State.[61] But even Oceania seems to recognize that it would be impossible to outlaw all forms altogether, and the State is thus more or less tolerant of lower and simpler forms of artistic expression amongst the proles; amongst Party members the right sort of higher form of poetry (Kipling's, for example) has not been ruled out altogether even if it is being (ineffectually) bowdlerized, as we know from Ampleforth's case (*1984*, 230–31). But, Orwell suggests, just as a line in Kipling proves untranslatable, aesthetic form itself ultimately proves uncontrollable. Even the simplest forms, forms that have been officially approved since they appear to be harmless, being nearly content-less, may prove unruly, unmanageable, and subversive; "the form"—of a nonsense rhyme, for example—"can conjure up another time, a possible alternative."[62] As W. B. Yeats put it late in life, "You can refute Hegel but not the Saint or the Song of Sixpence."[63] You can burn *Phänomenologie des Geistes* but not "Humpty Dumpty."

In *Nineteen Eighty-Four*, accordingly, it is that charming, more than charming *objet*, the coral paperweight, that changes things. It is a "vision of [it] mirrored by the surface of the gate-leg table" that gives Winston the idea of turning Charrington's upstairs room into a love nest—an idea upon which he acts (*1984*, 137). Later Winston reports having "the feeling that he could get inside it," this hemispheric paperweight, "that in fact he was inside it" when in the room; "the paperweight was the room he was in, and the coral was Julia's life and his own, fixed in a sort of eternity at the heart of the crystal" (*1984*, 147). One recalls that "eternity" is a key word in Keats's ode; it is crystal clear that Winston conceives of the love nest as a "sort of" aesthetic refuge;[64] entering into it is like somehow managing to join the figures on Keats's urn, melting into that sylvan scene, the notion being that in so doing you are yourself able to acquire some of the urn's tough, marble timelessness.[65] Indeed, as if wishing to link Winston's paperweight to Keats's urn explicitly and unmistakably, Orwell has Winston characterize the former as bearing "a message from a hundred years ago, if one knew how to read it," the latter of course declaring a famous message of its own (as Vendler asserts, it "finally speaks") (*1984*, 145).[66]

In the end, of course, the paperweight's "sort of eternity" proves just that, "sort of" eternal; for all its tenacity and longevity, the paperweight turns out to possess a sort of fragility. Winston does not use it to smash that party-operative whom he has mistaken for a member of the Thought Police; to the contrary, a party-operative, one of the Thought Policeman "Charrington"'s security thugs, smashes *it*, what Alex Zwerdling terms the "lust for power" triumphing in this instance over the instinct for beauty.[67] Yet even here and now, beauty pushes back. Note how the destruction of this *objet* "sharply" displeases Charrington: "'Pick up those pieces,' he s[ays] sharply" (*1984*, 224). Charrington is a member of the Thought Police; one would guess that he would be indifferent to paperweights, crystal or other. Why should he care? This reaction as well as his actions in a couple of earlier scenes suggest, I claim, that he has himself been taking strong aesthetic delight in this object and that, indeed, the "aesthetic," as a variety of experience, continues in totalitarian Oceania—continues in covert spaces and often twisted shapes, but continues nonetheless. It is easy to imagine that Charrington will soon be looking through new batches of antiques for an equally lovely specimen to take the shattered paperweight's former place in his shop (*1984*, 224).

A final, more general comment on art and the aesthetic in *Nineteen Eighty-Four* and in the later Orwell—for one can imagine readers at this point objecting, "Wait! You have been suggesting that Orwell like his characters cares about art, cares about beauty—you have been talking about *Orwell*? *George Orwell*, who once wrote that '[a]ll art is propaganda'—correct?"[68] Correct. I am arguing, both explicitly (here) and implicitly (in "From the Archives"), that Orwell's typical, oft-quoted statement on the aesthetic, that it is always already political, is more provocative, more rhetorical, and thus more equivocal than is usually recognized. Orwell's descriptions of art, "*all* art" (my emphasis), as propaganda are themselves propaganda. For no, Orwell could not truly believe that all artworks of whatever sort and scope are works of propaganda, pure and simple, not in the strict—which is to say, the recognizable—sense of the latter term. Garth S. Jowett and Valerie O'Donnell, for example, use the term to distinguish "deliberate, systematic attempt[s] to shape perceptions, manipulate cognitions, and direct behaviour to achieve [the propagandist's desired] response."[69] Orwell by contrast would include indeliberate, unsystematic, non-manipulative "attempts" made by artists indifferent to the "cognitions" and the "behaviour," if not the "perceptions," of others; he broadens the term to point far beyond what most would recognize as its clear instances. Everything from Lennon/McCartney's "Michelle" (1965) to Leni Riefenstahl's *Der Triumph des Willens* (1935) would qualify, and everything in between. Indeed, by Orwell's conflation nothing that falls into the aesthetic category, the realm of the artistic, is not propagandistic, even a child's impromptu drawing of a horse or a cow or a goose. A whimsical child walking by whistling some nameless tune that came to her on her walk—a little Eichmann...?

Orwell's refinements of the claim do little to render it less totalizing. Note Orwell-the-essayist's much-quoted characterization of the artist as "propagandist" in his 1940 BBC interview with Desmond Hawkins: "I have always maintained that every artist is a propagandist ... in the sense that he is trying, directly or indirectly, to impose a vision of life that seems to him desirable."[70] The motive, according to Orwell, is always the same, aesthetic "impos[ition]," no matter how "indirect" the motive of the imposer, however hazy, abstract, or indifferent to "life" the "vision," and whatever the object (the slice or segment, style or species of "life") envisaged, and we submit to imposition simply by paying aesthetic attention. Now Orwell's sense of imposition is not particularly absurd if we take the term to signify something like aesthetic *occupation*. That is, it could be argued that we "impose on" another aesthetically, or try to, every time we share a representation of an object (or non-object, in the case of the denizens of the "'twenties ... 'cultured' circles," the worst of whom Orwell lampoons as "merely dabbling with word-patterns"); we are imposed upon as readers or listeners or viewers, in a sense, simply by lending out our minds as pedestals, plinths, slates, canvases, theaters, so to speak, for an aesthetic performance produced by another.[71] The premise is that it is the nature of aesthetic experience to be captivating, moving, elevating; art is essentially transportive; it is essentially rapturous. Note the *Macmillan's British English Dictionary* definition of "rapt" as "completely interested and involved in something," indeed "rapt above" all circumambient non-aesthetic other things.[72] But here, too, Orwell's ostensible aesthetic proves more extreme upon closer examination. The artwork thus conceived is scarcely offered as such a vehicle of uplift. Rather, Orwell suggests a notion of art as just another relation of power in which something (in this case, the artist's "vision") is "imposed" from above, as it were, immobilizing us, bolting us to the floor—but a floor which moves, thereby moving us. We are not far from the image of the whale that Orwell employs in his essay on Henry Miller and modern fiction, "Inside the Whale" (discussed in detail just below). Orwell thus appears to eschew any notion of a more benign exercise in the aesthetic. Art itself, thus conceived, will not allow it. Instances of art are always already exercises in mastery. Certainly Orwell appears to disavow any notion of aesthetic *contemplation*. We who undergo aesthetic experience are absorbed by it; we surrender our own agency even as we suspend our disbelief. We are not theater-goers who can pay selective attention, who can stop paying attention and walk out at any time, and who can sustain critical distance even as—paying thorough attention—we allow ourselves to be moved by a performance; rather, scarcely freer than the seats in which we sit, we are the theater itself, a theme-park ride pitching and rolling on cue, and one whose doors lock from the outside permitting no exit once the performance has begun.

Again, it is hard to believe that Orwell, this great hater of orthodoxy and "orthodoxy sniffers," truly believed "all" of this—that all art really is propaganda, even an Orwell who, facing the twin totalitarianisms of Nazism and Sovietism, saw the need for the Western democracies to get into the propaganda game. It is much easier to think that these statements indeed represent a move in that game.[73] The claim is that Orwell was himself being propagandistic, tactical, rhetorical.

For he had at least two reasons to be so. On the one hand, he wanted certain of his readers, the more naive and trusting ones, to become more suspicious of works of art, less reflexively assimilative of their "message[s]."[74] Addressing these more naive readers, he deliberately, boldly overstates the case; facing those who think of art and politics as occupying separate spheres, when they think about the question at all, he characterizes art as reducible to its message, a message that is essentially a political one. The best way to get people thinking that art may be political, that it may be influencing their judgment in all sorts of subtle ways? Assure them in confidence that it always is such, always does such. On the other hand, Orwell also wanted others of his readers, the *less* naive and unsuspicious ones, to see him himself as such—as less naive, more suspicious, and thus to see him himself as one of them. That is, he wanted to avoid losing that more sophisticated part of his audience who might walk away should he fail to distinguish himself as sufficiently political in orientation—this, not in order to ingratiate himself with this audience but in order to enlist them in an attack on a certain element in their own ranks. The American literary critic and university administrator Stanley Fish is rumored to have coined the following motto: "never get outflanked to your Left." Orwell ran "Left" (which is to say, political) on the aesthetic question so as to enable a distinctly Left-political attack on a certain sort of Left-political writing.

By running Left he could attack Left excesses without being dismissed as a Rightist.

What Left excesses? Those of the Left sophisticate, in the pejorative sense of the term—those of the proudly jaded, the smugly cynical, someone like "Mr. Louis MacNeice" (according to Orwell). Such are they who appear to believe not just that all art is propaganda, but that "all [proper] propaganda is art" and, thus, that all an artist needs to do to be an artist and do creditable art is to speak from the heart, having once gotten his or her heart into the proper place. They may not be very "good" artists—good as in effective ("constructive")—but they will be real ones, just so long as the "keynote … is 'serious purpose.'"[75] Orwell did not favor frivolous purpose, or purposelessness, or even, ostensibly, Kantian "purposiveness without purpose."[76] But neither did he like Mr. Louis MacNeice, and here again we come upon the phenomenon of Orwell's opposition to orthodoxy (one which did not prevent his now and then adopting a confident, commanding tone). As he declares in "Inside the Whale" (1940), the particular orthodoxy that he found most objectionable in the run-up to the Second World War was precisely "the left-wing orthodoxy of the last few years" (since 1937), years which saw what he calls the "Marxis[ing of] literature."[77] But extreme right-wing orthodoxy would have been no better to the extent that it, say, (Adam) Smith-ized literature. The kind of orthodoxy did not matter; what mattered was orthodoxy itself. For orthodoxy, he was convinced, always spoils or at the least "damages" art (it is especially "ruinous" to the art of the novel, that "most anarchical of all forms of literature").[78] Art requires the liberty to cross lines (the novel demands it). Art of whatever sort is the free, unbounded expression of that "vision of life that seems to [the artist] desirable," often by contrasting it favorably with a conventional or collective—i.e., socially bounded—vision of life that seems to the artist undesirable. Seems to the artist: "[l]iterature is an individual thing"; art, literary or other, is individualistic. Orthodoxy, by contrast, is indeed social; orthodoxy requires that we "toe the line."[79] The propaganda which acts as its agent is the un-free expression of a vision of life that seems desirable to the collective, often by contrasting it with that which seems desirable to the unorthodox, the eccentric, the idiosyncratic, the individualistic.

Which at last brings us to the question of Orwell and modernism—which is, largely, the question of Orwell and precisely what orthodoxy will not allow, *autonomy*, both of the individual and of the artwork ("the idea of aesthetic autonomy—of art as a law unto itself—was a central preoccupation of modernism").[80] And such indeed remains a question, despite Orwell's now and then declaring the imminent death of both, at least "in the form in which we [have] know[n them]."[81] With totalitarianism creeping and liberalism withering away, as he prophesies in "Inside the Whale," "[t]he autonomous individual is going to be stamped out of existence"; intellectual autonomy, "freedom of thought," is doomed, and with it "literature, in the form in which we know it" ("the writer ... is merely an anachronism, a hangover from the bourgeois age, as surely doomed as the hippopotamus").[82] But for all the doomsaying Orwell does not seem to have been convinced. For one thing, and it is no small thing, Orwell carried on. He carried on acting the autonomous individual, carried on freely thinking, carried on writing. Subsequent virtually to declaring *himself* a liberal writer, a doomed hippopotamus, he did not behave hippopotamus-ly. The premise here is that, should what Orwell did and what he said be in conflict, we should go by what he did: which is, he went on saying (!). But even when we do not go by what he did, even when we focus on simply what he said, we may note little hints that the phenomenon of individual autonomy, that "hangover," was a phenomenon that was hanging on, hanging around. For what he said contains suggestions and intimations at odds with its own more oracular and apocalyptic declarations.

For just one example of such a suggestion, ignore Orwell's doomed hippo for the moment and consider his characterization of the titular whale, or, rather, of Henry Miller's particular whale: "in his case the whale happens to be transparent."[83] Of course, Jonah's whale happened not to be, and indeed Jonah was double-blind, having been blindfolded as well as swallowed whole ("the weeds were wrapped about my head").[84] The first thing to notice about Orwell's Miller's whale, then, is simply that it has been characterized; it has been given a particular character. That is, it is its (his, Miller's) own whale; or, if there is just one whale for all, "*the* whale" (my emphasis), how this whale is constituted somehow differs depending upon the individual "case." The point is that a quality of individuality has been inserted—and inserted into a symbol of the titanic (it is a large whale), of the totalizing (the whale engulfs one entirely), of that which is indifferent to whatever sort of human being or even whatever sort of animal you might be (the whale entirely engulfs one, no matter what is distinctive or special about one). Having constructed a satisfying image of indiscriminate engulfment ("admit you are in the whale—for you *are*, of course," no matter who you are), then, Orwell immediately modifies it so as to discriminate particular modes, conditions, "cases" of engulfment.[85] This move suggests an inability to shake one's belief in modes, conditions, and cases. It also suggests an ineradicable respect for the particular, an incapacity, finally, to allow its subsumption by the general. Where human beings are concerned, such respect signifies the intuition of an ineradicable individualism—an ineradicable belief in "the autonomous individual."

The exact same thing is signified by *how*, as opposed to the simple fact *that*, Orwell characterizes Miller's whale. Miller's whale is not unique—it does not constitute a special case—because it happens to be opaque, which it might have been. It is unique, rather, because it happens to be transparent; he can see through it to the "reality" beyond.[86] Miller's incorporation by the whale limits what he can do, to be sure, as Miller himself recognizes, according to Orwell; indeed, Miller "allow[s] himself to be swallowed, remaining passive, *accepting*."[87] But such does not limit what he can see and say, what he can observe and "record."[88] One would have thought that Orwell's central purpose in wheeling out this particular figure of titanic subsumption was in order to indicate Miller's total loss of autonomy, both of action and of mind, of perception and of expression. Such is suggested by his brief, quietly extravagant meditation on the prospect of life inside the whale: "the whale's own movements would be imperceptible to you. He might be wallowing along the surface waves or shooting down into the blackness of the middle seas (a mile deep, according to Herman Melville), but you would never notice the difference."[89] But Miller would notice the difference, as we immediately find (again, "in his case the whale happens to be transparent"). Ergo, it would appear to be possible to be entirely swallowed up by the whale even as one is... not entirely swallowed up by the whale, your perception and expression remaining free. Orwell cannot sustain a symbol of complete and total human *heteronomy*.[90] His commitment to an at least rudimentary notion of human autonomy proves ineradicable.

Modernism enters the picture, rather as visible (if nameless) form than ghostly presence, when we note an equally ineradicable commitment to (equally) rudimentary notions of aesthetic autonomy, of the so-called "autonomous art work."[91] This is so, as in the case of the autonomous individual, despite declarations of its imminent demise. That particular one of the central assumptions of what has come to be called High Modernism, that works of art, when they are successful, are autonomous, is one that Orwell can no more abandon than he can abandon the notion that humans, too, when they are relatively successful (i.e., more fully human), are autonomous.[92] An abiding if qualified commitment to aesthetic autonomy emerges in Orwell's discussions of both the modernists, whom he refers to as "writers of the 'twenties," and of their literary works.[93] That one has to get into the weeds to see it does not mean that it does not exist.

Getting into those weeds: as is well known, Orwell was particularly fascinated by James Joyce and *Ulysses*; T. S. Eliot and his "Prufrock" also impressed him.[94] Not that he celebrated Joyce and Eliot as avatars of autonomy; indeed, in "Inside the Whale" he distinguishes Joyce and Eliot and others whom we now think of as modernists from mere "dabbl[ers] with word patterns," sheer formalists who are so committed to art and art alone beyond any reference to the world outside it that their work becomes virtually immaterial, utterly lacking in "subject matter."[95] The premise is that it is possible to purify one's art without thus evacuating it, and that is exactly what the modernists, according to Orwell, did. To be sure, modernists like Joyce are often "quietis[ts]," Orwell feels, ones who would inculcate social, political, religious, and other, more personal sorts of dispassion.[96] But this does not make them formalists. The dispassionate have a distinct feeling about the feelings. Quietists do not lose touch with the world in encouraging us to be quiet about it; indeed, quietists impose their own particular vision of the world. Orwell distinguishes modernist "mysticism," in some extreme cases, the premise being that mystics communicate a very clear idea of the world which they would have us transcend; "stoicism" is another term that has been proposed (Hugh Kenner called Flaubert, Joyce, and Beckett "the stoic comedians").[97] In any event, we might thus conclude that Orwell's mystical or stoical or merely quietistic Joyce is not, in Orwell's words, a "pure artist," the very concept of which Orwell calls into question by putting the phrase in scare quotes.[98] Yet it is to Joyce that Orwell approvingly attaches the phrase, qualified as it is, and before long we find Orwell casually introducing a notion of a pure work of art, a pure "book"; he writes of books being good "as books" as opposed to... well, as something other than books (for example, as instruments of orthodoxy, works of propaganda).[99] Thus a specifically *literary* value would appear to be extant. A book can be of value even if it lacks "serious"—non-literary, that is—"purpose."

Now Orwell does not specify what a book must be to be a good book; he does not specify the criteria, the constituents, of literary value (mimetic fidelity? thematic coherence? formal complexity? figurative economy? beauty? balance? symmetry? "organic unity"?).[100] He does, however, say what a good book must *do*: it must "survive."[101] Orwell predicted that the works of the modernists would last as the books of the thirties, the ones favored by Mr. Louis MacNeice, would not. Orwell, in other words, was in possession of, or was possessed by, a notion of "the classic"—one perhaps at odds with the belief that all art = propaganda (!). Significantly, this notion of the classic was one that he may have picked up from none other than T. S. Eliot, who in 1944 gave a presidential address to London's Virgil Society entitled "What is a Classic?" Employing what J. M. Coetzee distinguishes as "Horatian terms," Eliot believed that a classic is among other things "a book which has lasted a long time (*est vetus atque probis, centum qui perfecit annos*)."[102] By praising modernist works as likely to endure, then, Orwell appears to be invoking much the same criterion, and by invoking that criterion he is revealing his possession of a literary value distinct from that of contemporary relevance, "serious purpose," and so forth. It is to the point that Orwell stops short of enunciating anything like the second Eliotic criterion distinguished by Coetzee: the classic is that which invites each era to reread it so as to address that era's own peculiar problems; it is "a book that will bear the weight of having read into it a meaning for [one's] own age."[103] For Orwell, the classics of the modernists appear to be books which will indeed shrug off this burden, resisting any such attempt to have read into them an exhaustively appropriative local meaning. A modernist work is what it is, compelling and strange, and so it will remain, so it will survive, even as a new generation takes it off the shelf, dusts it off, and, rather than absorbing it, becomes absorbed by it.

In so distinguishing books as books Orwell provides just another example of his unwillingness, in practice, in the vibrant round of discussion, in the heat of utterance, in the historical moment, even amidst the mess of a bombed-out culture, to abandon the aesthetic—books *as* books, art *as* art. And he felt the same way about books as books in a second, more material sense—not as the aesthetic experience contained, preserved, and presented by a bit of stitched cloth and pasteboard and paper and ink but the cloth-paste-paper-ink itself. Gordon Bowker writes of Orwell's rescue mission subsequent to a "doodle-bug" or V-1 rocket having paid a visit to his flat at 10A Mortimer Crescent: "Inez Holden remembered him scrabbling among the bomb-rubble to salvage his books and trundling them in a wheelbarrow back to the *Tribune* office in the Strand during his lunch break."[104] Though Holden's memory of the episode has been called into question, surely Bowker's inference is on target: "parted from his books he felt acutely deprived."[105] Orwell himself reports a passion for books as simple, sensuous material objects, as things-in-the-world; he loved the "sight and smell and feel" of them, the "peculiar flavor" that a mass of them might exude at some estate sale in the country, even "the sweet smell of decaying paper."[106] For Orwell, an attractive book, even an unattractive book (one of those "odd volumes of forgotten novels, bound numbers of ladies' magazines of the sixties"), was an end-in-itself.[107] It did not have to have anything to do with anything else. It stood alone and separate and wondrous, an object of surprising pleasure, of delight—an "autonomous" work of art, in the most material and irreducible sense of that word.

None of this is to claim by any means that Orwell was himself a modernist, simple and plain; it is to claim merely that he had a modernist motive and that it abided. Certainly his relationship to modernism, as well as to the individual authors whom he regarded as the major modernists (though again, he would not have used this term), was complex, as has been argued recently by a number of literary historians.[108] Drawing on the work of Keith Williams, Roger Fowler, and Michael Levenson, among others, Martha C. Carpentier, for example, writes of "Orwell's [1930s] quest for a new kind of realism that could work in conjunction with Joycean modernism"; over the course of the 1930s "he increasingly felt torn between the modernist formal experiments he loved and the ethical and political commitment to social realism he felt was necessary."[109] Orwell was no more simply a modernist than he was simply a realist, on the one hand, or simply an idealist, on the other (see section i). That he was a modernist at all, that his commitment to "social realism" was balanced by an abiding commitment to (as opposed to a brief fling at) "modernist formal experiment[ation]," is of course the claim that has most needed proposing and defending. And, again, it has indeed been defended by a number of critics, perhaps most resonantly by Levenson in his essay on Orwell's four novels of the 1930s. As Levenson argues, Orwell's 1930s novels "sustain the [modernist] formal commitment to the limited narrative perspective of the focalized individual."[110] Moreover, if "epiphany" is widely regarded as "the signature motif of modernism," as David James asserts, Orwell's 1930s "fiction of the ordinary world" is significantly epiphanic; it "mov[es] repeatedly toward exceptional events and states of mind."[111] It is, therefore, significantly if also problematically modernist.

Carpentier has discussed Orwell's final novel of the 1930s, *Coming Up for Air*, as a substantially Joycean and therefore modernist work. But no one has ever—to my knowledge—called his *final* final novel, *Nineteen Eighty-Four*, "Joycean." Nor will I do so here. As Carpentier asserts, "unlike *A Clergyman's Daughter* and *Coming Up for Air*, [*Nineteen Eighty-Four*] shows no conscious attempt at imitation."[112] What it does show, I would propose, is a less-than-fully conscious (I will not say unconscious) attempt at extirpation, correction, "perfect[ion]" (*1984*, 244). That is, it is itself a "show," a spectacle, a psychodrama wherein Orwell's disguised but painful, deep, and still-abiding fascination with Joyce both punishes, by way of O'Brien, and is punished, by way of Winston. The truncheon strikes on the Joycean's behalf; yet the body struck is its own, the body of the would-be Joycean modernist, vessel of both resignation and presumption.

Carpentier herself characterizes *Nineteen Eighty-Four* as "a last gasp of modernism"; it is, she suggests, a book in which we may witness modernism's expiration.[113] I would argue that it is more a work of painful expiation. As Carpentier claims, here "Orwell's fictional style ... remains the same, albeit more mature: a narrative of different states of consciousness—dream, reverie, and memory—underscored by a subtext of tragic oedipal conflict, all 'dovetailing ... into a huge, complex pattern.'"[114] I would argue that the novel does not just represent "oedipal conflict"; it enacts it. That is, Orwell has not so fully "internalized" or digested Joyce as Carpentier claims—so much so as to signify "his mastery over the master as he aged and drew nearer to the composition of his own masterpiece"; he has not "finally overcome or banished his oedipal anxiety of influence."[115] Rather, he has made of it a spectacle, the arresting power of whose surface is such as to conceal its animating motive. Carpentier keenly observes how Orwell, having even in the late 1930s "stood in awe" of Joyce, now "invests ... Winston" with an oedipal ambivalence; he "long[s] to return to the spirit of the father while opposing [his] oppressive law."[116] She imagines Orwell thereby *externalizing* Joyce, getting him out of his system. But the novel's uncanny echoing of Orwell's awe of Joyce in its characterization of O'Brien, or of Winston's conception of him, suggests that Orwell's own anxiety regarding Joyce's "paternal threat" has stuck around.[117] Joyce is stuck in Orwell's craw. As Orwell writes in his 1940 essay on Miller, also an essay on modernism,

> [t]he effect [of Joyce's writing] is to break down, at any rate momentarily, the solitude in which the human being lives. When you read certain passages in *Ulysses* you feel that Joyce's mind and your mind are one, that he knows all about you though he has never heard your name, that there exists some world outside time and space in which you and he are together.[118]

This same sense of a meeting and commingling of the minds, of a dissolution of any barrier between them, is given voice by Winston upon his and O'Brien's eyes meeting in the aftermath of the Two Minutes Hate: "it was as though their two minds had opened and the thoughts were flowing from one into the other through their eyes" (*1984*, 17). Looking at O'Brien, and being looked at by him, has the same "effect" on Winston as Orwell's reading Joyce has on him; "you feel that [his] mind and your mind are one." Later Winston will tell Julia "of the strange intimacy that existed, or seemed to exist, between himself and O'Brien" (*1984*, 152). Later still, subsequent to arrest and torture, Winston will note how "in some sense that went deeper than friendship, they were intimates; somewhere or other, although the actual words may never be spoken, there was a place where they could meet and talk" (*1984*, 252; "the place where there is no darkness"; *1984*, 25); that is, Winston says of O'Brien and himself just what Orwell says of Joyce and of himself as Joyce's reader: "there exists some world outside time and space in which you and he [Joyce] are together." Having entered that world (an interior in the Ministry of Love), Winston at one point has a thought and looks up to see O'Brien "looking down at him with an expression which suggested that the same thought might be in his own mind" (*1984*, 252). Winston is sure that "O'Brien [knows] everything"—"How intelligent, he thought, how intelligent! Never did O'Brien fail to understand what was said to him" (273). Joyce, similarly, "knows all about you," Orwell feels—knows all about Orwell himself, "though he has never heard [his] name."

J : O :: O'B : W. Joyce is to Orwell as O'Brien is to Winston. It is with a small shock that one makes this suggestive connection, this virtual analogy, between, on the one hand, Orwell's character Winston and his interrogator and torturer in *Nineteen Eighty-Four*, and on the other Orwell and his perhaps strongest single literary influence—James Joyce. The shock passing, one begins to explore the suggestions, one of which is the notion (mentioned above) that Orwell's own shock—the shock of the new, the shock of reading Joyce for the first time, so much on display in his 1930s letters to Brenda Salkeld—has not entirely dissipated by the time of *Nineteen Eighty-Four*.[119] Carpentier claims that Orwell is putting modernism and Joyce behind him in *Nineteen Eighty-Four*, or has already done so prior to its composition. If that were true, it is difficult to see how that explosive little parcel of affect makes it way, disguised or not, into the novel. Once it is there, would it not be dealt with so as to defuse it, or harmlessly explode it, or at the least more firmly contain it? A substantial portion of the novel's final one-third is devoted to a debate between Winston and O'Brien—between Orwell's own ego-character and the omniscient Joyce-figure. If Orwell were in this novel putting Joyce behind him, would not the Orwell character have to win the contest? Or, at least, play to a draw? Or, at the *very* least, lose but play well? One can imagine the novel having O'Brien persuaded or at least stymied by a more powerful interlocutor than we have in Winston, which is exactly to the point: just as Orwell felt that his 1930s novels were *contained* in or by Joyce in *Ulysses*, so does Winston here find his mind completely contained in or by O'Brien's: "O'Brien was a being in all ways larger than himself ... His mind *contained* Winston's mind" (*1984*, 256). Has, then, the paternal threat posed by Joyce been banished by or in *Nineteen Eighty-Four*? Winston says that he is "thirty-nine years old" with "varicose veins" and "five false teeth" (*1984*, 120). But, until his physical torture is complete, at which time he displays in O'Brien's mirror "the body of a man of sixty," he seems much younger; when he is in O'Brien's company, especially, and is "struck ... by the tiredness of O'Brien's face," how "old and worn ... [it] looks," he assumes the posture of the much younger man (*1984*, 263; at one point "he [clings] to O'Brien's body like a baby, curiously comforted by the heavy arm round his shoulders"; *1984*, 250). O'Brien, accordingly, is very ready to assume the posture of the older, wiser, more experienced man, if not The Father then the Big Brother. He is the perverse guardian who has "[f]or seven years ... watched over" Winston and now has Winston "in [his] keeping" (*1984*, 244). In O'Brien's company Winston is the much younger man being instructed by the older, ostensibly, but truly being informed of his own comparative lack of intellectual "originality" or even authenticity.[120] As he learns, "[t]here was no idea that he had ever had, or could have, that O'Brien had not long ago known, examined, and rejected" (*1984*, 256). The suggestion is that by creating this dynamic Orwell is giving voice to an abiding anguish at a certain dim but sharp realization: there is no aesthetic innovation that he has ever made, or could ever make, that Joyce has not long ago adopted, explored, and either rejected or perfected. At some level he knows that he will never be another Joyce; he also knows that he will never stop wanting to be, trying to be.

A second, supplementary suggestion, but the last one that we will explore here, is the suggestion that emerges when we recall Rorty's claim (discussed in section i) that Orwell deliberately "uses his own sadism to create the character of O'Brien."[121] This is the suggestion that Orwell invests as much of himself in O'Brien as he does in Winston, that O'Brien represents some curious, perhaps furious part of Orwell every bit as much as Winston does some other (anguished) part of him. What curious, furious part might that be? Having prompted this question, the suggestion turns into a suspicion: if Winston voices Orwell's pain at his own "squeak[y]" eunuch inferiority to Joyce, as I have been arguing, then O'Brien may well embody his commensurate contempt thereof.[122] I do not leave "thereof" vague: the suspicion bifurcates, yielding two seemingly contrary (but in fact supplementary) suspicions. Orwell, we may suspect, could be angry on either of two accounts—either because (1) he is inferior to his master Joyce, or (2) because he is anguished about it. (1) He is angry with himself for being inferior; (2) he is angry with himself for caring. Limiting ourselves to the first and simpler suspicion for the moment, we may derive thereby a sharper sense of *Nineteen Eighty-Four* as site of Orwellian inner conflict, as secular *psychomachia*. For when Orwell becomes O'Brien, as it were, he does not cease to be Winston. That is, our recognition of O'Brien as a projection of Orwellian affect does not negate our recognition of Winston as a like projection, though of a different affect. With this recognition, then, also comes a revision of Rorty's claim about Orwell's "own sadism"; perhaps it would be as well to speak of Orwell's own masochism. For the element of Orwell denominated "Winston" and punished in *Nineteen Eighty-Four* is punished by—Orwell, himself, or the part of Orwell, denominated "O'Brien," that is hostile to this other part of himself.

But that second possible suspicion, noted in passing above, remains to be explored, however briefly. This is the suspicion that Orwell in *Nineteen Eighty-Four* does not summon some alien specter of Joyce to occupy and animate its punisher (after all, it is not as if O'Brien resembles Joyce physically or ideologically); he does not go to the trouble of imagining how Joyce might have spoken to him as a fellow but, by his own account, failed Joycean novelist in every way Joyce's inferior. As we may suspect, he does not need to; he has plenty of hostile feeling closer to home (Roger Fowler notes in passing "Orwell's dominant discontent and anger").[123] Indeed, that hostile affect occupies a certain part of Orwell: not the part that is damned sure that he is not the next Joyce, but the part that is almost sure (maybe not quite) that he has put or is putting his aspirations to be the next Joyce behind him and is moving on to claim his own seat in the literary pantheon, perhaps right next to Joyce. Indeed, this is the part of Orwell angry with himself, not for failing to become Joyce, but for ever wanting and trying to be Joyce, to begin with—for having been a Joyce-manqué. Accordingly, he is not a modernist of the "twenties" but a novel sort of realist—a "neorealist," perhaps, or "hyperrealist" (as Roger Fowler calls him), and one who feels that he is now by way of *Nineteen Eighty-Four* "contain[ing]" or at least circumventing Joyce just as Joyce once contained him; he also feels that he is now by way of the novel containing that which Joyce contains, his own younger self.[124] Returning here is something close to Carpentier's claim that Orwell moves dialectically beyond realism (thesis) and modernism (antithesis) to a successful synthesis, "a new kind of realism that could work in conjunction with Joycean modernism."[125] The difference, as we have already noted, is that Carpentier's neorealist or hyperrealist Orwell is serene as Fowler's—and my own—never is. He, the Orwell of *Nineteen Eighty-Four*, is for Carpentier the calm and confident Orwell of the essays, one whose later (after 1942) "critical passages of disavowal" of Joyce "may represent," she asserts, Orwell's "mastery" of what we might call his Joyce problem.[126] The premise here is that one finds too much affect in the novel, too much "discontent and anger," and discontent and anger that point elliptically back to Joyce, for any such sense of Orwellian triumph. Modernism, we may conclude, modernism in the figure and form (aesthetic and other) of Joyce, remained for Orwell a great provocation.

iv. ORWELL'S ENLIGHTENING WOMAN—AND HIS WOMEN

As noted in the last section, "From the Archives" features an art object, the crystal paperweight figuring centrally in *Nineteen Eighty-Four*, at a critical moment in the plot. In a story about waiting and watching, one in which few opportunities for decisive action, aesthetic or other, arise, art plays a role. It is put to use. And it is worth pointing out that it is Avril O'Malley who is its user.

Justly is this opportunity handed to Avril, the original of whom, Avril Blair, has never gotten the biographical attention that she deserves. "None of the accounts of my father's time on Jura recognize [sic] how essential she was," writes Orwell's adopted son, Richard Blair.[127] Certainly Avril was cheerfully essential to the Orwell farming operation. As Davison comments, "She worked hard gardening and caring for the animals—indeed, keeping the small property going."[128] But now and then she also worked hard at something else—keeping Orwell's writerly activities going. A minor but perceptive character in Joyce's *Ulysses*, Lenehan, at one point in the story exclaims, "There's a touch of the artist about old Bloom."[129] Was there a touch of the artist about old Avril? A photograph of Avril on Jura, shovel in hand, survives, one which should be iconic; to render it iconic, to create a powerful image of Avril Blair as Orwell's constant gardener, so to speak, is one ambition of "From the Archives." But another is that of recognizing her contribution to Orwell's *literary* operation. For when Orwell was too ill to continue his diary, as he sometimes was, Avril would step in (as her first diary entry in "From the Archives" mentions). Indeed, one who reads through the diaries does not find it hard to imagine her at some point choosing to start a diary of her own, even a diary that could prove a rival to her brother's.[130]

"From the Archives" of course takes another step and imagines what that diary may have contained—Avril's independent view of Orwellian (and "Avrillian") things. Avril Blair was quite the reader. A photograph of her as a six-year-old poring over a large picture book, *My Big Book of Soldiers*, survives and indeed figures in one of Cedric's diary-entry recollections. But the Avril of this story turns out to be quite the writer, too, proving not just a complement to her brother but a competitor; her own independent diary, which as it were breaks out of and partitions itself apart from "Cedrician" discourse early on, comes to constitute over one-third of the novella. Orwell's quietly remarkable sister is thereby given a voice.

Orwell of course knew other remarkable women, some of them less quietly such. With this attention to Avril arises, then, the larger question of his sexual politics, which have on occasion been deplored. Orwell has been accused of tending to neglect feminine individuality and agency and doing so both within and without his fiction. What may be termed "the Spenderian consensus" has emerged, a position on the question of Orwell and women shared by several of Orwell's friends, colleagues, and commentators and one that is represented most thoroughly and academically by Daphne Patai's book-length statement, *The Orwell Mystique: A Study in Male Ideology*.[131] On the question of Orwell and his non-fictional women, Spender himself, for example, is curt: "Orwell was very misogynist. I don't know why ... he thought women were extremely inferior and stupid ... He really rather despised women."[132] Regarding Orwell's fictional women, on the other hand? According to Averil Gardner, for example, they may escape Orwell's disdain; they do not escape stereotype: "however sympathetically they may be presented, [women in Orwell's novels] play no more than a sexual and/or domestic role."[133] Such, then, is the Spenderian consensus, roughly. But we may identify a contrary, equally rough consensus that may be termed "the Salkeldian consensus": "He liked very strong women. Women who had an opinion. That is what attracted him."[134] By all accounts his first wife, Eileen O'Shaughnessy Blair, was such a woman, and that clergyman's daughter Brenda Salkeld was another. Certainly this "intelligent, handsome woman" was in a position to know something about Orwell's attitudes and conduct;[135] as one of Orwell's biographers puts it, she was the "gym mistress" who was for a time one of Orwell's chief interlocutors; she and Orwell "became good friends in the 1930s and remained in touch with each other all his life"; "[h]e respected her literary views and wanted her good opinion," going "to the trouble of annotating her presentation copy of *Down and Out*."[136] As we saw in the last section, several of his letters to Salkeld contain significant ruminations on Joyce and his literary-historical significance; as Richard Blair asserts, "the letters show that he used Salkeld as a sounding board for his ideas."[137] What did Salkeld, herself, say about Orwell—about Orwell and women? About Orwell and *herself*, as a possible married couple, she had no doubts: "marriage was not for us... he would have been impossible to live with."[138] On that larger question? She was silent. But some will agree with D. J. Taylor that, when all is said ("[i]n the end")

Orwell's women, real and fictional, "Eileen and Sonia, Brenda and Eleanor, Sally and Inez, Dorothy Rodgers walking home across Southwold Common and the sacking aproned-drudge of the Wigan backstreets"—they "are [all] sisters under the skin"; we should not "ignore ... the genuine imaginative sympathy that Orwell brought to" them.[139]

Could one say that on "the Woman Question," as the Victorians denominated it, Orwell as so often proves fundamentally ambivalent? In any event, before all is said in "From the Archives" Caroline O'Malley is given a say, and it would not be misleading to describe the novella as being every bit as much Caroline's story, as well as Avril's story, as it is Cedric's. As mentioned above, Avril's saying alone occupies roughly one-third of its pages; the premise is that most "sounding boards" may just have their own distinctive voices. Which is not to suggest that Avril Blair, in particular, or "Orwell's women," in general, have been submitted to some form of compensatory idealization in "From the Archives." It could be argued that Avril, for one, was not particularly Enlightened. She was said to be capable of harshness and clannishness— which survives in "From the Archives" in Avril's capacity for caustic, sardonic commentary as well as unflinching, at times cold scrutiny. She can be monitory, peering, peeping, even, at one point thereunto snatching up a hand-drill, and she can also be punitive, bordering upon cruel. She thinks of herself as offering corrective lenses to what she regards as Cedric's soft-hearted, soft-headed point of view, especially when Caroline, whom she regards as an interloper, is nearby, and she functions as a particularly fierce sort of "focalizer" climactically.[140]

v. ORWELL'S INDIVIDUALISM

If Avril is a focalizer, then upon what—or upon whom—does Avril tend to focus? Upon Cedric, of course, but even more so, as I may have suggested, it is indeed Caroline Pretzel O'Malley who earns her attention, and little wonder. A prominent pre-war and wartime novelist and intellectual who suffers an unspecified chronic respiratory complaint (perhaps Orwell's own tuberculosis), Caroline is the object of Avril's suspicions. Avril's preoccupation with the question of how Caroline spends her time to herself itself becomes a question. What Caroline is in fact doing at these times is one of the puzzles of the novella and for a number of reasons should not be clarified here. Suffice it to say that she is an "individualist" as well as an intellectual and that "From the Archives" addresses the established question of individuality ("*ownlife*" in Newspeak; *1984*, 82) in Orwell's late career.[141] Indeed, it explores the topic along the lines sketched by Gass in his influential review:

> If you are an individualist, as Orwell was on his sunny days, but also join forces with others to make a group, a group like POUM ... you will soon grow restive about certain rules .... You will become unreliable. Suspicious. The collective will begin to follow your friends to their assignations. Accusations will begin to fly. You can't swat all of them. You are accused of Trotskyism.[142]

Like their author, who "remained a solitary, individualistic writer," according to the biographer Jeffrey Meyers, all the particular characters in "From the Archives"—even a particular aeroplane (!)—are individualists; at the least, they all begin as such.[143] But Caroline is the most "restive" amongst them; even the minimal Jura cottage "rules" prompt her to turn "unreliable," and this is resented by brother and sister alike, though especially by sister, who has always distrusted her and who once secretly followed her around London and bore witness, as she imagines, to an "assignation."

vi. ORWELL AND THE JEWS

Caroline O'Malley is, as we have just seen, this and that; she's an artist, she's an intellectual, she's an individualist, et al.—and she is a *Jew*. The issue of Orwell's "possibly unresolved problems with 'the Jewish question'" stands out starkly across the array of his later writings; it remains unsettled and unsettling, despite the best efforts of, for just two examples, John Rodden and Christopher Hitchens to resolve it—indeed, in Hitchens's case, to contain it and even kill it, once and for all.[144] In his detailed discussion of "Orwell, the Catholics, and the Jews" Rodden claims that Orwell "saw Jews as non-doctrinaire in belief, free from a ruling hierarchy, radical-liberal in political tendency, and victimized by anti-Semitic prejudices."[145] Hitchens passionately and, some would say, uncritically presents an Orwell who is, if not Rodden's virtual pro-Semite, so to speak, a sort of anti-anti-Semite whose feelings and attitudes, though complicated, even contradictory, were always at the least trending in the correct direction.[146]

More recently and magisterially, and more neutrally, Michael G. Brennan has argued that Orwell did in fact in the "pre-war" years exhibit a certain tendency towards anti-Semitism, one from which issued "sometimes demeaning and apparently anti-Semitic depictions of Jewish figures"—but that such were "rapidly eradicated from his publications once intelligence about the horrors of Nazi persecution of the Jews began to circulate in England."[147] (D. J. Taylor notes an interesting example of such "self-censorship" in the emendation whereby "'an old fat Jew' trying to swim away from a pursuing helicopter in the propaganda film [discussed in section iii] becomes 'a great huge fat man.'"[148]) Note Brennan's choice of a passive voice construction; yes, Orwell would soon ("from 1945") adopt and "offer ... a strident public voice in the denunciation of anti-Semitism," but what of his private voice? Brennan also wonders that Orwell's "pathological hatred of the Catholic hierarchy" should persist unabated, unquestioned, unqualified after the war and the "intelligence" that it brought; one might think that in coming to question his own somewhat less-than-pathological but at times vibrant "kind of quick and casual prejudice against the Jews he encounters"—assuming that he really did come to question it—he would also come to question the hatred that was in a sense its twin.[149] All of which is to say that the larger question of "Orwell and the Jews" is one of those whipsaw issues difficult to avoid in any sustained consideration of Orwell.

Accordingly, Orwell's own Jewish Question informs "From the Archives," most centrally by way of Caroline, who is for several characters—and for herself—the official Jew of the story, representing Jerusalem, or made to do so by Cedric, as against Cedric's Athens (by way of Dublin). Little wonder that she should in certain uncertain ways wander, nowhere more significantly, even spectacularly, than in her dreams, three of which are reported in detail. In these dreams, especially, she may remind one of the "Wanderer Herodias" who may be found in Ceferino Tresserra's *La Judia Errante* (1862)[150] or of Eugène Sue's *Le Juif Errant* (1889), she who roams thirstily in search of something

> through the shadow thrown by the overhanging wood, which stretches far into endless depths ... It is a [human form, a] woman. She advances slowly towards the ruins ... She treads the once sacred ground. [She] is pale, her look sad, her long robe floats on the wind, her feet covered with dust. She walks with difficulty and pain. A block of stone is placed near the stream, almost at the foot of the statue of John the Baptist. Upon this stone she sinks breathless and exhausted, worn out with fatigue ... [H]er throat becomes dry, contracted, all on fire. She sees the stream, and throws herself on her knees, to quench her thirst in that crystal current, transparent as a mirror. What happens then?[151]

What happens then to Caroline, whose dream has taken her not to "a block of stone" but to a sort of obelisk sitting in the "endless depths" of a different dark forest? As readers will discover, she, too, has an encounter with a "crystal current," but one with decidedly fewer baptismal properties; she, too, looks in a kind of "mirror"; she, too, has a kind of revelation.

vii. ORWELL'S PASTORALISM

In "Why I Write" Orwell vowed to "continue ... to love the surface of the earth ... [s]o long as I remain alive and well."[152] That love is explored in "From the Archives," in its earlier pages, especially. What is also explored is the threat faced, the threat to both his love of the surface and to that surface itself.

As Cedric, something of an environmentalist, wonders at one point, "who would plant a missile in the heart of the rising sun, & the bluest September sky, & the quiet mind of humankind? Is not it because we humans ... want more than human history, ... we want to own the very weather, the seasons, the light, the law, to make time, itself, that famous Aeonian rhythm, pulse to our pulse, step to our tune?" One of "the two aims of the Party" Winston reads about in "Goldstein"'s *Theory and Practice* is "to conquer the whole surface of the earth" (*1984*, 193). "From the Archives" imagines "the Party" seeking a dominance that extends beyond and beneath the surface, as well. Hence, on the one hand, the slightly anachronistic reference to the Great Killer Fog of 1952, a kind of twentieth-century post-war embodiment of John Ruskin's "Storm-Cloud of the Nineteenth Century." Hence, too, on the other, the significant if seemingly casual mention late in the novella of the Party's plan to bomb Corryvreckan, itself. Corryvreckan keeps the trains—the troopships, rather—from running on time; worse, perhaps, it is an object of wonder. But the novella is even more interested in the Party's attack upon the human "love" of that surface. Cedric's encounters with various beloved features of the natural world as they are available on and around Jura are the substance of a number of his journal entries, and close attention to the latter will reveal an arc in his career as an impromptu, amateur naturalist and longtime nature lover.

Orwell's diary entry of 16 August 1947 provides the basis for what is perhaps the climax of this particular subplot of the novel: Orwell reports having seen "the northern lights for the first time" the night before and having noticed an "extraordinary flickering passing over them, as though a searchlight were playing upon them."[153] For Cedric, unlike Orwell, that searchlight signifies an invasion or, at the least, the failure of his own Jura strategy of evasion. His imagination, whether confronting supreme natural loveliness or just simple natural fact (D. G. Rossetti's woodspurge with its cup of three), has lost that healthy ability to carry him beyond wartime and general political concerns. Note Orwell's Jura diary entry of 22 July 1947: "Eagle over field again today. Crows mobbing him appeared to succeed in forcing him down to the ground."[154] Orwell appears to resist emblematizing either eagle or crow; "mobbed" as he may be, Orwell's eagle remains an eagle. Cedric, on the other hand, gradually loses the ability to see eagles as eagles, crows as crows. Rather, he gives way to insistent, comprehensive Social Allegory.

viii. ORWELL ON HISTORY AND MEMORY

According to Rodden and Rossi, one of Orwell's chief concerns in writing *Nineteen Eighty-Four* "was his fear that the very idea of historical truth was disappearing ... Orwell believed that a sense of history might cease to exist in the future."[155] Any such concern about historical truth is of course a subsidiary of a more general concern about objective truth, which I have treated at some length in section i above (cf. the paragraphs on "Orwell's realism"). Here I would like to add just a few comments on a subsidiary of that subsidiary, what we might term subjective truth—though less in the sense of a subjective (biased) collective history than in the sense of the subject's or self's own history. For, quite curiously, Orwell's fears that accounts of our collective, public past might prove frangible and fungible do not appear to have extended into the private sphere. That is, he does not seem to have been quite so worried about the personal or individual memory.

Recall Winston's interview with the old prole whom he meets in the pub. Memories of days long past are elicited by Winston, memories of what he dismisses as "a million useless things," "a quarrel with a workmate, a hunt for a lost bicycle pump, the expression on a long-dead sister's face, the swirls of dust on a windy morning seventy years ago," and so forth (*1984*, 93). Useless? Perhaps, as may be the memories of them, but unlike the former, the things themselves, the memories are no less tenacious than useless, unquestionably: just another windy morning from "seventy years ago" somehow resides in memory, indelible, ineradicable. The "things" pass away; the memories do not. We do not forget our dead sisters. We don't forget our dead brothers, either: even if Eileen Blair had lived another seventy years, she would never have forgotten her brother Laurence.[156] Nor do we forget the "expression." Winston has not forgotten the look on his mother's face as he dreams of her and his sister sinking beneath him "in the green waters," having sacrificed themselves on his behalf: "he could see the knowledge in their faces ... that they must die in order that he might remain alive" (*1984*, 29); as we discover in ch. 7 of Part Two, here in the very opening of Part One, ch. 3, Winston has slightly transformed his guilty memory of the childhood episode of stealing chocolate from his sister and ignoring his mother's rebuke (discussed in section ii; *1984*, 163); it is a dream, the "saloon of the sinking ship" being a particularly phantasmagoric image, but it is based upon "a memory that he must have deliberately pushed out of his consciousness over many years" (*1984*, 160):

> Exactly as his mother had sat on the dingy white-quilted bed, with the child clinging to her [whimpering over the stolen chocolate], so she had sat in the sunken ship, far underneath him, and drowning deeper every minute, but still looking up at him through the darkening water. (*1984*, 164)

That dingy, white-quilted bed memory has stuck around, somewhere, and in Part Two, ch. 7, it comes back, somehow (by way of a second dream in which "he had remembered his last glimpse of his mother"; *1984*, 160). In so doing it displays all of the athletic vigor *not* displayed by the *"great huge fat"* swimmer whom Winston sees machine-gunned in a flick one evening: it had "swum into his mind in the few seconds after waking" (*1984*, 8, 160).

The question arises, however, whether such remarkably tenacious personal memory in Orwell is, if not useless, *worse* than useless. Could it not be indeed, in at least one respect, positively harmful? Regarding the old prole's memories: do they serve anything other than an escapist, politically disabling sentimentalism? It is difficult to say, in part because Orwell's representation of prole memory is difficult to disentangle from his depiction of prole "consciousness" at large. Nevertheless, to the extent that one discounts the revolutionary potential of the latter it is hard to be hopeful about the former; it becomes hard to regard it as an untapped well of revolutionary substance. Winston himself, of course, momentarily loses all hope in the proles collectively upon this one old prole's finally truncating his unbroken stream of seemingly pointless recollections to run off to the loo: he concludes that the proles lack "the power of grasping that the world can be other than it is" (*1984*, 210). David Morgan Zehr puts the point well even though he attributes Winston's conclusion to Orwell: "[c]onvinced that history was on the verge of collapse, Orwell invested his last faith in an historical community [i.e., the proles], even though (and partly because) he believed it was a community without any historical consciousness."[157] According to Zehr and Winston alike, the possession of an indelible personal history does not entail "historical consciousness." Indeed, one can imagine it inculcating the opposite—the deliberate belief that the more things change, the more they stay the same: "It's no good ... There always will be rich and poor."[158] The escape from "passive unconsciousness" could lead to confirmed, conscious passivity.[159]

Moving from a member of the proletariat to a member of the Party: what about Winston, himself? Does, for example, the recollected memory of his mother's and sister's self-sacrifice (Part Two, ch. 7), which is also his last memory of them, do Winston any good? Or does it only further dismay, depress, disable? Such a thing is thinkable; note Thomas Hardy's undoing of Wordsworth's celebrated "myth of memory as salvation" in "The Voice" (1912), whose speaker's trip down memory lane ("as when I drew near to the town") ends with his yet sharper sense of past loss and present misery: "Thus I; faltering forward, / Leaves around me falling, / Wind oozing thin through the thorn...."[160] But it is difficult to dismiss Winstonian memory in such terms. Yes, his first dreamy encounter with this last memory of his mother, the sinking-ship dream, at first depresses; it only sharpens his sad, disabling sense that "[t]oday," unlike the yesterday of his childhood, "there were fear, hatred, and pain, but no dignity of emotion, no deep or complex sorrows" (*1984*, 30). But the dream gives way to, having prepared the way for, an auspicious "Golden Country" memory/fantasy in which the Party's existential dependence on sexual repression is revealed or at least brought into focus—thus prompting Winston's sexual rebellion. Still half-asleep, Winston finds himself in a sexualized landscape ("the boughs of the elm trees were swaying very faintly in the breeze, their leaves just stirring in dense masses like women's hair") into which a dream-Julia enters; as Julia approaches she "[tears] off her clothes and [flings] them disdainfully aside" with "what seemed a single movement," "a single splendid movement of the arm," a "gesture" which with "its grace and carelessness seemed to annihilate a whole culture, a whole system of thought" (*1984*, 31). And, crucially, this core gesture is not fantastical, even if the enveloping Golden Country episode might be; rather, it would appear to echo and transfigure, politically, "a gesture of the arm made by his mother," "an enveloping protective gesture of the arm" that she made on their last afternoon together and that Winston remembers only later (again, in Part Two, ch. 7)—when, significantly, he is waking up from the second dream in bed with Julia (Julia "roll[ing] sleepily against him"; *1984*, 159). His first encounter with the memory, thus, proves not depressing but enabling, at least potentially. Also enabling, moreover, is his second encounter with the memory, by way of the second dream. As we have already seen, this second dream leads to a full emergence of the originating memory; it also leads to an emotional and intellectual, even a potentially *political*, breakthrough. At the end of a complex meditative sequence gotten on foot by the dream and its animating memory lies Winston's discovery that the "proles are human beings ... We"—members of the Party—"are not human" (*1984*, 165). Again, it is hard not to see these moments of memory as salutary. To see them otherwise requires that we regard all Winston's breakthroughs as merely serving to make his ultimate annihilation the more painful—because giving the Party more to annihilate, the calf-self having been that much more fatted before slaughter.

In any event, it is clear that Orwell's fearful evocations of historical memory's being mutable and mortal in its public incarnations are balanced by signs of its immutability and longevity in the individual mind, ones which comfort, arguably. Which is just another way of asserting that history, personal or collective, is no less than a vital issue in the later Orwell. Suffice it to say, here, that "From the Archives" explores this issue thoroughly.

INCONCLUSION

A liberal humanist, realist, feminist, anti-anti-Semitic progressive who harbors salutary-if-traditional feelings for the English countryside even as he puts his young writer's pretension to High Art (aka, James Joyce) in its place? A perforce illiberal, caustically skeptical, casually anti-Semitic despiser of women who could not get Joyce out of his system and whose pastoral nostalgia was—surprise!—nationalistic?

Something in between, or somewhere, that "where" at which we arrive by some complex navigation between these antipodes?

Nothing so fixed and final as this last question assumes? Orwell at sea, not exactly lost but tacking back and forth, steering, coming about, exploring, risking whirlpools…?

William Gass gave his influential—it influenced one, at least—review of *George Orwell, Diaries*, "Double Vision," the subtitle "Orwell's Contradictions." Having surveyed and scrutinized that "Vision," having tried to counter those "contradictions," to solve them, dissolve them, critic turned acidic, I am still seeing "Double"—though sometimes Treble. And it is a good thing, too, despite the possibility that such trebleness and doubleness may be entered into the record as exhibit "X" in the prosecution of *Nineteen Eighty-Four* for Aesthetic Inadequacy, two counts. Orwell's final book "is, in fact, at best a good 'bad book,' inept as narrative [count #1], and [count #2] worse than that as characterization."[161] With regard to count #2, "worse than … inept" characterization, never mind that Orwell was, like the South African author J. M. Coetzee, writing a "less than fully human literature, unnaturally preoccupied with power and the torsions of power"; never mind that Winston's character suffers the "torsions" proper to life in an imagined totalitarian state; never mind Orwell's very theme: the State stunts the individual self and soul.[162] Never mind, too, the conditions of the book's composition—that is, Orwell's own physical condition, worse than stunted, while writing it (witness the particularly prim and grim refusal to hazard the Intentional Fallacy).[163] Consider Orwellian doubleness, trebleness, ambiguousness, ambivalence, multivalence: mushiness, squishiness, signs of something less than a tough mind, being mere conceptual, expository, and aesthetic flaws, one and all. Thomas Ricks intensely admires Orwell, putting him on a level with or even above Churchill as shaper of the post-war world in which we still live ("[a]ll told, in terms of contemporary influence, Orwell arguably has surpassed Churchill").[164] But note the form that such Ricksian admiration for *Nineteen Eighty-Four* assumes: "by the end of the first page, it is clear that he knows what he wants to say and how to say it."[165] Foreclosed by such an encomium is any admiration for an author who is not entirely sure he knows what he wants to say, not altogether, but who *says*, anyway, who says something, despite its provisional quality, its partiality, its insufficiency as definite message. Such an author may not be certain, entirely—and decidedly so, intentionally so, having submitted to uncertainty as the proper and necessary condition of her saying. Indeed risking "confusion and contradictions," she eschews the indicative, the declarative, the constative, preferring the suggestive.[166] Which is to say, finally, that such an author may be a "symbolist," in the broader sense of the word.[167]

Having read or reread *Nineteen Eighty-Four*, and having let a little time pass, what do we remember about the book? What abides, what lingers? Is it the book's argument, its chain of claims, its syllogisms, its enthymemes, premises, propositions, and conclusions? Is it the abstract contours, the truth trees and skeleton keys of the one-sided debate between O'Brien and Winston? Is it not, rather, the *symbols*, "as seen through Winston Smith's eyes but [in] patterns … unperceived by him"—the images, vibrant, bell-like in their resonance, mysterious, ineradicable, like the memories reported by the old prole in the pub?[168] For just one, perhaps preeminent example, (re)consider the faces, the principal of which is that of Big Brother, "black-haired, black mustachio'd," the face "full of power and mysterious calm, and so vast that it almost filled up the screen" (*1984*, 16); "enormous," "more than a meter wide" on its innumerable posters, it is "the face of a man of about forty-five, with a heavy black mustache and ruggedly handsome features," the eyes "follow[ing] you about when you move" (*1984*, 1–2). This is a face no less impenetrable to the understanding than it is ubiquitous, whether vast in size or tiny (Winston "slid a coin out of his pocket and looked at it. The face gazed up at him"; *1984*, 103–04). What does that mustache, multiplied endlessly on public walls throughout the city, mean? In the end Winston feels that he finally knows "what kind of smile was hidden beneath the dark mustache" (*1984*, 104, 297)—only after "[f]orty years" (*1984*, 297).

Curiously, as Orwell himself might have put it, he does not tell. Nor does the narrator.

And what of the eyes of Big Brother that "follow … you about," or those of O'Brien's servant Martin, the "little man" whose "dark eyes flicker[…] over… faces" (*1984*, 174), or those other, related eyes, denizens of the Ministry of Love, which do not follow or flicker about but grow "larger and more luminous" and become a sort of pool in which you imagine disappearing: "Suddenly he floated out of his seat, dived into the eyes, and was swallowed up" (*1984*, 243). What of those yet other, those unrelated and very different "eyes," those of Julia, which he has seen ("She looked him straight in the face," "[h]er eyes ... fixed on his"; *1984*, 100, 105) but cannot see during their brief assignation at Victory Square ("To turn his head and look at her would have been inconceivable folly"; *1984*, 117)? What of the eyes that he *does* see in Victory Square—those "of the aged prisoner gaz[ing] mournfully at Winston out of nests of hair"— "eyes look[ing] into Winston's... with strange intensity" (*1984*, 117, 116)? What do they signify? What kind of "meaning" is hidden, "nested" within that "mass of grizzled hair," egg-like, ready to be hatched, or fledged, ready to take flight (*1984*, 116)? Winston does not know; he knows only that they are meaningful, and the reader agrees. They may just be the most meaningful eyes in all the story.

Curiously, again, Orwell's narrator, for his part, does not say.

Notes

I. Introduction

1. Robert McCrum, "The Masterpiece That Killed George Orwell," *The Observer*, 9 May 2009 (https://www.theguardian.com/books/2009/may/10/1984-george-orwell); Stephen Miller, "Orwell Once More," *The Sewanee Review* 112.4 (Fall, 2004), 595; Jeffrey Meyers, *Orwell: Life and Art* (Urbana, Chicago, Springfield: University of Illinois Press, 2010), ix. In "Orwell: Sage of the Century" William Giraldi quotes Christopher Hitchens's apposite claim that Orwell "owns the twentieth century, as a writer about fascism and communism and imperialism, in a way that no other writer in English can claim" (*The New Republic*, 11 August 2013; https://newrepublic.com/article/114254/george-orwell-life-letters-reviewed-william-giraldi).
2. Richard Lance Keeble, "George Orwell: The Cultural Icon of Today," *The Orwell Society*, 10 September 2014 (https://orwellsociety.com/george-orwell-the-cultural-icon-of-today/); Thomas Cushman and John Rodden, eds., *George Orwell: Into the Twenty-First Century* (New York: Routledge, 2016), 1.
3. All references to *Nineteen Eighty-Four* will be to the widely available American "Signet" edition, *1984* (New York: American Library, 1950; 1977), and will be noted parenthetically. Regarding the novel's suddenly becoming a bestseller, see *https://www.nytimes.com/2017/01/25/books/1984-george-orwell-donald-trump.html*. Other reports on the book's recent resurgence may be found at *https://www.theguardian.com/*books/2017/feb/03/americanism-us-writers-imagine-fascist-future-fiction, https://www.arundelpatriot.org/2018/01/21/understand-trump-read-orwell/, http://www.bbc.com/culture/story/20180507-why-orwells-1984-could-be-about-now*—the beat goes on. So numerous are these recently published little reports of Orwell's newfound relevance that one could make a small book of them.
4. As Richard Lance Keeble notes, the term "Orwellian" has come to be "used as a pejorative adjective to evoke totalitarian terror, the falsification of history by state organised lying; the use of euphemistic language to camouflage morally outrageous ideas and actions."

"Occasionally," however, it is "used as a complimentary adjective to mean 'displaying outspoken intellectual honesty, like Orwell'" ("George Orwell: The Cultural Icon of Today"). Most often I use it as a neutral adjective signifying something of or relating to Orwell.

5. D. J. Taylor, *On Nineteen Eighty-Four: A Biography* (New York: Abrams Press, 2019), 8.
6. Robert Scholes writes of how "fabulators" "care for form" above all else (*The Fabulators* [Oxford: Oxford University Press, 1967], 41).
7. Scott R. Stroud helpfully cites Jürgen Habermas (*Postmetaphysical Thinking: Philosophical Essays* [Cambridge, MA: MIT Press, 1996]) and the duo Peter Lamarque and Stein Haugom Olsen (*Truth, Fiction, and Literature: A Philosophical Perspective* [Oxford: Clarendon Press, 1984]), among others, as offering strong challenges to the notion of "narrative argument": "In a similar vein to Habermas, [Lamarque and Olsen] argue that the fact that narratives may present us with situations that refine or reconstruct a concept does not mean that they argue for that conception. In other words, even though narratives might spur readers to *recognize* a certain position or claim, they do not function as arguments insofar as they lack any force that pushes for a reader's *adoption* of that concept as normatively better than alternatives" ("The Complex Relationship Among Truth, Argument, and Narrative," *The Journal of Speculative Philosophy* 34.4 [2020], 511). Stroud goes on to clarify some of the arguments against the notion that fiction provides "evidence" (note its common practice of evidentiary fabrication complemented by inferential error, e.g. "hasty generalization," 512). But Stroud ends up arguing that we should "accept [narratives] as a valid part of argumentative appeals from others" (512).
8. That is, much of the "evidence" (see Stroud, note 7) presented in the novella has been found in Orwell's work rather than having been found, as in conventional fiction, from a variety of sources. To an unusual degree, perhaps, this novella culls and collects from the writings of a single author. The premise is that fiction typically gathers its evidence more broadly—culls and collects it from that seeming universe of evidentiary material loosely called "experience" as well as from that seeming universe constituted by art and literature.
9. Will Self would surely regard such Orwellian lapses as signs of literary inaptitude, given the position he adopts in his provocation "A Point of View: Why Orwell was a Literary Mediocrity," *BBC Magazine*, 31 August 2014. For a balanced account of the media "kerfuffle" that Self instigated by way of this attack, see Richard Lance Keeble, "The Orwell/Self Spat: What It Reveals About Contemporary Culture," *The*

Orwell Society, 7 September 2014 (https://orwellsociety.com/the-orwellself-spat-what-it-reveals-about-contemporary-culture/).

10. In "Charles Dickens" Orwell asserts that "every writer, especially every novelist, *has* a 'message,' whether he admits it or not" (*George Orwell: A Collection of Essays* [New York: Houghton Mifflin Harcourt, 1946], 90).
11. McCrum, "The Masterpiece That Killed George Orwell."
12. Ibid.
13. Thomas E. Ricks, *Churchill and Orwell: The Fight for Freedom* (New York: Penguin, 2017), 235. For an evocative account of how the dying Orwell began to write a novella set in what is now Myanmar, see Emma Larkin, *Finding George Orwell in Burma* (New York: Penguin, 2005).
14. Alex Zwerdling, *Orwell and the Left* (New Haven: Yale University Press, 1974), 209. Orwell sometimes became openly disparaging. For example, he "thought [*Keep the Aspidistra Flying*] a failure, dismissing it (along with *A Clergyman's Daughter*) as a 'silly potboiler'" (John Rodden and John Rossi, *The Cambridge Introduction to George Orwell* [Cambridge: Cambridge University Press, 2012], 41).
15. George Orwell, "Why I Write," in *The Complete Works of George Orwell*, Volume 18, ed. Peter Davison (London: Secker and Warburg, 2000), 320.
16. Anthony Burgess, *1985* (New York: Little, Brown and Company, 1978). Martin Amis: Burgess "dismisses '1984,'" preferring "a stoked-up 1976" (see "A Stoked-Up 1976," *New York Times*, 19 November 1978 (https://archive.nytimes.com/www.nytimes.com/books/97/11/30/home/burgess-1985.html). Like this book, Burgess's *1985* is one-half critical. But Burgess's critical reactions to *Nineteen Eighty-Four* take the form of mock interviews, parodies, screeds, and, yes, a few essays fairly standard in form if brief and tony. On the whole Burgess's book on Orwell, unlike his work on James Joyce, proves of greater interest to students of Burgess than to students of the major author in question.
17. David Peace, *GB84: A Novel* (New York: Melville House, 2014).
18. Andrew Ervin, *Burning Down George Orwell's House* (New York: Soho Press, 2016).
19. Dom Shaw, *Eric is Awake* (Anonymous Press, 2013).
20. Hermione Lee, "Great Extrapolations," *The Guardian*, 28 September 1997 (*https://www.theguardian.com/books/1997/sep/28/fiction.petercarey*).
21. See Michael D. Shear, "Trump Will Withdraw U.S. from Paris Climate Agreement," *New York Times*, 1 June 2017 (*https://www.nytimes.com/2017/06/01/climate/trump-paris-climate-agreement.html*).

22. See Jon Henley, "Antisemitism on Rise across Europe 'in Worst Times since the Nazis,'" *The Guardian*, 7 August 2014 (*https://www.theguardian.com/society/2014/aug/07/antisemitism-rise-europe-worst-since-nazis*).
23. Steven Pinker, *Enlightenment Now: The Case for Reason, Science, Humanism, and Progress* (New York: Viking, 2018). The website for The Re:Enlightenment Project may be found at *http://www.reenlightenment.org/*.
24. "complement," *Collins Dictionary* (*https://www.collinsdictionary.com/us/dictionary/english/complement*).
25. "Reception study" is a critical approach that abolishes "the classic priority of the work over the reader" (Hans Robert Jauss, "Theses on the Transition from Literary Works to a Theory of Aesthetic Experience," in *Interpretation of Narrative*, ed. Mario J. Valdes and Owen J. Miller [Toronto: University of Toronto Press, 1978], 138). Readers interested in reception should consult James L. Machor and Philip Goldstein's excellent reader, *Reception Study: From Literary Theory to Cultural Studies* (New York: Routledge, 2000).
26. Keith Williams, "'The Unpaid Agitator': Joyce's Influence on George Orwell and James Agee," *James Joyce Quarterly* 36.4 (Summer, 1999), 730.
27. Michael Levenson, "The Fictional Realist: Novels of the 1930s," in *The Cambridge Companion to George Orwell*, ed. John Rodden (Cambridge: Cambridge University Press, 2007), 59.
28. Caroline Rody, "Burning Down the House: The Revisionary Paradigm of Jean Rhys's *Wide Sargasso Sea*," in Jean Rhys, *Wide Sargasso Sea*, ed. Judith Raiskin (New York: Norton Critical Edition, 1999): 217-24; Hermione Lee, "Great Extrapolations."
29. In "The Metaphysics of Logical Atomism" (2000) Bernard Linsky, for example, writes of logical atomism as a "metaphysical view" (2; *http://www.sfu.ca/~jeffpell/Phil467/LinskyLogAtom.pdf*); Dan Rather, "Dan Rather Facebook Post," Facebook, retrieved 28 January 2022.
30. On reception theory, see note 25 of this introduction.
31. George Orwell, *George Orwell, Diaries*, ed. Peter Davison (New York: Liveright, W. W. Norton and Co., 2012).
32. See "Orwell Diaries 1938–1942": *https://orwelldiaries.wordpress.com/*.
33. William H. Gass, "Double Vision: George Orwell's Contradictions," *Harper's Magazine* 325.1949 (October 2012), 79 (*http://harpers.org/archive/2012/10/double-vision/*).
34. Orwell, *George Orwell, Diaries*, 515–16.
35. As readers will see in Orwell's own diaries, the egg-count became so obligatory that Avril kept it up when she took over the diary upon Orwell's being hospitalized in 1947.
36. Ellen Malenas Ledoux, *Social Reform in Gothic Writing: Fantastic Forms of Change, 1764–1834* (New York: Palgrave, 2013), 178.

III. Teaching Supplement

1. Sigmund Freud, *The Interpretation of Dreams*, *The Standard Edition of the Psychological Works of Sigmund Freud*, trans. James Strachey (London: Hogarth Press, 1953–73), 195.
2. George Orwell, "Why I Write," 319.
3. Cf. Elaine Scarry, "A Defense of Poesy (The Treatise of Julia)," in *On Nineteen Eighty-Four: Orwell and Our Future*, ed. Abbott Gleason, Jack Goldsmith, and Martha C. Nussbaum (Princeton, NJ: Princeton University Press, 2005), 13–28 (*https://muse.jhu.edu/chapter/1179762*).
4. Orwell, "Charles Dickens," 90.
5. Stanley Fish, "Literature in the Reader: Affective Stylistics," *New Literary History; A Symposium on Literary History* 2.1 (Autumn, 1970), 125 (*https://www.jstor.org/stable/pdf/468593.pdf*).
6. Steven Mailloux, "Evaluation and Reader Response Criticism: Values Implicit in Affective Stylistics," *Style* 10.3 (Summer, 1976), 329 (*https://digitalcommons.lmu.edu/cgi/viewcontent.cgi?article=1020&context=engl_fac*).
7. Hans Robert Jauss, *Literaturge-schichte als Provokation der Literaturwissenschaft* (1967; reprint edn Frankfurt/Main: Suhrkamp, 1970), as quoted by Syndy McMillen Conger in "Hans Robert Jauss's 'REZEPTIONSÄSTHETIK' and England's Reception of Eighteenth-Century Literature," *The Eighteenth Century; A Special Issue on Translation* 22.1 (Winter, 1981), 76. Conger is quoting Elizabeth Benzinger's translation of Jauss ("Literary History as a Challenge to Literary Theory") as published in *New Literary History* 2 (1970): 7–37.
8. Conger, "Hans Robert Jauss's 'REZEPTIONSÄSTHETIK'," 76.
9. Ibid., 75.
10. Ibid.; Hans Robert Jauss, "Der Leser als Instanz einer neuen Geschichte der Literatur," *Poetica* 7 (1975), 325, as quoted (in translation) by Conger, "Hans Robert Jauss's 'REZEPTIONSÄSTHETIK'," 75.
11. An online copy of James's "Preface" is available at *http://www.online-literature.com/henry_james/ambassadors/0/*.
12. An online copy of Shaw's "Preface" is available at *https://www.gutenberg.org/files/3789/3789-h/3789-h.htm*.
13. *Early Letters of William and Dorothy Wordsworth*, Volume I, ed. Ernest de Selincourt (London: Oxford University Press, 1941), 63.
14. In a pithy discussion of the diary ending James Joyce's *Portrait of the Artist as a Young Man*, Michael Levenson specifies several features of the genre which taken together may compose a gesture at its fundamental animating motive or motives. Among these features are the modes of "fidelity" (1018), "intimacy and periodicity" (1018), "sincerity" (1020), and "regularity" (1019); one consequence of

periodicity or regularity is the quality of being incompletable (once you start a diary, how and why should you stop or end it?). See "Stephen's Diary in Joyce's *Portrait*—The Shape of Life," *ELH* 52.4 (Winter, 1985): 1017–35 (https://www.jstor.org/stable/3039476).

15. Cf. Steven Shapin and Simon Schaffer, *Leviathan and the Air-Pump: Hobbes, Boyle, and the Experimental Life* (Princeton, NJ: Princeton University Press, 1985); David Wootton, *The Invention of Science: A New History of the Scientific Revolution* (New York: Harper, 2015); Barbara J. Shapiro, *A Culture of Fact: England, 1550–1720* (Ithaca and London: Cornell University Press, 2000); and Mary Poovey, *A History of the Modern Fact: Problems of Knowledge in the Sciences of Wealth and Society* (Chicago: University of Chicago Press, 1998).

16. In *Churchill and Orwell: The Fight for Freedom*, Thomas E. Ricks makes perhaps the strongest possible case for fact—and for the claim that Orwell, too, makes that case. To Orwell and to us, "the facts of the matter" matter indeed; respect for and deference to them matter, since the "struggle to see things as they are is perhaps the fundamental driver of Western civilization … the agreement that objective reality exists, that people of goodwill can perceive it, and that other people will change their views when presented with the facts of the matter" (269–70).

IV. Critical Supplement: "Orwell Agonistes"

1. Gass, "Double Vision," 79.
2. Ibid., 78.
3. As Richard Joseph Voorhees characterizes "Rosenfeld's theory of suicide," "Orwell's retirement to the island in Scotland not only led to his death, but was designed to do so. In effect, he committed suicide in protest against the horrors of contemporary history" (*The Paradox of George Orwell* [West Lafayette, IN: Purdue University Studies, 1961], 33). See Isaac Rosenfeld, *Preserving the Hunger: An Isaac Rosenfeld Reader* (Detroit: Wayne State University Press, 1988). Jeffrey Meyers stops short of ascribing suicidal designs even as he recognizes the "powerful sense of impending and then actual disaster that dominated Orwell's life and mind in the thirties and forties" (*Orwell: Life and Art*, 129).
4. Orwell, "Why I Write," 319.
5. Martin Martin, *Description of the Western Isles of Scotland* (1703); quoted in Jeffrey Meyers, *Orwell: Wintry Conscience of a Generation* (New York: W. W. Norton and Company, 2000), 272.
6. As Richard Rorty notes, "O'Brien is a curious, perceptive intellectual—much like us"; he is also "as terrifying a character as we are likely to meet in a book." See *Contingency, Irony, and Solidarity* (Cambridge:

Cambridge University Press, 1989), 183. Curiously, Rorty does not call him a philosopher. Indeed, Orwell himself was not much of a philosopher, precisely speaking, even if he were a curious and perceptive intellectual, according to Abbott Gleason ("Orwell's commitment to the principle of 'objectivity' was not really an epistemological position at all," being a—commonsensical—"commitment to the reality of ordinary things") et al. ("Puritanism and Power Politics during the Cold War: George Orwell and Historical Objectivity," *On Nineteen Eighty-Four: Orwell and Our Future*, ed. Abbott Gleason, Jack Goldsmith, and Martha C. Nussbaum [Princeton, NJ: Princeton University Press, 2005], 85). The question of Orwell's realism as well as the philosophical debate that has grown up around it are discussed below.

7. Here I echo Richard Rorty's suspicion that Orwell "use[d] his own sadism to create the character of O'Brien," something that Rorty regards as "a triumph of self-knowledge and self-overcoming" (*Contingency, Irony, and Solidarity*, 184, n.16).

8. George Orwell, *The Collected Essays, Journalism and Letters of George Orwell*, Volume II: *My Country Right or Left, 1940–1943*, ed. Sonia Brownell and Ian Angus (London: Secker and Warburg, 1968), 172. Here Rorty quotes Orwell to characterize Orwell (*Contingency, Irony, and Solidarity*, 184). Like Rorty, Richard A. Epstein "think[s] that [Orwell] is both repelled by and attracted to O'Brien" ("Does Literature Work as Social Science? The Case of George Orwell," in *On Nineteen Eighty-Four: Orwell and Our Future*, ed. Abbott Gleason, Jack Goldsmith, and Martha C. Nussbaum [Princeton, NJ: Princeton University Press, 2005], 66).

9. Elizabeth Vreeland, "Jean Rhys: The Art of Fiction LXIV," *Paris Review* 76 (1979), 235.

10. William Bristow, "Enlightenment," *The Stanford Encyclopedia of Philosophy*, Fall 2017 edn, ed. Edward N. Zalta (*https://plato.stanford.edu/archives/fall2017/entries/enlightenment*).

11. As Jennifer Mensch asserts, it "is hardly unusual to remark on the centrality of 'progress'—and of the conceptually related notions of optimism, providentialism, and human perfectibility—to Enlightenment discussions of history and politics. In France, belief in human progress was endorsed by Turgot and Condorcet, by d'Holbach and Helvétius, and by Diderot and Montesquieu. Even Voltaire, who famously penned *Candide, or Optimism* as an antidote to such claims, concluded that mankind's rational faculties at least gave hope for the possible improvement of the human race. This approach was mirrored by Gibbon in England." See "What's Wrong with Inevitable Progress? Notes on Kant's Anthropology Today," *Cogent Arts and Humanities* 4.1

(2017) (*https://www.tandfonline.com/doi/full/10.1080/23311983.2017.13 90917*).

12. Isaiah Berlin, *The Crooked Timber of Humanity: Chapters in the History of Ideas*, 2nd edn, ed. Henry Hardy (Princeton, NJ: Princeton University Press, 2013). Immanuel Kant's famous phrase appears in his "Idea for a Universal History with a Cosmopolitan Intent," in *The Philosophy of Kant: Immanuel Kant's Moral and Political Writings*, ed. Carl J. Friedrich (New York: Random House, 1977), 123 ("crooked ... wood").
13. D. H. Lawrence, *Women in Love* (Cambridge: Cambridge University Press, 1987), 126.
14. Max Horkheimer and Theodor W. Adorno, *Dialectic of Enlightenment: Philosophical Fragments*, ed. Gunzelin Schmid Noerr, trans. Edmund Jephcott (Stanford, CA: Stanford University Press, 2002), 1.
15. See the Amazon advertisement for Justin E. H. Smith, *Irrationality: A History of the Dark Side of the Reason* (Princeton, NJ: Princeton University Press, 2019): https://www.amazon.com/Irrationality-Justin-E-H-Smith-audiobook/dp/B07NGN6RR5/ref=sr_1_1?keywords=irrationality&qid =1690820844&sr=8-1.
16. Kwame Anthony Appiah, "Dialectics of Enlightenment," *New York Review of Books* 66.8 (9 May 2019) (*https://www.nybooks.com/ issues/2019/05/09/*). (Another excellent review of Smith's book is Jonathan Egid, "Maths Rules: Where the Dialectic Takes Us," *TLS* [5 June 2020], 28.) As Smith himself puts it, "the harder we struggle for reason, it seems, the more we lapse into unreason." See Smith, *Irrationality*, 13. All further reference to Smith's book will be noted parenthetically.
17. Smith asserts that irrationality "encompasses the greater part of human life and has probably governed most periods of human history" (12). It is "humanly ineradicable," as "ineliminable" as sleep (14).
18. Paul Roazen, "Orwell, Freud and 1984," *VQR* 54.4 (Autumn, 1978) (*https://www.vqronline.org/essay/orwell-freud-and-1984*).
19. Rorty, *Contingency, Irony, and Solidarity*, 175.
20. Gordon B. Beadle, "George Orwell and the Victorian Radical Tradition," *Albion: A Quarterly Journal Concerned with British Studies* 7.4 (Winter, 1975), 298.
21. Roazen, "Orwell, Freud and 1984."
22. Patricia Hill, "Religion and Myth in Orwell's *1984*," *Social Theory and Practice, A Special Issue: Orwell's 1984* 10.3 (Fall, 1984), 273.
23. Christopher Hitchens, *Why Orwell Matters* (New York: Basic Books, 2002), 53, 52.
24. Orwell, "Charles Dickens," 104.
25. Alan Sandison, *The Last Man in Europe: An Essay on George Orwell* (New York: Macmillan, 1974), 6.

26. James Wood, "A Fine Rage: George Orwell's Revolutions," *The New Yorker* (13 April 2009) (https://www.newyorker.com/magazine/2009/04/13/a-fine-rage).
27. Gleason, "Puritanism and Power Politics," 80; R. H. Tawney is quoted by Alan Sandison in *The Last Man in Europe* (New York: Barnes and Noble, 1974), 115.
28. Wood, "A Fine Rage."
29. Like Wood, Richard Rees, for example, finds Orwell a "romantic, a lover of the past, of ... old-fashioned virtues ... of old-fashioned customs and old-fashioned people ... Dickensian streets and homes ... quiet fishing streams" (*George Orwell: Fugitive from the Camp of Victory* [Carbondale, IL: Southern Illinois University Press, 1961], 6)—but he also, in Gordon B. Beadle's judgment, "rightly insist[s] that this was only one aspect of a very complex character and temperament" ("George Orwell and the Victorian Radical Tradition," 288).
30. Orwell, "Why I Write," 316.
31. Ritchie Robertson, "Pick Your Teams: Eighteenth-Century Political Thought, Catalogued," *TLS* (5 June 2020), 12; Beadle, "George Orwell and the Victorian Radical Tradition," 298.
32. James Conant, "Freedom, Cruelty, and Truth: Rorty versus Orwell," in *Rorty and His Critics*, ed. Robert B. Brandom (Oxford: Blackwell, 2000), 272.
33. Orwell, "Why I Write," 316. In "For George Orwell" Christopher Hitchens endorses and explains Orwell's preference for the term "power" over the term "ability" and argues that this phrase is "oddly well put" (*Grand Street* 3.2 [Winter, 1984], 125).
34. T. S. Eliot, "Burnt Norton," in *Four Quartets* (New York: Harvest/HBJ, 1971), 40.
35. These words appear in a letter Jefferson wrote to William Roscoe dated 27 December 1820 (*https://rotunda*.upress.virginia.edu/founders/default.xqy?keys=FOEA-print-04-02-02-1712).
36. Peter van Inwagen, "Was George Orwell a Metaphysical Realist?," *Philosophia Scientiæ—Travaux d'histoire et de philosophie des sciences. (Anti-)Realisms: The Metaphysical Issue* 12.1 (2008), 166.
37. Rorty, *Contingency, Irony, and Solidarity*, 173.
38. James Conant, "Rorty and Orwell on Truth," in *On Nineteen Eighty-Four: Orwell and Our Future*, ed. Abbott Gleason, Jack Goldsmith, and Martha C. Nussbaum (Princeton, NJ: Princeton University Press, 2005), 101.
39. Richard Rorty, "Response to James Conant," in *Rorty and His Critics*, ed. Robert B. Brandom (Oxford: Blackwell, 2000), 343. Though it may seem unfair to lump Conant and van Inwagen together when the former explicitly resists being identified as a realist, Rorty

compellingly asserts that it is difficult "to figure out how [Conant] differs from van Inwagen" (343). Rorty complains that Conant vaguely gestures at a third sort of "space" of "justification," an "intervening space between the rejection of Realist theses and the affirmation of their Rortian counterparts," one whose nimble occupant avoids both (realist) "justification in the light of facts" and (non- or anti-realist) "ordinary intersubjective justification." Presumably Conant has something like what we might call Putnamian normativity in mind (see Conant, "Rorty and Orwell on Truth," footnote 36 [102]).

40. Rorty, "Response to James Conant," 343.
41. van Inwagen, "Was George Orwell a Metaphysical Realist?," 166. Conant discusses those "extended verbal shrugs" whereby Rorty says, in effect, "Yeah, yeah, you want to accuse me of [among other things] being out of touch with *reality*; but don't you see that that sort of criticism is only effective against someone who *cares* about ... being in touch with reality, and so on; and don't you see that my whole goal is to try to get you to stop caring about ... the sorts of problems that philosophers say we have to care about" ("Rorty and Orwell on Truth," 86).
42. van Inwagen, "Was George Orwell a Metaphysical Realist?," 163.
43. Gregory Claeys, *Dystopia: A Natural History* (Oxford: Oxford University Press, 2017), 413.
44. See Elaine Scarry, "A Defense of Poesy (The Treatise of Julia)," in *On Nineteen Eighty-Four: Orwell and Our Future*, ed. Abbott Gleason, Jack Goldsmith, and Martha C. Nussbaum (Princeton, NJ: Princeton University Press, 2005), 13–28.
45. Claeys, *Dystopia*, 413.
46. Ibid., 412.
47. A brief, non-technical account of "the invention of fact"—"fact" as a concept that arose in Western culture at a certain time and place and in response to certain intellectual and historical exigencies—is offered by David Wootton ("A Brief History of Facts," *History Today* [13 February 2017] [*https://www.historytoday.com/*history-matters/brief-history-facts]): "[f]acts developed with a conviction that knowledge could progress." Wootton reports a consensus view when he characterizes "David Hume (1711–1776) [as] the first 'philosopher of the fact'"; facts as we know them did not emerge until the eighteenth century (with the Enlightenment). Wootton develops his narrative of the fact's emergence in *The Invention of Science: A New History of the Scientific Revolution* (New York: Harper Perennial, 2016). For a significantly contrary account of the history of fact, see Mary Poovey's *A History of the Modern Fact: Problems of Knowledge in the Sciences of Wealth and Society* (Chicago: University of Chicago Press, 1998), which the

historian Margaret C. Jacob reviews at length in "Factoring Mary Poovey's *History of the Modern Fact*," *History and Theory* 40 (May 2001), 280–89 ("strange and provocative" [280], "eccentric" [281], "postmodern" [289], "ahistorici[st]" [282], "anti-realist" [284]).

48. One of the at least conceivably fortunate, salutary, or edifying—i.e., "good"—ways in which the fact/value opposition might erode could mean a return to what we might call the Aristotelian unity. As Alasdair MacIntyre puts it, "within the Aristotelian framework the one task," deciding "what acts are to be done," "cannot be discharged without discharging the other," deciding "how human action is to be explained and understood." Once we abandon that framework, and MacIntyre is sure that Enlightenment thinkers since David Hume have abandoned it, "'[f]act' becomes value-free, 'is' becomes a stranger to 'ought' and explanation, as well as evaluation, changes its character," all manner of baleful changes following apace. See *After Virtue: A Study in Moral Theory*, 3rd edn (Notre Dame, IN: University of Notre Dame Press, 2007), 82, 84.
49. Egid, "Maths Rules," 28.
50. William Shakespeare, *The Arden Shakespeare: King Lear*, ed. Kenneth Muir (London: Methuen & Company, 1952), I.i.93, I.i.113–14.
51. Hitchens, *Why Orwell Matters*, 52.
52. For example, in *Orwell: The Authorized Biography* (New York: HarperCollins, 1991) Michael Shelden recounts Orwell's "relatively active social life" in 1943–44 at Mortimer Crescent while composing *Animal Farm* and notes that Orwell "began to yearn more than ever before to have a child of his own … in the months that followed his mother's death" (362).
53. William Morris, *News from Nowhere and Other Writings*, ed. Clive Wilmer (New York: Penguin, 1993). Of course, it might be objected that the institution's survival of totalitarian revolution indicates Orwell's doubts about it rather than faith in it; it may appear to adapt itself to Oceania's new order all too well. As Winston reports, commenting upon how the children had been "systematically turned against their parents and taught to spy on them and report their deviations," "[t]he family had become in effect an extension of the Thought Police. It was a device by means of which everyone could be surrounded night and day by informers who knew him intimately" (*1984*, 133). But by this measure, that of an institution's malleability, would any institution in Oceania not be an "extension" of state in one way or another?
54. *King Lear*, I.i.113.
55. Apposite is the filmmaker George Stevens, who filmed the liberation of Dachau in 1945: "When a poor man, hungry and unseeing because

his eyesight is failing, grabs me and starts begging, I feel the Nazi, because I abhor him, I want him to keep his hands off me. And the reason I want him to keep his hands off me is because I see myself capable of arrogance and brutality to keep him off me. That's a fierce thing, to discover within yourself that which you despise the most in others" (see *http://www.tcm.com/this-month/article/236927%7C0/ George-Stevens-A-Filmmaker-s-Journey.html*).

56. In *Coming Up for Air*, George "Fatty" Bowling discourses memorably on the topic of the fat man in Part One, ch. 3: "I'm fat, but I'm thin inside. Has it ever struck you that there's a thin man inside every fat man, just as they say there's a statue inside every block of stone?" (*http://gutenberg.net.au/ebooks02/0200031.txt*). The sense of fat as, figuratively speaking, an aesthetic impediment is balanced by the more favorable suggestion that fat men possess a unique degree of aesthetic raw material and thus offer the artist a richness of opportunity denied them by the already-thin man.

57. In *George Orwell* (Boston: Twayne Publishers, 1987) Averil Gardner writes of how O'Brien aims to reduce Winston to "a condition of irreversible nonhumanity" (121).

58. Friedrich Schiller, *The Aesthetic Letters, Essays, and the Philosophical Letters of Schiller*, translated and introduced by J. Weiss (Boston: Charles C. Little and James Brown, 1845), 241.

59. Matthew Arnold, "Literature and Science," *Nineteenth Century* 12 (August 1882), 225.

60. William Blake, *The Complete Poetry and Prose of William Blake*, ed. David V. Erdman (New York: Anchor Books, 1988), 36.

61. Ian Slater, *Orwell: The Road to Airstrip One* (Montreal and Kingston: McGill-Queen's University Press), 214.

62. Slater, *Orwell*, 214. Slater correctly claims that *Nineteen Eighty-Four* contains notions of poetry, song, and art more generally as intrinsically subversive of social control: "verse *forms*," even, may "remind the singer or singers of another time, of history, of an alternative way of life, and in so doing constitute a threat to the state's supposed infallibility" (213–14).

63. Quoted in Richard Ellmann, *Yeats: The Man and the Masks* (New York: Norton, 1948), 289.

64. Here in particular we should pause to disallow Zwerdling's confident declaration—"Orwell accepts certain basic elements of Marxist aesthetics"—from misleading (Zwerdling, *Orwell and the Left*, 185). Zwerdling is talking about Orwell's essays, of course, and his careful choice of adjectives indicates that he would agree that Orwell, in his literary criticism as well as his literary practice, does not accept certain basic elements of Marxist aesthetics. Not that all agree with the premise

that the literary-critical Orwell is bound to be more declarative and doctrinaire than is the novelist Orwell, given the nature of literature as conceived of by, for example, Tzvetan Todorov, who by 2007 was finding that "literature makes us live unique experiences; philosophy, on the other hand, manipulates concepts. The first preserves the richness and diversity of what is lived, the second favors abstraction, which allows the formulation of general laws" ("What is Literature For," *New Literary History* 38 [2007], 25). Matthew Hart, for example, asserts that "Orwell the novelist is a more ideological writer than Orwell the journalist"—or at least such is suggested by "reading [Raymond] Williams and [Christopher] Hitchens alongside one another" ("The Measure of All That Has Been Lost: Hitchens, Orwell, and the Price of Political Relevance," *PMC* 13.3 [May 2003], para. 20 [http://pmc.iath.virginia.edu/issue.503/13.3hart.html]). Zwerdling largely agrees to the (considerable) extent that he sees Orwell as "rescu[ing] the essay from [the propagandistic] sort of thinking" ("all of Orwell's essays grow out of his quarrel with doctrinal thinking") even as he often succumbs to "rigid ... schematization" in the late "fantasies" (Zwerdling, *Orwell and the Left*, 184, 190, 199, 198).

65. "[W]e may say that in the ode [Keats] sees the urn as a refuge as well as a passion, as a friend to man in woe ... conscious representational artifice [i]s [here] a refuge, enabling man to 'enter into the existence' of other modes of being" (Helen Vendler, "Truth the Best Music: The 'Ode on a Grecian Urn,'" in *English Romantic Poetry*, ed. Harold Bloom [New York: Chelsea House, 2004], 78).

66. "Beauty is truth, truth beauty,—that is all / Ye know on earth, and all ye need to know" (*https://www.poetryfoundation.org/poems/44477/ode-on-a-grecian-urn*). Vendler, "Truth the Best Music," 78.

67. Zwerdling, *Orwell and the Left*, 180. Note, too, how the telescreen in Winston's and Julia's love nest is concealed by an artwork, a "picture" (*1984*, 145; an old "steel engraving" of St Clement's Dane framed in "rosewood"; *1984*, 97), which is detached from the wall in the moment of their arrest ("as though a catch had been turned back") and allowed to fall to the ground; they hear "a crash of breaking glass" (*1984*, 221–22).

68. George Orwell, quoted in J. P. O'Flinn, "Orwell on Literature and Society," *College English* 31.6 (March 1970), 608.

69. Garth Jowett and Valerie O'Donnell, *Propaganda and Persuasion* (Thousand Oaks, CA: Sage Publications, 2006), 7. For Jowett and O'Donnell, the judgment of authentic propaganda requires that the propagandist make a "[d]eliberate attempt," one "linked with clear institutional ideology and objective" (3). "To identify a message as propaganda is to suggest something negative and dishonest" (2).

70. George Orwell, *The Collected Essays, Journalism and Letters of George Orwell*, Volume 2, ed. Sonia Orwell and Ian Angus (New York: Harcourt, Brace & World, 1968), 41.
71. George Orwell, "Inside the Whale," in *George Orwell: A Collection of Essays* (New York: Harcourt, 1946), 228.
72. The phrase "rapt above" I borrow from John Milton's *Paradise Lost*: "Standing on earth, not rapt above the pole,/ More safe I sing with mortal voice" (VII.23–24; https://www.macmillandictionary.com/us/dictionary/american/rapt).
73. Orwell, "Inside the Whale," 241.
74. In "Charles Dickens" Orwell asserts that "every writer, especially every novelist, *has* a 'message,' whether he admits it or not" (90).
75. Orwell, "Inside the Whale," 231.
76. Immanuel Kant, *Critique of Judgement*, trans. J. H. Bernard (New York: Hafner Press, MacMillan Publishing Co., 1951), e.g., §§V–VIII & §17.
77. Orwell, "Inside the Whale," 240, 233.
78. Ibid., 241.
79. Ibid.
80. Andrew Goldstone, *Fictions of Autonomy from Wilde to de Man* (Oxford: Oxford University Press, 2013), "Abstract" (https://academic.oup.com/book/6584).
81. Orwell, "Inside the Whale," 249.
82. Ibid., 249, 249, 249, 250.
83. Ibid., 245.
84. "Jonah," *King James Bible*, ii.5.
85. Orwell, "Inside the Whale," 250, 245.
86. Ibid., 244.
87. Ibid., 245.
88. Ibid., 250.
89. Ibid., 244.
90. Cf. *Oxford Reference*: "Agents are heteronomous if their will is under the control of another" (*https://www.oxfordreference.com/view/10.1093/oi/authority*.20110803095436286).
91. Charles Altieri, "Why Modernist Claims for Autonomy Matter," *Journal of Modern Literature* 22.3 (Spring, 2009), 2.
92. As Altieri asserts, "Modernist artists and writers had to take very seriously the idea of the autonomous art work and had to develop means of turning that idea into formal possibilities for a new art, and into a new way of imagining how subjects and objects might be inseparable from one another" (Ibid., 2). Perhaps the most philosophically influential defense of the modernist idea of aesthetic autonomy may be found in Theodor Adorno's *Aesthetic Theory* (1970). For an account of the central role played by various concepts of autonomy

in the extended drama of Enlightenment "modernity," see Robert Pippin, *Modernism as a Philosophical Problem: On the Dissatisfactions of European High Culture*, 2nd edn (Malden, MA: Blackwell, 1999).

93. Orwell, "Inside the Whale," 230.
94. For an illuminating account of Orwell's great admiration for yet another modernist, D. H. Lawrence, see Richard Lance Keeble, "Orwell's Love of Lawrence," *The Orwell Society* (14 November 2020) (*https://orwellsociety.com*/orwells-love-of-lawrence/). As Keeble notes, Orwell especially admired Lawrence's short fiction.
95. Orwell, "Inside the Whale," 228, 229.
96. Ibid., 245.
97. Ibid.; Hugh Kenner, *The Stoic Comedians: Flaubert, Joyce and Beckett* (Berkeley: University of California Press, 1975).
98. Orwell, "Inside the Whale," 228.
99. Ibid., 231.
100. In "Some Theories of Aesthetic Judgment" Harold Osborne roundly declares that the "feature which aesthetic objects have in common is 'organic unity,' which takes the place of subjective purposiveness in Kant's system" (*The Journal of Aesthetics and Art Criticism* 38.2 [winter, 1979], 142).
101. Orwell, "Inside the Whale," 231.
102. J. M. Coetzee, *Stranger Shores: Literary Essays, 1986–1999* (New York: Viking, 2001), 5.
103. Ibid.
104. See Gordon Bowker, "Orwell's Library," The Orwell Foundation (*https://www*.orwellfoundation.com/the-orwell-foundation/orwell/articles/gordon-bowker-orwells-library/).
105. Ibid.
106. George Orwell, "Bookshop Memories," in *The Complete Works of George Orwell*, Volume 10: *A Kind of Compulsion 1903–1936*, ed. Peter Davison (London: Secker and Warburg, 1998), 513.
107. Ibid.
108. Orwell's reactions to Joyce and to *Ulysses*, in particular, were complex, and they evolved. In a letter to Brenda Salkeld upon first reading a contraband copy of *Ulysses*, Orwell does not celebrate Joyce's attempts to achieve aesthetic autonomy; rather, he is struck by the book's realism: "Joyce [in *Ulysses*] is attempting to select and represent events and thoughts as they occur in life and not as they occur in fiction." See his letter "To Brenda Salkeld, Sunday [10(?) December 1933]," *The Complete Works of George Orwell*, Volume 10: *A Kind of Compulsion 1903–1936*, ed. Peter Davison (London: Secker and Warburg, 1998), 327.
109. Martha C. Carpentier, "Orwell's Joyce and *Coming Up for Air*," *Joyce Studies Annual* (2012), 134, 133.

110. Levenson, "The Fictional Realist," 67. Roger Fowler similarly distinguishes in Orwell's fiction such modernist practices as "stream of consciousness, free direct and indirect thought, [and] verbs of perception and of mental process" (*The Language of George Orwell* [Basingstoke, Hampshire: Macmillan, 1995], 185). Martha C. Carpentier explores "Orwell's [Joycean] portrayal of latent dream content, fantasy, perception, and memory"; Joyce "profoundly shap[ed Orwell's] rendering of male subjectivity and identity formation by oedipal loss and guilt" ("Orwell's Joyce and *Coming Up for Air*," 135).

111. David James, *The Legacies of Modernism: Historicizing Postwar and Contemporary Fiction* (Cambridge: Cambridge University Press, 2012), 85; Levenson, "The Fictional Realist," 67.

112. Carpentier, "Orwell's Joyce and *Coming Up for Air*," 150.

113. Ibid.

114. Ibid.

115. Ibid. In a letter to Brenda Salkeld Orwell notes how reading *Ulysses* makes him "feel like a eunuch who has taken a course in voice production ... but if you listen closely you can hear the good old squeak just the same as ever." See his letter "To Brenda Salkeld, Wed. night [early September? 1934]," in *The Complete Works of George Orwell*, Volume 10: *A Kind of Compulsion 1903–1936*, ed. Peter Davison (London: Secker and Warburg, 1998), 348.

116. Carpentier, "Orwell's Joyce and *Coming Up for Air*," 150.

117. Ibid., 131.

118. Orwell, "Inside the Whale," 213.

119. Martha C. Carpentier claims that "Orwell's letters to Brenda Salkeld of 1933 and 1934, while he was working on *A Clergyman's Daughter* and desperately trying to establish himself as a novelist, demonstrate Orwell's tremendous enthusiasm for Joyce, as well as the paternal threat of Joyce's mastery to his own fledgling efforts" ("Orwell's Joyce and *Coming Up for Air*," 131).

120. In a letter to Brenda Salkeld that Orwell wrote during his extended period of early 1930s fascination with Joyce's *Ulysses*, he notes "how extraordinarily original [Joyce's] mind is." See letter 186, "To Brenda Salkeld Sunday [10(?) December 1933]," in *The Complete Works of George Orwell*, Volume 10: *A Kind of Compulsion 1903–1936* (London: Secker and Warburg, 1998), 326–28.

121. Rorty, *Contingency, Irony, and Solidarity*, 184, n.16.

122. See note 115.

123. Roger Fowler, "Versions of Realism," in *George Orwell: Bloom's Modern Critical Views, Updated Edition*, ed. Harold Bloom (New York: Chelsea House, 2007), 27.

124. For Keith Williams, Orwell's "neorealism," his putatively 1930s Marxist-inflected "documentary" realism, was beset by a saving "ambivalence" (729) rooted in his reading of Joyce and suspicious of "facile polarizations," "simple Platonic oppositions between appearance and actuality" (742). In his last two full novels, *Coming Up for Air* and *Nineteen Eighty-Four*, "an object from the past" (i.e., the crystal paperweight in the latter) proves difficult to know apart from his "symbolic investment" in it (743). See "'The Unpaid Agitator': Joyce's Influence on George Orwell and James Agee," 729–63. Roger Fowler writes of Orwell's "hyperrealism" in "Versions of Realism," 27.
125. Carpentier, "Orwell's Joyce and *Coming Up for Air*," 134. Fowler persuasively explores what he calls Orwell's "descriptive realism," a realism of "physical particularity" one step short of "sordid naturalism," which creates the "illusion of clarity and precision" by way of "certain linguistic techniques including focus on detail or 'microscopism'; the enumeration of facts; and a preoccupation with textures, spatial dimensions, and other material considerations" ("Versions of Realism," 26–27). According to Fowler, Orwell in the end achieves a "hyperrealism," "a stage beyond naturalism" (of the sordid variety) as well as descriptive realism in which "the assault upon the senses" constitutive of sordid realism is "intensified and diversified, and there are odd juxtapositions of images," "[m]etaphors and similes, often unusual and opaque," and "symbolism," all suggestive of an "alien world" (27). It is in these passages, if anywhere, that Orwell would be transcending Joyce, perhaps by presenting an objective reality both more politically and ideologically fashioned and simply far more hostile than any we find in *Ulysses*.
126. Carpentier, "Orwell's Joyce and *Coming Up for Air*," 150.
127. Orwell, *George Orwell, Diaries*, 533.
128. Ibid.
129. James Joyce, *Ulysses: The Corrected Text* (New York: Random House, 1986), 583.
130. Peter Davison offers an exact, detailed account of Avril's contribution to Orwell's diary project (*George Orwell, Diaries*, 533–34).
131. Daphne Patai, *The Orwell Mystique: A Study in Male Ideology* (Amherst: University of Massachusetts Press, 1984).
132. Stephen Spender, "The Truth About Orwell," *New York Review of Books*, 16 November 1972.
133. Gardner, *George Orwell*, 128.
134. *Hindustan Times*, 21 January 2020 (*https://www.hindustantimes.com/books/letters-claim-that-george-orwell-s-wife-let-him-offer-sex-to-female-friend/story-9YIRp0huLVPezhJDoP4DfO.html*).

135. Shelden, *Orwell: The Authorized Biography*, 143. Orwell's "authorized" (approved by Sonia Brownell Orwell) biographer Shelden briefly explores Eileen's possible hand in the composition of *Animal Farm* ("It is possible that some of the wry bits of humor in the book were ... her inventions"; *Orwell: The Authorized Biography*, 372).
136. Bernard Crick, *George Orwell, A Life* (Boston: Little, Brown and Company, 1981), 150; Shelden, *Orwell: The Authorized Biography*, 144.
137. Richard Blair, quoted in the *Hindustan Times*, 21 January 2020.
138. Brenda Salkeld, quoted in Shelden, *Orwell: The Authorized Biography*, 144.
139. D. J. Taylor, "Brief Encounters and Romps in the Park: George Orwell Pursued Women with Enthusiasm and Varying Degrees of Success," *The Critic*, March 2020 (https://thecritic.co.uk/issues/march-2020/brief-encounters-and-romps-in-the-park/).
140. Cf. Gerard Genette, *Narrative Discourse: An Essay in Method* (Oxford: Blackwell, 1972 [1980]).
141. Jeffrey Meyers, for example, mentions Orwell's sense of "the importance of the individual mind" (*Orwell: Life and Art*, 145).
142. Gass, "Double Vision," 81.
143. Meyers, *Orwell: Wintry Conscience of a Generation*, 325. "Like [his] author," as Thomas Pynchon says of O'Brien in his introduction to the Penguin edition of *1984* ("Foreword," *1984* [New York: Penguin, 2003]), "it is his individuality, compelling and self-contradicting, that we remember," not his sense of himself as a "mere cell of the greater organism of the State" (xii).
144. Thomas F. Veale, *The Banality of Virtue: A Multifaceted View of George Orwell as Champion of the Common Man* (Lawrence, KS: University of Kansas, 2007). See Hitchens's introduction to *George Orwell, Diaries*, xiv–xv.
145. John Rodden, *Scenes from an Afterlife: The Legacy of George Orwell* (Wilmington, DE: ISI Books, 2003), 198. Rodden's Orwell sees British Jews as by and large "a common people, many of them refugees clinging to standards of craftsmanship and to a dissenting tradition—two signal characteristics of nineteenth-century English Nonconformity" (200). Rodden's Orwell thus places the Jews of Britain amongst the enemies of orthodoxy, one of which he was himself (see section i).
146. Indeed, some have said: "According to Hitchens, Orwell's antipathy toward Jews was a passing phase, an adolescent misdemeanor that he outgrew ... But [Hitchens's] admiration seems to have clouded partly his critical faculty, for Orwell never fully grew out of his ill feelings toward Jews." See Anshel Pfeffer, "Was Orwell an Anti-Semite?," *Haaretz*, 3 August 2012 (https://www.haaretz.com/was-orwell-an-anti-semite-1.5276759).

147. Michael G. Brennan, *George Orwell and Religion* (London: Bloomsbury, 2017), 16, 15.
148. Taylor, *On Nineteen Eighty-Four: A Biography*, 170.
149. Brennan, *George Orwell and Religion*, 15, 15; Ricks, *Churchill and Orwell*, 35.
150. Ceferino Tresserra, *La Judia Errante* (Barcelona: Libreria de Salvador Manera, 1862).
151. Eugène Sue, *The Wandering Jew* (London and New York: George Routledge and Sons, 1889), 312, 314. Not to be identified with Wagner's Kundry (*Parsifal*), Caroline nevertheless shares in her history.
152. Orwell, "Why I Write," 319.
153. Orwell, *George Orwell, Diaries*, 515.
154. Ibid., 507.
155. Rodden and Rossi, *The Cambridge Introduction to George Orwell*, 81.
156. Cf. Michael Shelden's account of Eileen's response to her brother Laurence O'Shaughnessy's death at Dunkirk in *Orwell: The Authorized Biography*, 330–33.
157. David Morgan Zehr, "Orwell and the Proles: Revolutionary or Middle-class Voyeur?," *The Centennial Review* 27.1 (Winter, 1983), 40.
158. E. M. Forster, *Howards End* (New York: W.W. Norton and Company, 1998), 163.
159. Zehr, "Orwell and the Proles," 39.
160. Harold Bloom, *The Visionary Company: A Reading of English Romantic Poetry* (Ithaca, NY: Cornell University Press, 1971), 140; Thomas Hardy, "The Voice," The Poetry Foundation (*https://www.poetryfoundation.org/poems/52333/the-voice-56d230b56eb7c*).
161. Harold Bloom, *Bloom's Guides: Orwell's 1984* (New York: Chelsea House, 2004), 7.
162. J. M. Coetzee, *Doubling the Point: Essays and Interviews* (Cambridge: Harvard University Press, 1992), 98.
163. See McCrum, "The Masterpiece That Killed George Orwell."
164. Ricks, *Churchill and Orwell*, 261.
165. Ibid., 226.
166. Ibid., 43.
167. Students are told that symbols in novels "gesture beyond events to their greater significance, detecting what is essential or eternal in the particular" (John Mullen, *How Novels Work* [Oxford: Oxford University Press, 2006], 295). The American novelist Flannery O'Connor offers a similarly useful non-symbolic definition of symbols as "details that, while having their essential place in the literal level of the story, operate in depth as well as on the surface, increasing the story in every direction"; "the truer the symbol, the deeper it leads you, the more meaning it opens up" (*Mystery and Manners: Occasional Prose*

[New York: Farrar, Straus & Giroux, 1969], 71, 72). It is wise to distinguish between the "symbolist" in the sense of the purveyor of symbols to be found in many genres, many national literatures, and many eras, on the one hand, and on the other the "Symboliste," capital "S," represented by poets such as W. B. Yeats, Lionel Johnson, Stéphane Mallarmé, Paul Verlaine, and others who occupied the European later nineteenth century and *fin de siècle* and wrote so-called "Symbolist" poems. The original theorist of the "Symbol," the creation of which was the aim of such poets, was Jean Moréas, who defined "Symbols" as the "concrete phenomena ... presented [not as such but] as the sensitive appearance destined to represent their esoteric affinity with primordial Ideas." "Enemy of education, declamation, wrong feelings, objective description, symbolist poetry tries to dress the Idea in a sensitive form which, however ... would remain subjective ... the essential character of symbolic art consists in never approaching the concentrated kernel of the Idea in itself [any more than its concrete instance]." See "The Symbolist Manifesto," *Le Figaro*, 18 September 1886 (*https://theoria.art-zoo.com/symbolist-manifesto-jean-moreas/*).
168. Langdon Elsbree, "The Structured Nightmare of *1984*," *Twentieth Century Literature* 5.3 (October 1959), 135.

Index

Note: Page numbers followed by 'n' indicate notes.

Adorno, Theodor W. 117
aestheticism and modernism, Orwell's 132–50
aesthetic *contemplation* 137
Altieri, Charles 178nn91–2
Ambassadors, The (Henry James) 109
Amis, Martin 167n16
Appiah, Kwame Anthony 117
"From the Archives of Oceania" 19–104
　composition of 9
　diary form of 14–17
　interpretive contexts for 107–10
　Nineteen Eighty-Four and, connecting 105–7
　rationale for 4–7
　reading 12–13
　revisionary dimension of 12–13
　teaching 13–14
　see also Avril O'Malley's Diary; Cedric O'Malley's Diary
Arnold, Matthew 29, 120, 134
Atwood, Margaret 107
Avril O'Malley's Diary, 23–5, 28–9, 33–6, 39–40, 45, 47–9, 50–1, 58–63, 64–8, 69–77, 77–9, 80–4, 86–9

Beadle, Gordon B. 118, 173n29
Beowulf 12
Berlin, Isaiah 172n12
Blair, Avril 3, 9, 151, 153

Blair, Eileen O'Shaughnessy 152–3, 158, 182n135
Blair, Richard 151–2
Blake, William 133–4
Bloom, Harold 162, 183n160
Bowker, Gordon 144
Bradley, F. H. 127
Brennan, Michael G. 155
Bristow, William 171n10
Brontë, Charlotte 12
Bunyan, John 121
Burgess, Anthony 6, 167n16
Burning Down George Orwell's House (Andrew Ervin) 6

Carey, Peter 7
Caroline O'Malley's Letter 89–96
Carpentier, Martha C. 12, 145–6, 150, 180n110, 180n119
Cedric O'Malley's Diary 20–2, 26–8, 29–33, 37–9, 40–6, 49–61, 63–4, 66–9, 77, 79–80, 85–6, 96–104
Césaire, Aimé 12
Claeys, Gregory 125–6
Clergyman's Daughter, A (George Orwell) 145
Conger, Syndy McMillen 169n7
Coetzee, J. M. 12, 143, 162
Coming Up for Air (George Orwell) 3, 145, 176n56
Conant, James 123–26, 173n32, 173n39, 174n41

Contingency, Irony, and Solidarity
    (Richard Rorty) 123
Crick, Bernard 182n136
Culture of Fact, A (Barbara J.
    Shapiro) 110
Cushman, Thomas 165n2

Davison, Peter 14, 181n30
Defoe, Daniel, 12
Der Triumph des Willens (Leni
    Riefenstahl) 136
Dialectic of Enlightenment (Max
    Horkheimer and Theodor
    Adorno) 117
Diaries (George Orwell) 10, 14,
    111–12, 162
Down and Out in Paris and London
    (George Orwell) 152

Egid, Jonathan 172n16, 175n49
Eliot, George 120
Eliot, T. S. 32, 122, 142–3
Ellmann, Richard 176n63
Elsbree, Langdon 184n168
enlightening woman, Orwell's
    150–3
*Enlightenment Now: The Case for
    Reason, Science, Humanism,
    and Progress* (Steven
    Pinker) 10
Epstein, Richard A. 171n8
Eric is Awake (Dom Shaw) 7
Ervin, Andrew 6

family, Orwell on 127–31
Fish, Stanley 107–8, 138
Foe (J. M. Coetzee) 12
Fowler, Roger 12, 145, 150,
    180n110, 180n123, 181n125
Freud, Sigmund 105–6, 120

Gardner, Averil 152, 176n57
Gardner, John 12

Gass, William H. 16, 111,
    154, 162
GB84 (David Peace) 6
Genette, Gerard 182n140
Giraldi, William 165n1
Gleason, Abbott 121, 171n6
Goldstein, Philip 168n25
Goldstone, Andrew 178n80
Grendel (John Gardner) 12

Handmaid's Tale, A (Margaret
    Atwood) 107
Hardy, Thomas 160
Hart, Matthew 177n64
Hawkins, Desmond 137
Henley, Jon 168n22
Hill, Patricia 120–1
history and memory, Orwell on
    158–61
Hitchens, Christopher 120, 129,
    154–5, 165n1, 173n33
Holden, Inez 3, 144
Horkheimer, Max 117
Huxley, Aldous 130

individualism, Orwell's 153–4
*Irrationality: A History of the Dark
    Side of Reason* (Justin E. H.
    Smith) 117

Jack Maggs (Peter Carey) 7
Jacob, Margaret C. 175n47
James, David 145
James, Henry 109
Jane Eyre (Charlotte Brontë) 12
Jauss, Hans Robert 14, 108, 168n25
Jefferson, Thomas 123
Jews, Orwell and 154–6, 182n145
Jowett, Garth S. 136
Joyce, James 12, 142, 143, 145–51,
    161, 169n14, 179n108,
    179nn119–20, 180nn124–5
"Jura diaries" 3

Index

Kant, Immanuel 115–6, 139
Keats, John 135
Keeble, Richard Lance 165n2, 165n4, 166n9, 179n94
Kenner, Hugh 143
King James Bible 178n84
King Lear (Shakespeare) 175n50

La Judia Errante (Ceferino Tresserra) 156
Larkin, Emma 167n13
Lawrence, D. H. 116, 179n94
Ledoux, Ellen Malenas 168n36
Lee, Hermione 7
Le Juif Errant (Eugène Sue) 156
Levenson, Michael 12, 145–6, 168n27, 169n14, 180n110
Linsky, Bernard 168n29

Machor, James L. 168n25
MacIntyre, Alasdair 175n48
Mailloux, Steven 169n6
Major Barbara (George Bernard Shaw) 109
Martin, Martin 170n5
McCrum, Robert 5, 165n1
McCartney, Paul 136
McTaggart, J. M. E. 127
Mensch, Jennifer 171n11
Meyers, Jeffrey 154, 165n1, 182n141
Miller, Henry 137
Milton, John 178n72
modernism, Orwell and 140–50
Moréas, Jean 184n167
Morris, William 130, 175n53
Miller, Stephen 165n1
Mullen, John 183n167
My Big Book of Soldiers 151

1948 described 4–9
    philosophical issues taken up by 10

navigating 1948 10–17
why *1948* 4–9
why *1948* now? 9–10
see also Nineteen Eighty-Four (George Orwell)
1985 (Anthony Burgess) 6
Nineteen Eighty-Four (George Orwell) 1–3
    on reading *Nineteen Eighty-Four* 12–13
    see also 1948
Nussbaum, Martha 123

Observer (Robert McCrum) 5
O'Connor, Flannery 183n167
O'Donnell, Valerie 136
O'Flinn, J. P. 177n68
"Orwell Agonistes" 111–61
    capital-"p" Puritanism 121
    as a critical supplement to "From the Archives" 8–9
    enlightening woman 150–3
    issues addressed by 9
    Orwell and modernism 140–50
    Orwell and the Jews 154–6
    Orwell on history and memory 158–61
    Orwell, enlightenment, counter-enlightenment 115–27
    Orwell's pastoralism 156–7
    Orwell's individualism 153–4
    on rationality 117
    reading 11–12
    small-"p" puritanism 121
Orwell Mystique: A Study in Male Ideology, The (Daphne Patai) 152
Orwell, Sonia 3
Osbourne, Harold 179n100

Pamela (Samuel Richardson) 110
Paradise Lost (John Milton) 178n72
Peace, David 6

pastoralism, Orwell's 156–7
Patai, Daphne 152
Pfeffer, Anshel 182n146
Pinker, Steven 10
Pippen, Robert 179n92
Poovey, Mary 110, 174n47
Pynchon, Thomas 182n143

Rather, Dan 14
Rees, Richard 173n29
Rhys, Jean 12, 115
Richardson, Samuel 110
Ricks, Thomas 162, 167n13, 170n16
Riefenstahl, Leni 136
Roazen, Paul 118, 120
Robertson, Ritchie 173n31
Robinson Crusoe (Daniel Defoe) 12
Rodden, John 154–5, 158, 165n2, 167n14, 182n145
Rody, Caroline 12
Rorty, Richard 115, 118, 123–6, 149, 170n6, 171n7
Rosenfeld, Isaac 112
Rossetti, D. G. 157
Rossi, John 158, 167n14
Ruskin, John 157
Russell, Bertrand, 14, 127

Salkeld, Brenda 147, 152
Sandison, Alan 121
Scarry, Elaine 107, 123
Schaffer, Simon 110
Schiller, Friedrich 133
Scholes, Robert 166n6
Self, Will 166n9
Shakespeare, William 12, 129, 175n50
Shapin, Steven 110
Shapiro, Barbara J. 110
Shaw, Dom 7
Shaw, George Bernard 109

Shear, Michael 167n21
Shelden, Michael 175n52, 182nn135–36, 183n156
Shklar, Judith 123
Slater, Ian 134, 176n62
Smith, Justin E. H. 117–19, 127–8, 172n17
Spender, Stephen 152
Stevens, George 175n55
Stroud, Scott R. 166n7
Sue, Eugène 156

Tawney, R. H. 121
Taylor, D. J. 1, 152–3, 155
Tempest, The (William Shakespeare) 12
Todorov, Tzvetan 177n64
Tresserra, Ceferino 156

Ulysses (James Joyce) 142, 148, 151
Une Tempête (Aimé Césaire) 12

van Inwagen, Peter 123–6, 173n39
Veale, Thomas F. 182n144
Vendler, Helen 177n65
Voorhees, Richard Joseph 170n3

Wide Sargasso Sea (Jean Rhys) 12
Williams, Keith 12, 145, 168n26, 181n124
Williams, Raymond 120
Wittgenstein, Ludwig 127
Wood, James 121
Wootton, David 110, 174n47
Wordsworth, William 109

Yeats, W. B. 134

Zehr, David Morgan 159–60
Zwerdling, Alex 5, 135, 176n64

www.ingramcontent.com/pod-product-compliance
Lightning Source LLC
Chambersburg PA
CBHW020800160426
43192CB00006B/392